THREE LITTLE WORDS

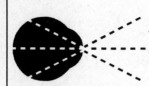

This Large Print Book carries the
Seal of Approval of N.A.V.H.

THREE LITTLE WORDS

SUSAN MALLERY

WHEELER PUBLISHING
A part of Gale, Cengage Learning

GALE
CENGAGE Learning·

Detroit • New York • San Francisco • New Haven, Conn • Waterville, Maine • London

GALE
CENGAGE Learning

LIBRARY OF CONGRESS CATALOGING-IN-PUBLICATION DATA

Mallery, Susan.
   Three Little Words / by Susan Mallery.
      pages cm. — (A Fool's Gold Romance Series) (Wheeler Publishing Large Print Hardcover)
      ISBN 978-1-4104-6206-0 (hardcover) — ISBN 1-4104-6206-4 (hardcover) 1. Large type books. I. Title.
   PS3613.A453T475 2013
   813'.6—dc23
                                                    2013018325

Published in 2013 by arrangement with Harlequin Books S.A.

Printed in Mexico
4 5 6 7 17 16 15 14 13

To Jenel, my amazing assistant, without whom I would be lost. Seriously. You keep me organized and together. You handle all the crazy stuff that comes with the writing world so I can lose myself in my stories. Without you there would be a lot less magic in Fool's Gold and very likely one less book a year. Thank you for all that you do.

Dear Ford, I can't believe my sister was stupid enough to cheat on you with your best friend two weeks before your wedding. With you joining the navy so suddenly, I didn't get a chance to confess in person. I know I'm only fourteen, but I love you. I'll love you forever and write you every day. Or at least once a week. I cried and cried when you left. Maeve wasn't happy. She said I was making a scene. I got right in her face and told her she was a bitch for cheating on you. Then I got in trouble for swearing at my sister. But I don't care. I wish you didn't have to leave. I really will love you forever, Ford. I promise. Stay safe, okay?

Dear Ford, I'm going to the prom! I know I'm just a sophomore, but Warren asked me and I said yes. My mom is practically more excited than me. We're going to San Francisco to buy a dress. My grandmother offered me one of the bridesmaid dresses from her store. OMG. As if. But Mom was cool and said we could get something from one of the big department stores. Yay! I'll send a picture of me in the dress. Stay safe, okay?

Dear Ford, I know I haven't written in a while. It was too awful. Prom, I mean. Warren wasn't who I thought and he got drunk. He and his friends had hotel rooms. I thought we were going to a party, you know, but that's not what he had in mind. He said he thought I understood. What is it with guys and sex? Explain it to me, please. Not that you ever write me back, but if you ever do. I kicked him like Dad taught me and then he threw up on my dress, which made me throw up. I wish you'd been here to take me to the dance. Stay safe, okay?

Dear Ford, I'm sorry I haven't written again for so long. My grandma died. She wasn't sick or anything. Just one day, she didn't wake up. I can't seem to stop crying. I miss her so much. Mom is sad and it's really hard. I'm trying to be there for my mom, doing my chores and cooking dinner a couple of nights a week. Sometimes, when I'm having fun with my friends, I feel guilty. Like I'm never supposed to smile again. Dad took me out to lunch and said it was okay for me to be a teenager. I wish I knew that was true. I hope you're okay out there. I worry about you, you know.

Dear Ford, I'm graduating. I'm enclosing a picture because, I don't know. Is it weird that I write? You never answer, and that's okay. I don't even know if you read these letters. But it's what I do because, in a way, I still miss you. Writing you has become this thing I do. Anyway, I'm going to UCLA. I'm set to major in marketing. Mom keeps pushing accounting, but with my math skills, we all know that's not going to happen. I'm excited and happy, except I still miss my grandma. Are you in Iraq? Sometimes when I hear the news on TV about the war, I wonder where you are.

Dear Ford, I love college. I'm just saying. Westwood is completely amazing and wonderful and we go to the beach most weekends. I'm dating a surfer. Billy. He's teaching me to surf. I'm not going to class as much as I should, but I'll make it up soon. I got highlights and I'm tan and this is the coolest my life has ever been. I love everything. I hope all is well over there, too.

Dear Ford, Fool's Gold Community College isn't so bad. I miss my friends and Westwood, but this is okay, too. My parents still aren't speaking to me except for the long conversations every week about how disappointed they are with me, that I wasn't mature enough to handle UCLA. I feel really bad about being so stupid and irresponsible, but me saying that doesn't stop the lectures. Still, I know I deserve them. Billy broke up with me a couple of weeks ago. I'm not surprised. He wasn't exactly long-term boyfriend material. I'm going to pay attention to my classes and work on being more mature. Sometimes I think about you going off to war around my age. That must have been incredibly hard. I'm still learning how to stand on my own two feet. Thinking of you and hoping you're well and staying safe.

Dear Ford, I have a job in NYC. Can you believe it? A marketing job. Do you know how many marketing students graduate every year? Like a million and there are maybe two jobs and I got one of them! Me! Mom and I are going to find me an apartment. I've been looking online and basically what I can afford is about two hundred square feet with a toilet. But I don't care. It's New York. I'm really doing it. Little Isabel from Fool's Gold is going to the Big Apple. By the way, do you know why they call New York that? Why is it like an apple? I'm not sure you're even getting these letters, but I wanted to tell you the good news. Maybe someday when you're back in the States you'll come visit me.

Dear Ford, Sorry I haven't written in so long. I've been crazy busy. We're working on a campaign for a new tequila brand. We've teamed them up with MTV and I'm involved. It's really exciting. I'm meeting all kinds of people and I even get to go to the MTV Awards! I love New York and I love my job, even though dating here is as dismal as I heard it would be. Too many single girls. But I'm not desperate. I love my work and if a guy doesn't treat me right, then I walk away. Hey, look — I finally grew up. I saw your mom last time I was home and she says you're okay. I'm glad. Fleet Week was last month and I thought of you. Hope you're staying safe, Ford.

Dear Ford, Eric is the guy I told you about before. He works on Wall Street and is very cute and funny. Smart, too. One of his friends hinted that he's about to ask me to marry him, which is exciting, of course. The thing is, he doesn't know that I write you. I know, I know, you never answer and it's more like writing my diary, only I think I need to stop. Because when I write you, I'm not just writing a diary entry. I'm wondering who you are and what you're like now. It's been forever. Ten years. Maeve is still popping out babies every couple of years. I'm sure you're over her. At least, I hope you are. I know you're still serving our country. No one knows what you do, but I can't help thinking you're in danger sometimes. I'm not that fourteen-year-old kid who swore she would love you forever anymore, but as silly as it sounds, you'll always have a

piece of my heart. Take care, Ford.
Goodbye.

CHAPTER ONE

"Death by lace and tulle," Isabel Beebe said as she waved the nozzle of the steamer.

"I'm so sorry," Madeline told her, then winced as she studied the front of the wedding gown.

"Brides-to-be are determined." Isabel lifted up the front layers of the white dress and carefully clipped them to the portable clothesline in the back room of the boutique. With a dress like this — multiple layers of flowing chiffon — she would start on the inside and work her way out.

Isabel focused the steam on the wrinkles. An excited bride had wanted to find out if her potential wedding dress was comfortable to sit in. So she'd sat. For half an hour while on the phone with a girlfriend. Now the sample had to be steamed back into perfection for the next interested customer.

"Should I stop them next time?" Madeline asked.

15

Isabel shook her head. "Would that we could. But no. Brides are fragile and emotional. As long as they're not tossing paint on the dresses or reaching for scissors, let them sit, twirl and dance away. We are here to serve."

She showed Madeline how to hold the chiffon so the steam flowed through evenly and then explained about the layers and the time to let the dress cool and dry before being put back with the other sample dresses.

"It helps if you think of each wedding gown as a very delicate princess," Isabel said with a grin. "From a family with a lot of inbreeding. At any second, there could be disaster. We're here to keep that from happening."

Madeline had only been working at Paper Moon Wedding Gowns for three weeks, but Isabel already liked her. She showed up early for her shift and was endlessly patient with the brides *and* their mothers.

Isabel passed over the steamer. "Your turn."

She watched until she was sure Madeline knew what she was doing, then returned to the front of the store. She replaced sample shoes, straightened a couple of veils, then gave in to the inevitable and admitted she was stalling. What had to be done had to be

16

done. Putting it off wouldn't change reality. Oh, but how she wanted it to.

After sucking in a breath for strength, she went into the small office, grabbed her purse and stepped into the workroom and smiled at Madeline. "I'll be back in an hour."

"Okay. See you then."

Isabel left the shop and walked purposefully to her car. Fool's Gold was small enough that she generally walked everywhere, but her current destination was just far enough to warrant a car. That and the fact that driving meant a faster and cleaner getaway. If things went badly, she didn't want to have to run like a frightened bunny. Not that she could in her four-inch heels, but still. With a car, there might be a spray of gravel and she could disappear in a cloud of dust, like in the movies.

"Things are not going to go badly," she told herself. "Things are going to go great. I'm visualizing greatness." She nearly closed her eyes, then remembered she was driving. "I'm wearing my tiara of greatness even as I turn."

She went left on Eighth Street, then right, and before she was ready, she found herself driving into the parking lot of CDS.

Cerberus Defense Sector was the new

security firm in town. They trained body-guards and offered classes in self-defense and other manly things. Isabel wasn't clear on the details. She found that she and exercise had a much better relationship if they avoided each other.

She parked next to a wicked-looking muscle car from maybe the 1960s, a large black Jeep tragically painted with flames and a monster Harley. Her Prius looked desperately out of place. Not to mention small.

Now that she wasn't driving, it was safe for her to close her eyes. She did and tried to visualize, but her stomach was churning too much for her to do much more than worry about throwing up.

"This is stupid!" she announced and opened her eyes. "I can do it. I can have a reasonable conversation with an old friend."

Only Ford Hendrix wasn't an old friend and the talk was going to be about how, despite her vow to love him forever, the ten years she'd spent writing him, not to mention the pictures she'd sent, he had no reason to be afraid of her. Because she thought that he might be. Just a little.

She doubted it was anything he would admit. The man had been a SEAL. She knew that, in addition, he'd been part of a special joint task force that had been even more dangerous. She also knew he'd returned to Fool's Gold nearly three months ago, and in all that time, they'd managed to avoid each other. But that wasn't possible anymore.

"I am not a stalker," she said, then groaned. Bad way to start a conversation. And not one designed to get him to believe her.

"Whatever," she muttered and got out of her car.

She paused to smooth the front of her black dress. It was fitted without being tight and skimmed all the lumpy bits. As much as she loved clothes, a reasonable person might assume she would be obsessed with working out to fit into designer samples. But for Isabel, the call of the cookie was hard to ignore. So she was really good at draping her curves and still looking stylish. Or so she told herself.

She adjusted her sleeves, paused to brush off a bit of dust from her shoes and then prepared to face the lion in his den. Or warrior in his cave. Whichever.

She walked into CDS. No one sat at the reception desk, so she started down the hall toward the sound of music and a weird thumping noise. She saw double doors standing open and stepped through them into the biggest workout room she'd ever seen.

The ceiling had to be thirty feet high. Ropes hung from beams at one end of the room. There were all kinds of scary-looking exercise machines, boxing bags and other weights and equipment she couldn't name. In the center of the room a petite woman with long dark hair pulled back in a ponytail was fighting a much larger man. Fighting him and maybe even winning.

They both wore protective headgear and had tape around their hands. It took her a second to recognize her friend Consuelo Ly as the woman.

Isabel watched as Consuelo swung out her leg. The guy moved, but not quick enough. Her heel caught him behind the knee and down he went. Isabel winced, but then the guy was up faster than she would have thought possible and he had the woman in a headlock. Consuelo flailed around, trying to kick him or punch him. Her elbow connected with his midsection. He grunted but didn't let go.

"You two know what you're doing, right?" Isabel asked. "Is someone going to get hurt? Should I call nine-one-one?"

The man turned toward her. Consuelo didn't. One second he was standing, then next he was flat on his back and she had her foot pressed against his throat.

"Sucker," the woman said and pulled off her protective headgear. She glared at her victim. "Are you that stupid on a mission?"

"Not usually."

She held out her hand. The guy took it and she pulled him to his feet. Consuelo turned to Isabel.

"Thanks. I owe you."

"I didn't mean to be a distraction," Isabel said. "You're so small and he's so . . ."

The man removed his headgear and turned to her. Isabel felt her mouth go dry, which was a much better reaction than the sudden flipping going on in her stomach. She had a feeling she'd gone either pale or red and kind of hoped for the former. It would be less embarrassing.

The man — all six feet of muscles in a T-shirt and sweatpants — was just as handsome as she remembered. His eyes were just as dark, his hair as thick. Fourteen years away had no doubt changed Ford Hendrix on the inside, but on the outside, he was better than ever.

She still remembered him standing in her parents' living room, confronting her sister. Isabel had been told to stay in her room, but she'd crept out to listen. She remembered crouching in the hall, crying as the man she'd loved as much as her fourteen-year-old heart could allow had asked why Maeve had cheated on him and if she really loved Leonard.

Maeve had cried, too, and apologized, but said it was all true. That she was ending things with Ford, that she should have ended them weeks before. As their wedding was in less than ten days, Isabel couldn't help agreeing. There'd been more fighting — mostly yelling on his part — then he'd stalked out.

Isabel had run after him, begging him not to go. He'd ignored her, had kept on walking. Two days later, he'd joined the navy and left Fool's Gold. She'd declared her love in an endless stream of letters but had never come face-to-face with him again until this second.

As an aside, he hadn't answered her letters. Not a single one.

"Hello, Ford," she said.

"Isabel."

Consuelo glanced between the two of them. "Okay," she said at last. "I'm sensing tension. I'm outta here."

Isabel shook her head slightly to try to clear her brain. "No tension. I'm tension free. I'm practically a noodle." She pressed her lips together. Was it possible for that statement to sound *more* stupid? A noodle?

Consuelo gave her a look that clearly stated she thought Isabel should investigate a local mental health clinic, grabbed two towels from a stack by the mats, tossed one to Ford and walked out.

Ford wiped his face, then draped the towel over one shoulder. "What brings you here?"

An excellent question. "I thought we should talk. What with our new living arrangements."

A single dark eyebrow rose. "Living arrangements?"

"Yes. As of last week, you're renting the apartment over my parents' garage. I haven't seen you coming and going and I thought maybe it was because you were avoiding me."

She drew in a breath. "I'm back in Fool's Gold for a few months to manage my parents' store while they're traveling. They want to sell Paper Moon and I'm helping update the inventory and maybe the interior. As I'm only here temporarily and they're on their world tour, it made sense for me to stay in the house. So I guess I'm house-sitting, too."

Because house-sitting sounded better than being twenty-eight years old and moving

23

back into her parents' house.

"They told me they'd rented out the apartment above the garage but didn't say to whom. I just found out it was to you, which is nice because you're not a serial killer and I don't want to live next to one."

The other eyebrow rose as his expression changed from mild interest to confusion. Probably time for her to get to the point.

"What I'm trying to say is that I'm not fourteen anymore. I'm not that crazy kid who swore she was in love with you. I've moved on and you don't have to be afraid of me."

His eyebrows relaxed and one corner of his mouth turned up. "I wasn't afraid."

His voice was confident, his half smile sexy, and he looked better than any guy ever had in the history of the universe. She was sure of it. Because even as she stood there, nerves all over her body were whispering about the *man* so tantalizingly close. As a rule, she wasn't one who believed in instant attraction. She had always thought that sexual interest required a meeting of the minds before there was any body-to-body contact. In this case, she might very well be wrong.

"That's good," she said slowly. "I don't want you to think I'm a stalker. I'm not.

I'm totally over you."

"Damn."

She stared at him. "Excuse me?"

The half smile turned into a grin. "I was the only guy in my unit to have a stalker. It made me famous."

She felt instant heat on her cheeks and knew she was blushing. "No," she breathed. "You didn't tell people about my letters."

The smile faded. "No, I didn't."

Thank God! "But you got them?"

"Yeah. I got them."

And? And? Had he read them? Liked them? Considered them the least bit meaningful?

She waited, but he didn't say anything.

"Okay, then," she murmured. "So we're clear. You're, um, safe around me and you're not avoiding me or anything."

"Yes."

"Yes, you're not avoiding me?"

"Yes."

Was it her or was he difficult to talk to? "I'm glad we got that cleared up. The apartment is okay? I checked it before you moved in. Not that I knew who you were, which was weird. Although now that I think about it, I wonder if my parents didn't tell me on purpose. Because of . . . before."

"You mean your promise to love me

forever? The promise you broke?" He said the last part with a smirk.

"It wasn't a real promise," she protested.

"It was to me."

She saw the amusement in his dark eyes. "Oh, please. You barely knew who I was. You were desperately in love with my sister and she —"

Isabel slapped her hand over her mouth. "I'm sorry. I didn't mean to say that."

He shrugged. "It was a long time ago." He moved toward her. "I got over Maeve a lot faster than I should have. She might not have handled it all that great, but she made the right decision for both of us."

"You're not still in love with her?"

"Nope." He hesitated, as if he were going to say more, then grabbed the towel and pulled it off his shoulder. "Anything else? I need to shower."

Want help?

She was reasonably confident she didn't ask the question out loud, but that didn't make the inquiry any less sincere. She would bet Ford looked great in a shower. All wet and soapy. And, um, well, naked. Which was really strange, because she couldn't remember the last time she'd speculated about a man's body. She just wasn't that interested in the whole naked-sex thing. She preferred quiet conversation to passion, and cuddling to groping. Of course, that went a long way toward explaining what had gone wrong between her and her ex.

"Interesting journey," Ford said.

"Excuse me?"

"You went from imagining me naked to some other place."

Her mouth dropped open. "I didn't imagine you . . . that way. What are you saying? I'd never do that." Heat burned hot and bright on her cheeks. "That would be rude."

The sexy smile returned. "So's lying. Don't sweat it. I'll take the compliment in the spirit you meant it." He raised one shoulder. "It's the danger. Knowing I'm a dark, dangerous guy makes me irresistible."

The Ford she remembered had been funny and charming and flirty, but he'd been a kid from a small town. Untested. Unchallenged.

The man in front of her had been honed by war. He was still charming, but he was also right about his appeal. There was something indefinable that made her both want to follow him into the shower and take off running.

She managed to swallow. "You're saying women want you?"

"All the time."

"How that must annoy you."

"I'm used to it. Mostly I consider taking care of them my patriotic duty."

She felt her mouth drop open. "Your duty?"

"*Patriotic* duty. It would be un-American to leave a woman in need."

Her gaze narrowed. So much for having to worry that Ford was uncomfortable around her. Or that her letters had bothered him. No doubt he'd considered them his God-given right.

"Just so we're clear," she said. "I'm over you."

"You mentioned that. You're not going to love me forever. It's disappointing."

"You'll survive."

"I don't know. I'm surprisingly sensitive."

"Oh, please. Like I believe that."

He winced. "You're mocking a hero?"

"With every fiber of my being."

"Better not let my mother hear that. She's still trying to convince me to let the town hold a parade in my honor. She wouldn't like knowing you're not appreciative of my personal sacrifice."

"This would be the same mother who took a booth at the Fourth of July festival so she could find you a wife?"

For the first time since she'd walked into the gym, Isabel saw a flicker of discomfort in Ford's steady gaze.

"That would be the one," he murmured. "Thanks for reminding me."

"She was taking applications."

"Yeah, she mentioned that." He shifted and turned his head, as if searching for an exit.

Now it was her turn to smile. "Not so big and bad when it comes to your mother, are you?"

He swore under his breath. "Yeah, well, so sue me. I can't help it. She's my mom. Can you stand up to yours?"

"No," she admitted. "But mine is half a world away, so I can pretend to be tough."

"So could I, when I was on another continent. Now I'm back."

She almost felt sorry for him. Almost. "I'll make you a deal," she said impulsively. "You stop talking about how you seduce women in the name of being a good soldier, and I won't bring up your mother."

"Done."

They looked at each other. Isabel was still conscious of his strength and chiseled good looks, but she was a lot less nervous now. Maybe because she'd figured out his weakness. That knowledge would keep the playing field even.

"So we're good?" she asked. "The letters, my sister, your mother, all of it?"

He nodded. "The best." His gaze sharpened. "You didn't apply, did you?"

She grinned. "To be your wife? No, I didn't. Technically, I wasn't qualified. What with me not staying in town permanently."

"Lucky you."

She pretended concern. "Oh, Ford, don't worry. I'm sure she'll find someone for you. A nice girl who appreciates your giving nature."

"Very funny." He paused and the grin returned. "About that shower . . ."

"Thanks, but no."

She waved and started for the door. The meeting hadn't gone at all like what she'd imagined, but she was leaving with the belief that Ford wouldn't avoid her in the future. Assuming he ever had. And she didn't have to worry that he thought she was stalking him.

She stepped into the hallway. Consuelo walked out of the locker room, a gym bag in one hand, her car keys in another.

"You two finished?" her friend asked.

"Order is restored."

Consuelo was one of those petite women who always made Isabel feel as if she were all arms and legs, with massive boat-long feet. The fact that Consuelo could easily wrestle an alligator into submission should have helped Isabel feel more feminine, but oddly it didn't. Maybe it was because on Consuelo, muscles looked sexy.

"Should I believe you?" Consuelo asked. "You've been avoiding Ford for most of the summer."

"I know and it was silly of me. I should have talked with him before."

"Uh-huh." Consuelo sighed. "You're not going to start following him around now, are you? Women tend to do that. They also show up in his bed without an invitation. Not that he usually sends them away."

"I heard about that. Not the women, but that it's his patriotic duty to satisfy them."

"You don't sound upset."

"I'm not. The guy I had a crush on wasn't this Ford. He was sweet and funny and caring. This more mature version is all that and sexy, too."

Consuelo waited.

"Not my type," Isabel said. "Too flashy. I like quiet guys who are thoughtful and smart. The whole sexual attraction thing is highly overrated."

Except for the chance at seeing Ford in the shower, she thought briefly. That would be exciting. But she was sure her interest was more about curiosity than temptation.

"You've had sex, right?" Consuelo asked. "More than once?"

"Of course. I was married. It's fine." Sort of. "But I don't see it as a driving force in my life. Ford's the fling guy and I'm not a fling girl. Not that he was asking."

Consuelo looked her over. "He would have been. Eventually. He might not be your type, but you're sure his."

"He likes blondes?"

Consuelo's mouth twisted. "He likes women."

Isabel had friends in New York who were all about the thrill of the chase. Sex was important to them, which was fine. But she was different. She wanted someone she could talk to. Someone she could hang out with. Which was probably why she'd ended up with Eric, she thought sadly. They got along great, had the same interests. Their relationship had been one incredible friendship. Unfortunately, they'd both mistaken it for more.

"I have to get back to work," Isabel said. "I have two brides coming in this afternoon to try on gowns. Let's have lunch this week."

"You're on."

■ ■ ■ ■

Ford Hendrix could disappear into the mountains of Afghanistan for months at a time. He could live within a mile of a village and no one would guess he'd ever been there. He'd traveled the world for his country, fought, killed and been wounded. More than once, he'd stared down death and won. But nothing in his fourteen-year career with the military had prepared him to have to deal with the determined, stubborn woman that was his mother.

"Are you dating?" Denise Hendrix asked as she filled a mug with fresh coffee and handed it to him.

It was barely six in the morning. Normally Ford would have been up and heading for work, but he was a civilian now and starting his day at O-dark-thirty was no longer necessary. He'd stumbled into his kitchen, only to find his mother had shown up and started coffee. Without warning.

He glanced around the small furnished upstairs apartment he'd rented and tried to make sense of it all.

"Mom, did I give you a key?"

His mother smiled and took a second mug for herself, then settled at the small table in the corner. "Marian gave me keys to the apartment and the house before she and John left on their vacation. In case something happened."

"Like you thinking I can't make my own coffee?"

"I'm worried about you."

He was worried, too. Worried that coming back home had been a mistake.

When he'd first arrived, he'd stayed in the family home because it had been easy. Only he'd awakened more than once to find his mother hovering. What she couldn't possibly know was that with his military training, he didn't react well to people hovering while he slept. Sneaking around like that was a good way to get dead.

So he'd moved out and into a house with Consuelo and Angel. Only he and Angel were too competitive for that kind of arrangement, so he'd been forced to move again. Technically, Consuelo had threatened to gut him if he didn't, but he was going to ignore that. In a fair fight, he could take her. The problem was Consuelo didn't fight fair.

He'd found what he thought was the perfect apartment. Close to work, quiet and away from his mother.

He sat across from the woman who had

given birth to him and held out his hand.

She blinked at him. "What?"

"The key."

Denise was in her mid-fifties. Pretty, with highlighted hair and eyes. She'd survived six kids, including triplet girls, and the death of her husband. A couple of years ago, she'd fallen in love with a guy she'd known in high school. Or maybe after. His sisters had written Ford about the romance. As far as he was concerned, his mom had been a faithful widow over a decade. If she found someone else at this stage in her life, he was happy for her.

"You mean the key to the —"

"Apartment," he finished. "Hand it over."

"But, Ford, I'm your mother."

"I've known who you are for a while now. Mom, you can't keep doing this. Dropping in on me. You have grandkids. Go freak *them* out."

Her dark eyes filled with emotion. "But you've been gone for so long. You almost never came home. I had to travel to other places to see you, and you didn't even let me do that very often."

He wanted to point out that she was the reason why. She smothered him. He knew that of the three boys, he was the youngest, but he'd grown up a long time ago.

"Mom, I was a SEAL. I know how to take care of myself. Give me the key."

"What if you lock yourself out? What if there's an emergency?"

He didn't say anything. He kept his gaze steady and determined. She was no more threatening than a Kalashnikov, and he'd faced plenty of those in his day.

"Fine," she said, her voice small. She pulled a key from her jeans pocket and dropped it into his palm. He closed his fingers around it.

The part of him that knew his family wanted to ask if she'd made a copy. He figured he would wait to see if that turned out to be a problem. For now it was enough that she wasn't going to pop in when he least expected her.

"You probably want me to go," she whispered.

"Mom, don't be a martyr. I love you. I'm home. Can't that be enough for now?"

She sniffed, then nodded. "You're right. I'm glad you're home and staying in Fool's Gold. I'll give you a couple of days to settle in, then call. We can go to lunch or you can come over to dinner. How's that?"

"Perfect."

She rose. He did the same. He put his arm around her and kissed the top of her head.

They headed for the door. She opened it and stepped onto the small landing at the top of the stairs. He'd nearly breathed the sweet air of freedom when she turned back to him.

"Did you get a chance to look at those files I sent you?" she asked. "There are several lovely girls."

"Mom," he began, his voice warning.

She faced him. "Honey, no. You've been on your own for too long. You need to get married and start a family. You're not getting any younger, you know."

"I love you, too," he said, gently pushing her out the door and closing it before she could say anything else he would regret.

"I want you married, Ford," she yelled through the closed door. "I have the applications on my computer, if you want to go through them. They're on a spreadsheet so you can sort them by different criteria."

She was still yelling when he reached the bedroom and closed that door, as well.

CHAPTER TWO

Isabel turned her cart down an aisle and knew a lack of inspiration would be a problem later. If she didn't figure out what she wanted for dinner, she would be starving in a couple of hours. Ordering a pizza at eight-thirty, then eating the whole thing was very bad for her hips and thighs. Remembering that the women in her family eased toward pear-shaped as they aged, she headed for the produce section and virtuously chose a bag of salad. Great. She had salad and red wine and a very small container of ice cream. Disparate elements that did not a dinner make.

She started purposefully toward the meat section, not sure what she would do when she got there. As she turned the corner, she nearly ran into another shopper.

"Sorry," she said automatically, only to find herself staring into a pair of dark eyes. "Ford."

He smiled. It was the same slow, sexy smile he'd used before. The one that made it hard for her to catch her breath. Telling herself that he tossed that smile around like empty peanut shells at a ball game didn't make her chest any less tight. Which was so very strange. She'd never been one to quiver in the presence of a man.

"Hey," he said. He raised his basket. "Food shopping."

"Me, too." She glanced at the package of steaks and the six-pack of beer. "That's your idea of dinner?"

"You have ice cream and red wine."

"I have salad," she said with a sniff. "That makes me virtuous."

"It makes you a rabbit. And hungry." The smile turned to a grin. "I saw a grill on your patio the other day. Why don't we pool our resources?"

A tempting offer. "You want the wine and the ice cream."

"True, but I'll eat the salad, just to be polite."

"Such a guy. Do you know how to use the grill? It's big and seems complicated."

One eyebrow rose. "I was born knowing how. It's in my DNA."

"Which seems like a waste of genetic material."

Somehow they were walking. She didn't remember making a decision about accepting his offer, but there they were, in line to pay. Five minutes later they were in the parking lot and heading to their cars.

They got to his first.

"Seriously?" she asked, staring at the black Jeep.

"It's a classic."

She pointed to the gold paint on the side. "It has flames. Jeeps have a long history of faithful service. Why would you torture yours like that?"

"You don't like it? Why not? The flames are cool."

"No. Consuelo's car is cool. Yours is kind of embarrassing."

"I bought it right after your sister dumped me for my best friend. I wasn't myself."

"That was fourteen years ago. Why haven't you sold it?"

"I never drive it and it's in great condition. When I decided to move back, Ethan got it ready for me."

"Being seen near it must have humiliated him," she teased, knowing Ford's brother would have been happy to help. "Doesn't Angel drive a Harley?"

Ford frowned at the mention of his business partner. "How do you know that?"

40

"It's hard to miss a guy like him in black leather and driving a motorcycle in Fool's Gold."

"You drive a Prius," he said. "You don't get to make judgments."

"You mean because I drive a safe, sensible, environmentally friendly car?"

"Logic," he muttered. "Just like a woman."

He helped her load her groceries, which consisted of a single bag. Something she could have handled herself. Still, it was kind of nice to have a man do that for her. Eric had supported her desire for equality, letting her lug her half of the groceries when they went shopping. Which was perfectly fair, she reminded herself. If not especially romantic.

Ford followed her home. She couldn't escape his hideously painted Jeep in her rearview mirror. Even a broken heart was no excuse to mutilate such a hardworking vehicle.

She pulled into the driveway. He parked next to her and climbed out. "I'll go put the beer in my refrigerator," he said. "Then be down to start the steaks."

"Works for me."

She went into her house and set everything on the counter in the kitchen. The sun had dipped to the other side of the house, leaving this part mostly in shadow. She flipped on overhead lights. The oak cabinets were only a few years old and the yellow tile she remembered from her childhood had been replaced with granite.

She thought briefly about dashing into her bathroom and fluffing her appearance. After a long day at the store, she was sure she had mascara under her eyes and very flat hair. Plus, her dress was plain. Not only had she worked in New York, where wearing black was practically the law, she now had a job in a bridal gown store. It was important to look professional while never, ever outshining the bride. She had a wardrobe of simple, stylish black dresses — the "office appropriate" kind, not the LBD kind.

Not that she was looking to slip into an evening gown or anything, but still. She settled on kicking off her heels and rolling up the long sleeves of her dress. That was plenty. She was only having dinner with her neighbor. There was no reason to spruce. Besides, until a couple of days ago, his last memory of her was of a fourteen-year-old girl, chasing him down the street while sobbing and begging him not to go. After that, nearly anything would be an improvement.

She unpacked her bag and slipped the ice cream into the freezer. Setting the outdoor table took all of three minutes. She was about to tackle the salad when he returned.

"I have three messages from my mother," he grumbled as he walked to the counter and pulled open a drawer. He dug through an assortment of can openers, measuring spoons and spatulas until he found the wine opener. Next he pulled two wineglasses from an upper cupboard shelf. "She wants to talk about the applicants."

Isabel was more interested in how he knew his way around her kitchen. Did the man case the place while she was gone? Was he —

Maeve, she thought. He'd dated her sister for three years and had spent hours here every week. He'd often stayed for dinner and helped her sister set the table. While the kitchen had been updated, the layout was the same. Flatware was still in the top drawer by the sink, and glasses were above the dishwasher.

"Future-wife applicants?" she asked.

"That would be them."

"Have you bothered to meet any of the women? They might be lovely."

He gave her a look that implied the corkscrew had more intelligence than her.

"No," he said firmly. "I'm not interested in anyone who would fill out an application."

"You're very critical and your mother is just trying to help."

"Are you in on this?" he demanded. "Is there a plan to torture me?"

"No. Any torture is just a happy by-product."

"Funny. Very funny. I don't remember you having this much attitude fourteen years ago. I liked you better then." He poured the red wine she'd bought and passed her a glass.

"You didn't know me then," she reminded him. "I was your girlfriend's little sister. You barely spoke to me."

"We had a special relationship that didn't require conventional communication."

She laughed. "You're so full of crap."

His dark eyes crinkled with amusement. "And you're not the first woman to tell me that." He touched his glass to hers. "To me being idiotic enough to come home."

"You'll settle in and your mother will calm down."

"I hope so. I know she's excited about having me back, but this is ridiculous."

Isabel thought about the time after Ford left — when she knew her heart was going to break. "You almost never came back to town. Was that because of Maeve?"

He leaned against the counter. "At first,"

he admitted. "Mostly I stayed away because being around my family was too complicated. They wanted to get involved in everything — especially my mom. I became a SEAL my third year and that was intense. I couldn't talk about what I did or tell them where I was going. I took the easy way out and avoided the situation."

He sipped the wine. "Maeve wasn't wrong to break up with me. When it happened I would have told you I'd miss her forever. But within a few weeks, I realized she was right. We were kids, playing at being in love. I guess she has the real thing with Leonard."

Isabel tried to read emotion into his words. She couldn't tell if he really didn't mind that his ex-girlfriend had married the guy who'd come between them or not.

"They've been married twelve years now," she said.

"The kids are more impressive. What's she up to now?"

"Four with another on the way."

He swore. "That many? I didn't know Leonard had it in him."

"Me, either. He's an accountant now. He started his own company and has several impressive clients. He's doing well."

"With a family that big, he'd better be.

How do you feel about being an aunt that many times over?"

"It can be overwhelming," she said, which was mostly accurate. In truth, she'd been living in New York for the past six years and hadn't been around her family all that much. She doubted Maeve's youngest could pick her out of a lineup. She and her sister didn't talk much, either. They'd both been busy and they didn't have all that much in common.

Guilt poked at her, making her think she should call her sister and arrange a visit.

"You okay?" Ford asked, studying her.

"Fine. You're not the only one with family issues."

"Probably, but I'm the only one with a mother who set up a booth at a Fool's Gold festival with the sole purpose of finding me and my brother wives."

She laughed. "That you are."

They pulled together dinner pretty quickly. In addition to the steaks, Ford had provided two russet potatoes. Isabel popped them in the microwave, then made the salad. She carried both their glasses of wine outside while he heated the grill and put on the steaks.

"You can use the grill anytime you want,"

she said. "I don't mind."

Ford flipped the steaks, then closed the lid. "Thanks. I may take you up on that."

"Meat good?" she asked.

He grinned. "Meat and fire. And beer." He reached for his glass. "Or wine."

She studied him, taking in the broad shoulders and easy smile. She searched for some hint he was still dealing with his time in the military, that he'd been scarred by all he'd seen, but there was no indication at all. If he had ghosts, they were the kind only he saw.

"Did you like being a SEAL?" she asked.

"Yeah. I liked being on a team. I also liked that we never knew what was going to happen next."

"Certainty and variety. Two key components to happiness."

He raised his eyebrows.

She shrugged. "I have a marketing degree, but I also have a minor in psychology. People like a sense of security. It's hard to have fun if you're starving or homeless. But we also like variety. Positive change engages the brain."

"Pretty and smart. Impressive."

She told herself he was a natural-born flirt and if she believed anything he said, she was an idiot. But that didn't stop the tingles.

47

"Why did you retire?" she asked.

"The last five years I was on a joint task force. Important work, but more stressful."

"Dangerous?"

He grinned. "Danger is my middle name."

She smiled. "I'm sure that's not true, and I can easily get confirmation from one of your sisters."

"Damn small town." He sipped his wine. "The work was intense and I was moved around a lot. The team changed. After a while it started to get to me. Justice called about CDS and I said yes."

"Were you worried about coming home?"

"I was worried about my mother." He grimaced. "With good reason."

Because it would be easier if he didn't have family or didn't get along with his. It was hard to tell a parent no when she was as loving and supportive as Denise.

"You should send her on a cruise around the world," she suggested. "It worked for me."

"If only she'd go." His dark gaze settled on her face. "What about you? You're back because you're divorced?"

"Uh-huh. The paperwork is final, so I'm a free woman."

"You okay?"

"I'm fine. Eric and I didn't contest anything. We owned an apartment together. He bought me out, so I have that money to help start my business."

"The one you're starting when Paper Moon sells?"

"Right. So it's all good."

"No hard feelings?" he asked.

She'd told the almost-true version of the story so many times, the words came out automatically. "No. Eric's a great guy, but we grew apart. We're better as friends."

He turned and checked the steaks, then flipped them again and closed the lid.

"It all sounds civilized," he said. "Better than hating each other at the end."

That would have required more energy than either of them had for the relationship, she thought sadly.

"I admire how you handled the situation," Ford said.

Praise she didn't deserve. She opened her mouth to say it was nothing, but what came out instead was "I thought everything was fine. I thought we had a great marriage. We were best friends with each other. We went to restaurants and gallery openings and estate sales on weekends. He supported my dreams and I supported his."

Their sex life had been nonexistent, but as sex wasn't important to her, she hadn't minded. In a way it had been freeing to simply be herself with a man.

"I liked spending time with him," she continued. "It was easy." She paused. "But it wasn't love."

"Doesn't sound like it," Ford said quietly.

She looked at him, then away before putting her wine down on the outdoor table. She was holding the glass so tightly she was afraid she was going to break it.

"He fell in love with someone else," she admitted, still remembering the shock when he'd told her. He'd sat her down, taken her hands in his and admitted he'd fallen in love.

"He was so excited. So happy. There was an energy I'd never seen before. I think that shocked me more than the infidelity. The enthusiasm. He'd never acted that way about me."

"He was gay."

She snapped her attention back to Ford and struggled to keep her mouth from falling open. "How did you know?"

"No straight guy goes to estate sales."

She managed a strangled laugh. "Of course they do, but you're right. He'd fallen in love with another man. He said it had never happened before, but I didn't know if I could believe him."

How could he not have known? How could he have lied to her for all those years? She'd been forced to grapple with the end of her marriage and worry about her health. If Eric had cheated with one person, who was to say there hadn't been others?

All the tests had come back fine and she was able to relax about sexually transmitted diseases, but then she'd still had the end of her marriage to get through.

"I missed him," she admitted. "We were friends and then he was gone. I had to figure out what to do next. Sonia and I had always talked about opening a store together and suddenly we were making real plans. I came here to help out my folks, earn some money and deal with everything."

She drew in a breath. "I never saw it coming. That's what I wrestle with. I had no clue. I mean we rarely had sex, but I figured everyone was different. He wasn't that interested and I was good with that. Only, what if it was me?"

"If he's gay, then it's not you. It's every woman."

He watched her with friendly concern. If there was judgment, he was keeping it hidden, which she appreciated.

"You didn't do anything wrong," he said. "He wasn't honest with you or himself. You had no part of that."

"I guess."

He lightly touched her under the chin, forcing her to raise her head and meet his steady gaze. "There's no 'I guess' on this."

"What if I turned him gay?"

Ford smiled. "You didn't."

"You can't know that. Maybe I was so horrible in bed he had to go be with a guy."

"I don't think it works that way. Isn't sexual preference biological? Sorry to disappoint, but you don't have that much power."

He was being so kind, she thought. Gentle and sweet. The unexpected support made her want to lean into him. "I feel stupid. Like I should have known."

"You trusted him, Isabel. You believed in him and he used you."

"You make it sound so simple."

"Because it is." The smile returned. "I'm always right."

"Oh, please." She felt herself start to smile back at him.

"Better," he said, then leaned forward and lightly touched his mouth to hers.

The kiss was brief. More comfort than seduction. Even so, she felt a distinct jolt deep in her belly. She told herself it was a combination of wine — even though she'd barely had a sip — and embarrassment. No one knew the truth about Eric. She'd been too humiliated to share what had really happened. Now she wondered why she'd been so reluctant to trust the people who loved her.

"Thank you," she said when he straightened. "For listening and not laughing."

"Your story wasn't funny."

"I was thinking more of being laughed *at* rather than with."

"Not my style," he told her.

What was his style? Who was this man who drove a ridiculous vehicle and claimed to be God's gift to women, yet offered comfort and knew the exact right thing to say?

Before she could ask, he turned away and checked on the steaks. "They're about done," he said.

"I'll get the potatoes and salad."

She walked into the house and drew in a breath. She felt better for having told the truth. As if the secret of why her marriage had ended had been weighing on her.

What she hadn't said, what she wondered if Ford or anyone else would guess, was that the sadness she felt was for the loss of a friend. Not of a husband or a lover. She didn't feel as if she'd ended things with her one true love. Which meant the marriage had been a fake from the beginning and somehow she'd never noticed.

Ford leaned back in his chair and propped his feet on the desk. "Two more accounts," he said, nodding at the folders on the desk.

Consuelo pushed his boots off the desk. "You're smug. I hate smug."

"I'm good at my job," he corrected, then drank his coffee.

Angel's expression turned pained. "You get the glory because you're in sales. We're all working just as hard."

"Do you hear anything?" Ford asked Justice. "I'm getting a buzzing sound in my ear."

Justice turned from his laptop and opened the folders. He glanced at the printed copies of emails, along with the signed contracts.

The workload at CDS was divided equally. Justice, who had pulled the business together, coordinated all their activities and kept everything running smoothly. Consuelo was in charge of classes and training. Angel put together custom programs for their security clients and the corporate customers, while Ford was in charge of sales.

"Don't make trouble," Justice said mildly as he reviewed the documents. He was tall and broad shouldered, and the only one of them wearing a suit. Ford, Angel and Consuelo had on cargo pants and T-shirts, which in Consuelo's case was really a tank top. The influence of their military training. The clothes provided for easy movement in any situation.

"Nice," Justice said, looking up. He turned to Angel. "I'll touch base with the companies to find out the details of what they're looking for. Then you can start designing the programs."

Angel looked disgusted. "How are you doing that? You have new clients nearly every week and we've only been open a month."

"Jealous? I'm good at what I do."

"Don't make me separate you two," Consuelo said.

"I've got style, bro," Ford said, ignoring her. "Real style."

There were three parts to the CDS business plan. The first types of client were ones already in the security business. CDS provided advanced training for senior operatives and basic training for new hires. Most companies found it cheaper to outsource instruction.

The second source of income came from corporate clients looking for a unique team-building experience. Using the town as a selling point, Ford presented the idea of a simple series of survival exercises to grow trust in a group. Most of the corporate clients picked weeks of festivals for their dates, bringing in the employees on Monday and flying in family members to join them on Thursday. At the end, there would be a group hug and a round of "Kumbaya." Or some crap like that.

The final source of income was from classes held for locals. Self-defense and basic exercise. It was good for the town, good for CDS, and that was all he cared about.

"You don't have style," Angel grumbled. "Look at that thing you drive."

"It's a classic."

"It's an embarrassment to Jeeps everywhere. The company should come take it away from you."

His friend's comment made him think about what Isabel had said. Which made him think about last night and the feel of his mouth on hers.

Nice. More than nice. He'd been aware of wanting to pull her close and do a lot more than kiss. Sometime while he'd been gone, his ex-girlfriend's little sister had grown up. Now she was funny, sexy and completely off-limits. Isabel was troubled and he didn't do troubled. She was also the commitment type, which, again, was not him. But a guy could sure dream.

"If we could get back to business," Justice said. He went through the rest of the schedule. "Angel's getting more work than he can handle."

"Thanks to me." Ford grinned. "Damn, I'm good."

Consuelo rolled her eyes.

"Don't ask him to help me," Angel demanded. "Don't even think about it."

"You can't design all the curriculum yourself," Justice reminded him. "Not at the beginning when it's all new. We'll all help."

"But I'll be the most help," Ford said.

Angel lunged for him. They tumbled to the floor, wrestling and punching each other.

Neither of them was trying very hard. If either of them put in any effort, there would be a fairly serious injury . . . or seven. Justice had already lectured them on not doing anything to increase their health insurance premiums.

"Are we done?" Consuelo asked.

"Apparently," Justice said and turned back to his computer.

Angel rolled Ford a couple of times and

tried to get an arm around his neck. Ford twisted and got away, only to have his friend pull him back to the mat. Consuelo grabbed her coffee and stepped over them.

At the door, she paused and looked back. "The Maá-zib Festival is coming up. The highlight is a man getting his heart cut out. I'm volunteering both of you for the sacrifice. Don't worry about thanking me."

CHAPTER THREE

Ford walked down the stairs by the garage and headed to his Jeep. He glanced toward the kitchen and wondered if Isabel was up yet. It was early by civilian standards and he knew the store didn't open until ten or eleven, so she had no reason to be. Oddly, he found himself wanting to go inside anyway, to make coffee and wait for her. An urge he couldn't explain or justify. He guessed she would be as freaked by his unexpected arrival as he'd been by his mother's.

There were elements about coming home that were more difficult than he'd expected. Not his mother — she was as much a pain as usual. He knew her actions were born in love, but honest to God, the woman needed a hobby. He'd seen his brothers and they were fine. Low-key. Welcoming but not so much with the hugging and worrying. His sisters were another matter and he didn't look forward to hanging out with them.

But Isabel was different. Being around her was fun. He could relax and enjoy listening to her talk or tease her. Probably because of the letters. She'd written him for years. He'd watched her grow up, had been privy to her secrets and had slept better knowing that while he was in hell, there were still good people going about their lives.

He doubted she knew what her letters had meant to him. How her words had kept him grounded. He'd never answered, and over time, the letters had changed. They'd become more of a diary and less of a correspondence. He'd liked that part, too.

He'd laughed over the funny things and felt for her when she'd gone through life's lessons. He'd been changing, too, and in a way, it was as if they'd gone through both together.

Seeing her was different than reading about her. Better. Three-D, grown-up Isabel was a lot more intriguing than the teen had been. She was pretty enough to tempt him but, as he'd been reminding himself, not someone he should pursue. He wasn't a good bet romantically, and she deserved a good guy in her life. He was more the good-time type. He felt bad about her ex. That had to set a girl back. If there were —

He stopped halfway down the stairs.

Someone was standing by his Jeep. He'd seen movement and then it had stilled, as if whoever was there was trying to stay in the shadows. Ford went on alert. He reached for his sidearm, only to remember this was Fool's Gold and he didn't have a gun.

Not a problem. He would take out his stalker the old-fashioned way.

He continued down the stairs, careful not to make a sound. He circled the vehicle and came up behind the guy. Ford had to consciously lower his arms to his sides as he recognized the man loitering.

"Leonard?"

Leonard, all five feet eight inches of him, jumped. "Ford! You startled me."

Leonard had dark hair and glasses. He wore slacks and a white shirt, along with a tie. Ford saw the white SUV parked on the street and guessed there was a suit jacket lying neatly in the backseat. Or worse, hung on a hanger.

Leonard held out his hand. "It's good to see you. Welcome home."

"Thanks." They shook. "What are you doing here?"

Leonard pushed up his glasses. "I thought we should talk. We need to settle our differences."

Ford held in a laugh. "It was all a long time ago, bro. There's nothing to discuss."

"I disagree. I was wrong to do what I did." Leonard's expression turned guilty. "You and Maeve were engaged. I had no right to get in the middle of that. You were my best friend." He paused to clear his throat. "I've never forgiven myself for hurting you."

Ford remembered being stunned when he'd found Maeve with Leonard. He was sure he'd been upset, but it was a long time ago. It was like recalling a movie he'd seen rather than reliving an emotional event.

"The better man won."

"No," Leonard said earnestly. "I'm not the better man. I can't be until I apologize and you accept." He squared his shoulders. "We should have told you. We should have explained we were falling in love."

"Yeah, you should have. So you have and we're good, right?"

Leonard shook his head. "No. That's not enough. Maeve and I were young and foolish. You have to see that."

"I do." He could also see the beginnings of a headache.

"Sure, we're married now, with four kids and another on the way, but so what? Our happy marriage doesn't make what we did right. You deserve your pound of flesh."

Ford sighed. "Do I have to?"

Leonard stepped closer. "Hit me."

Ford held in a groan. "Seriously?"

"Yes. Hit me. Then we'll be even."

"I appreciate the offer, but get real. I'm a highly trained SEAL. You don't want to go up against me."

"I'm not. I'm standing here as the man who wronged you. Hit me. I can take my punishment. I deserve it."

Ford wondered how long Leonard had been waiting for this moment, planning it. Then he realized he knew the answer. Fourteen years. He saw the determination in his friend's eyes and figured there was no other way out of it.

"All right," he said slowly. "If you're sure."

Leonard nodded and carefully removed his glasses. "I'm ready."

Ford pulled out his cell phone and dialed 9-1-1.

"Fool's Gold nine-one-one. What is your emergency?"

"There's an unconscious man on the ground. Send an ambulance."

"Wh—"

Leonard started to speak, but that was all he got out before Ford hit him and he crashed to the ground.

■ ■ ■ ■

Kent walked toward the CDS building. It was a warehouse south of the convention center and east of downtown. He'd never been there before. Although he'd seen his brother Ford several times since Ford's return, they'd always met at a restaurant, or their mom's house.

As he entered the large building, he wasn't thinking about his reason for being there. Instead he was mulling over his work schedule for the day. Although he had several weeks until school started, he'd already begun working on his lesson plans. This year he was determined to take his math-letes all the way to nationals. The kids worked hard and they deserved the opportunity. He was also going to be teaching a new advanced calculus class, which would challenge both him and his students.

"Kent, right?"

"Huh?" He realized he was in a hallway, with a large man standing in front of him. His gaze flickered between the cold gray eyes and the scar on the guy's neck.

"Angel," he said as the name came to him. "Kent Hendrix. Ford's brother. We've met a couple of times."

"Sure." Angel shook hands with him. "Ford's not here. There was some kind of trouble and he's at the hospital."

"He's hurt?"

Angel grinned. "No. It's the other guy."

Which sounded like Ford, Kent thought, wishing he could be a little more like his brother. Not the fighting. He didn't want to do whatever it was his brother had learned while in the military. But the ability to go for what he wanted, to not give a damn about convention or other people's opinions. That would be nice.

"I'm here to see Consuelo. About my son."

Angel's grin turned knowing. "Right," he said, drawing out the word. "That's a new one."

"New one what?"

"The kid. It's a good story, though. Original. You might get points for that."

Kent shook his head. "What are you talking about?"

"You seeing Consuelo."

Kent wondered if the other man had taken a few too many blows to the head. "My son is taking a martial arts class with her. He wants to take more and that means he doesn't have time for soccer. He's been with the team for a couple of years now, so I want

65

to make sure he's making the right decision."

The grin faded. "Oh. You're really here about your kid."

"Why else would I come here?"

Angel slapped him on the back. "You've never met Consuelo."

It wasn't a question, but Kent answered it anyway. "No. I registered Reese by phone after checking it out with Ford."

Angel chuckled. "You need to brace yourself. She's hot."

"Thanks for the warning."

He wanted to point out that he didn't actually care about Consuelo except as her classes related to his son, but he doubted Angel would believe him.

Dating seemed impossible, he thought grimly. It wasn't that he didn't want to; it was that he didn't trust himself to get it right. His previous marriage had been the very definition of a disaster. He'd been completely stupid and then he'd perpetuated the mistake by thinking he was still in love with his ex years after she'd left. He hadn't been. In truth he'd been unable to accept the end of his marriage until he'd accepted the truth about his ex-wife. But finally figuring out the problem didn't make him any less of an idiot.

"Just remember she could kill you where you stand and never blink."

Kent wasn't sure what blinking had to do with anything. "Does she do that often?"

Angel grinned. "Often enough."

Kent was fairly sure he was being played, so he didn't react. Angel led the way into the main workout room and yelled, "Consuelo. Kent Hendrix to see you. He's Ford's brother, so you shouldn't kill him."

A woman stepped out from a small office and shook her head. "What's wrong with you? Stop saying crap like that or I swear I'll turn you into a eunuch so fast you won't have time to scream."

She continued speaking, at least Kent assumed so. Her lips were moving. But he couldn't hear, couldn't think, and he was pretty sure he'd stopped breathing.

It wasn't that she was beautiful. The word didn't do her justice. Nor did *hot* or *incredible*. He was pretty sure there wasn't a word significant enough to describe the petite, brunette *goddess* walking toward him.

She wore cargo pants and a tank top. Neither left anything to the imagination. Her body was the perfect combination of curves and muscles, but it was her face that captured his attention. She had large eyes and a full mouth. Her long hair seemed to move with every step. She epitomized both sex and femininity.

He felt as if he'd been kicked in the gut by a pack mule. There wasn't a cell in his body that hadn't noticed her, and for the first time since high school, he was terrified of getting an erection and embarrassing himself.

Angel started laughing. "Told you," he said, not bothering to keep his voice down. He walked toward the exit, then paused to yell back, "Be gentle. He's a civilian."

Kent swore under his breath.

Consuelo scowled. "He's annoying and later I'll punish him." She shook her head, then looked at Kent. "Hi. I'm not sure we've actually met. I'm Consuelo Ly."

She held out her hand. Kent didn't want to take it in his. Oh, he *wanted* to, but he was terrified about what would happen. He thought he could either grab her and try to kiss her or actually ejaculate in his pants. Neither scenario had a positive outcome.

"Kent Hendrix," he said, then braced himself for the onslaught and shook hands with her.

The second their skin touched, he felt as if he'd been set on fire. The good news was the sudden shock of heat was so intense he wasn't in danger of getting hard. The bad news was his brain went completely blank and he was relatively sure he'd lost the ability to speak.

"I've known Ford for years," she said, releasing his fingers. She smiled. "I won't hold that against you."

He swore silently as the perfection of her smile cut him to the bone. The flash of teeth, the happy crinkle by her eyes, made her even more beautiful.

"Ah, thanks," he managed.

"You're Reese's father, right? He's a good kid. He has some talent. He and Carter are always trying to do more than they should. Typical for kids their age." She flashed the smile again. "I would say for *boys* their age, but you might take offense at that."

She was nice, he realized. Beautiful and nice. Talk about lethal.

He forced himself to concentrate. "Reese would like to take more classes here. Start training for a black belt. I worry he's too young. He's been playing soccer for years now and he's talking about giving it up."

Consuelo frowned. "Dumb-ass kid," she grumbled, then winced. "Sorry. I meant, sometimes students get caught up in the initial excitement of what they're doing and get overly enthused."

The realization that she was human, just

like everyone else, caused him to relax. He managed a full breath before saying, with pretend concern, "Did you just say 'dumb-ass kid'?"

"I, uh . . ."

"Is that how you talk to my son and your other students?"

She raised her chin. "Sometimes. When they need to hear it. Look, Mr. Hendrix, this is a dangerous sport and there has to be complete discipline. I work with military experts and trained assassins. I also work with civilians and every now and then I forget who has delicate sensibilities and who doesn't. If that gets your panties in a twist, then I'm probably not the best instructor for Reese."

"My panties in a twist?"

She flushed. "I probably shouldn't have said that, either."

"Probably not."

He folded his arms across his chest, aware that he was much taller than her. Not that it would help him in any kind of altercation. He was a math teacher and she was a . . . He realized he had no idea what she'd done before she'd moved to Fool's Gold to work for CDS.

Regardless, he felt a little less out of control.

She looked up at him. "Reese is good. He's athletic and coordinated. Does he have that incredible talent that comes along once in a generation? No. Sure, he could get his black belt and he probably will. But to give up everything else to focus on this?" She shrugged. "I'd make him wait a year and see if it's still what he wants to do. Maybe add one more class a week. He's a kid — he should have fun, not make a lifestyle choice."

"I appreciate the advice."

"It's worth what you paid for." She shifted on her feet. "Are you mad about what I said?"

"Will you hurt me if I say yes?"

It took her a second to realize he was kidding; then the smile returned. So did the sensation of being kicked in the gut. So much for being in control.

"I'm not good with parents," she admitted. "I've gotten used to saying what I think."

"Threatening people, and when that doesn't work, beating the crap out of them?"

The smile broadened. "Exactly. Civilized conversation is highly overrated."

"I agree. Unfortunately, I don't have the freedom you do to say what I think."

As soon as he made the statement, he saw

the danger of it. Whatever connection he'd established with her was about to disintegrate like cotton candy in the rain.

She tilted her head and her layered, dark, shiny hair slipped over one shoulder. "You're a math teacher, right?"

"In high school."

She laughed softly and then put her hand on his forearm. He felt the heat of her touch clear down to his groin. "You're far more brave than I could ever be. Teaching teenagers math."

At least she hadn't run screaming into another room. "Not just math. Algebra and geometry. Calculus."

Her expression flashed with an emotion he couldn't read. She withdrew her hand. "Tough gig," she murmured.

He knew something had shifted, but he couldn't say what. Why was she okay with him being a math teacher yet she retreated when he'd mentioned the specifics?

"I like it," he admitted. "I like my kids and I know what they learn in my class can help them later in life. I have a special program for underachieving students. To bring them up to grade and convince them they can go to college."

He told himself to stop talking — that he sounded like the neighborhood nerd showing off his homemade rocket.

"A worthy goal," she said and took a step back.

A clear dismissal, he thought grimly, knowing he'd never had a chance and wondering where he'd gone so very wrong.

"I appreciate your time," he said. "Thanks for the advice."

"You're welcome. He's a great kid. You're obviously a good dad."

Kent nodded and left. As he walked to his car, he was conscious of the irony of the situation. After years of thinking he was still desperately in love with his ex-wife, despite the fact that she'd left him, he'd finally been willing to admit the truth. That she had abandoned him and her son and he'd been a fool to marry her in the first place. Determined to get on with his life, he wanted to start dating. To find someone special and fall in love.

Just his luck the first woman to capture his attention wanted absolutely nothing to do with him.

Ford stood in the emergency room's waiting area of the Fool's Gold Hospital wondering why this kind of thing always happened to him. He'd only meant to do what Leonard asked. A friendly tap to the jaw.

73

He'd figured the other man would drop to the ground, what with never having been in a fight in his life. He would guess Leonard's idea of physical toughness was to wash the car without putting on gloves.

As expected, Leonard's legs had collapsed immediately. Unfortunately, as he'd gone down, he'd hit his head on the side of the Jeep and been knocked out cold. Which meant the 9-1-1 call had been a good idea. Only Ford had meant it to be preventive, not necessary.

"There you are!"

He turned and saw a medium-height woman with blue eyes and shoulder-length blond hair walking purposefully toward him. She was curvier than he remembered, and obviously pregnant, but otherwise pretty much the same. Except the last time he'd seen Maeve, she'd been in tears, and this time she looked as if she could spit fire.

"What is wrong with you?" she demanded. "What kind of moron goes around hitting other people?"

"I —"

"Tell me he's okay. Damn it, Ford, I can't believe you did this."

"He —"

"Oh, sure. Blame it on Leonard. Do you think I don't know why he went to see you?"

She poked him in the chest. "Since you've been back in town, you're all he could talk about. How he wanted to apologize and make things right. It's been fourteen *years.* How on earth could anyone still be holding a grudge?"

"I —"

She glared at him. "You *are* over what happened, aren't you?"

"Yes." He paused to assess the truth of the statement. "Very."

She raised her eyebrows.

He cleared his throat. "Not that you're not lovely."

She shoved him back a couple of steps. For a woman of her size and pregnancy trimester, she packed a punch. "You *hit* him!"

"He asked me to. He insisted. I didn't hit him that hard. He hit his head on the way down. It wasn't my fault." He moved back voluntarily, thinking the more room between him and Maeve, the better.

"He's a responsible person, unlike you," she snapped. "The father of four and a half children. Did you think of that when you tried to kill him?"

"I didn't try to kill him. Look, Leonard came to me."

"Yes, and I expected you to be the adult

in the situation. I see that was wrong. You're exactly who you were when you left."

"Hey, that's not fair."

She narrowed her gaze. "I'll tell you what's not fair. That my husband and the father of my children is in the hospital with a concussion because of what you did."

"He hit his head," Ford repeated helplessly.

The door to the waiting room opened and two uniformed officers walked in. The taller of the two women moved toward him. "Ford Hendrix?" she asked.

He nodded.

"We're going to have to take a statement."

"Serves you right," Maeve told him. "I hope they lock you away forever."

She stalked off. Ford followed the police officers to a quiet corner of the waiting area and knew his life couldn't get any worse.

Only he was wrong because, just when he was explaining what had happened, his mother arrived. She hurried over to him.

"See?" she said, her voice oddly triumphant. "None of this would have happened if you'd just gotten married like I told you."

Ford paced the length of Isabel's kitchen. She watched him move, feeling a little like watching one of the powerful cats at the zoo.

She was standing close enough to sense his frustration and energy, but she didn't have to worry about him turning on her and expecting her to be dinner.

The analogy made her smile. Now that she knew her brother-in-law was going to be fine, she could see the humor in the situation. Not that Ford had gotten there yet.

"It's not my fault," he muttered for maybe the thousandth time since he'd arrived. "He wanted me to hit him. He begged me."

"Next time you shouldn't listen."

He turned to her. "Thanks for the news flash."

"Hey, don't take your temper out on me. I'm not the one who coldcocked a guy six inches shorter and fifty pounds lighter. A guy who wears glasses."

Ford groaned. "He took them off and put them in his pocket. It's so Leonard."

She stepped in front of him. "Look, he's going to be fine. He explained what happened and his story matched yours. He's not pressing charges. You're right. It's not your fault he hit his head."

"Tell Maeve that."

Isabel had heard that her sister had gone a little crazy when she'd been told what had happened.

"She and Leonard have been together a

long time. She loves him. She didn't expect her ex-fiancé to beat the crap out of him and leave him for dead."

Ford flinched.

She grabbed him by the upper arms. "Sorry. I'm teasing. Everything is okay."

"They're keeping him overnight for observation."

"A precaution."

"Maeve is pregnant. She has four other kids."

"I come from a long line of good breeders."

His dark eyes remained troubled. "I could have killed him."

"He's going to be fine. Obviously he's been waiting for this moment for years. You've given him closure and a great story. In the future, keep your bullying ways for your tough friends."

"I know," he muttered, then shook his head. "I thought I was making things better for Leonard. I thought . . ."

Not knowing what else to do, Isabel tried to pull Ford close. He was about as movable as a house, so instead she stepped close and wrapped her arms around him.

He was taller than her, broader and solid muscle. But he was also warm and in need, so she hung on, even when he just stood there.

After a couple of seconds, he put his arms around her and hugged her back. She rested her cheek on his shoulder, thinking this was nice. This was —

Without wanting to, she noticed her breasts were nestled right against his chest. And that her thighs were brushing his. She found herself getting a little tingly and thinking it would be nice if he kissed her again. Only this time, with a little passion and maybe some tongue.

The concept was so shocking she jumped back. Fortunately, Ford didn't seem to notice her retreat or her panic.

"If you'd heard my mother," he said, bracing his hand on the granite countertops. "She lit into me something fierce. She kept going on and on about how I needed to settle down, and if I would just get married, she could be happy. She brought up those women she'd found. She wants me to look at the applications."

"I don't think having a girlfriend would have stopped you from hitting Leonard."

"Probably not. Still, it would get my mother off my back." He turned his head and looked at her. "You're a woman."

She held up both hands. "Thanks for

noticing, but no."

His gaze didn't waver. "You're leaving, so there'd be no misunderstanding between us. You wouldn't want me to fall in love with you."

She was pretty sure he was suggesting some kind of fake relationship, and the answer to that was a very firm "No."

"Come on, Isabel, I'm desperate. Look at what's happening to me."

"You hit a guy. You did that yourself. Nothing is happening." She made air quotes about the last word. "Leonard is fine. Do a better job of hiding from your mother. It'll be okay."

He straightened and turned toward her. Funny how, until right this second, she hadn't been aware of how much Ford filled up her kitchen.

"It's more than that," he said, sounding defeated. "Everybody said I'd been in too long. That I would have trouble adjusting to civilian life. I didn't believe them, but they were right."

She wanted to stomp her foot. How was she supposed to fight against the "I've been off serving my country" card?

"You're adjusting very well. This is a teeny, tiny setback."

"And there's my mother."

"I'll admit that Denise is a challenge."

"More than a challenge." His dark gaze settled on her face. "All this time I've been away, keeping you safe."

She took a step back. "No," she said firmly. "You're not going to try that again."

"Risking my life while you went to prom and got laid in college."

She covered her ears with her hands and started to hum. He raised his voice.

"You promised to love me forever. I have proof. In writing."

She lowered her hands. "Stop it right now."

"You went back on your word and broke my heart." He hung his head, as if defeated.

She stared at him. For a second she allowed herself to wonder what it would be like if he were actually speaking the truth. If he did love her, the way Leonard loved Maeve — with his entire being. Or if not Ford, then someone. Because Eric had never loved her. Not as more than a good friend.

She gathered her resolve and smiled at him. "You're going to have to solve this another way because I'm not going to be your fake girlfriend."

He sighed heavily. "I'm doomed."

"So it would seem. Want a beer?"

His head came up and he grinned. "Sure."
"And like that, he's healed."
"Hey, I'm a simple guy."

CHAPTER FOUR

Two days later, Ford walked into Leonard's spacious office. His friend sat behind a large desk. There was a big window behind him and bookcases on both sides. The space belonged to a successful man with plenty of money. Little Leonard had come a long way.

The man in question rose when he saw Ford and walked around his desk.

"Good to see you," Ford told him as they shook hands.

Leonard pointed to a sofa and leather chairs opposite the window. "I appreciate you stopping by."

When they were seated, Ford studied his friend. "You okay?"

Leonard pushed up his glasses, then touched the side of his head. "It only hurts when I breathe." He smiled. "I'm kidding. I'm fine."

"How's the jaw?"

"Painful."

Ford felt like shit. "I'm sorry I hit you."

"I asked you to. I begged for it." Leonard smiled as he spoke. "Come on, Ford. We both know I had it coming."

"I should have said no."

"You did the right thing. You gave me closure. I hit my head all on my own."

"Did you tell that to Maeve?"

"More than once. She's considering forgiving you. I wouldn't expect a Christmas card, though."

Ford nodded. "She was pissed at the hospital."

"Maeve takes our relationship seriously. She's explained she's not ready for me to die."

"That's nice," Ford said, knowing there wasn't anyone who felt that way about him. Not romantically. If he did die, he didn't doubt his mother would travel to the afterlife and drag him back, if she could. But the caring between a man and his wife — that was different.

He'd thought he'd loved Maeve once. Enough that he'd proposed. But after she'd ended things, he'd gotten over her faster than he should have. The other day, at the hospital, he'd felt nothing. More proof of what he'd always suspected.

He wasn't an "in love" kind of guy. He

liked women. He liked being with them and most of the time he enjoyed dating. But then they got serious and he got itchy feet. Having a woman say "Let's take this to the next level" was the fastest way to get him gone. He would request a transfer, move on and start the whole damn process again. Unlike Leonard, who'd been with the same woman over a decade.

"You've got those kids," Ford said. "Big family."

Leonard's shoulders went back as his expression filled with pride. "Two boys, two girls. We swore we were done and I was about to get a vasectomy when Maeve said she wanted one more. This time I'm going under the knife while she's still recovering. That way she'll be too distracted to stop me. Five kids is plenty."

"Must be loud," he said, remembering what it was like when he'd been growing up. He was one of six.

"I want to say controlled chaos," Leonard admitted. "But it's more uncontrolled. Maeve knows what's going on, though. She's terrific."

"Still a beauty."

"You know it." Leonard looked at him. "I feel guilty for staying here and living my life while you were off serving. I appreciate what you've done."

Ford waved away the thanks. "I took a different path. I'm glad you're okay."

They stood and shook hands again. "We should get together sometime," Leonard said. "Grab a beer."

"I'd like that."

His friend smiled. "I know this sounds strange, but thanks for hitting me. It made things right between us. I know Maeve will never understand, but I'm hoping you do."

Ford nodded. "We're even, bro. Next time, don't fall on your head."

"Next time I'm kicking your ass."

"Sure you are," Ford said, holding in a grin.

Consuelo strolled through the center of Fool's Gold. The Máa-zib Festival was in full swing. Around her, booths sold everything from jewelry to Celtic music. There was a food court and later the promise of live music by the park.

She'd been in town only a few months, but she'd quickly learned that the rhythm of life here was measured by the steady parade of festivals. The obvious pun made her smile as she ducked around a family walking along the sidewalk. Every month there were at least a couple of festivals and even more around the holidays. There were tourists everywhere, but she'd met enough locals to be able to offer plenty of waves and smiles.

She was on her own today. Something she was used to, but since moving here she'd made lots of female friends. A change she appreciated. But Patience was busy working at Brew-haha and Saturdays were busy for Isabel at Paper Moon. Felicia was running the festival and Noelle had realized that her plans to open *her* new store — the Christmas Attic — on Labor Day weekend meant days spent unpacking stock. Consuelo had offered to help. Noelle had promised to take her up on that soon, but this weekend she wanted to be by herself to figure out where everything went.

Leaving her at loose ends, Consuelo thought. Funny how in such a short period of time she'd gotten used to hanging out with her peeps.

She turned a corner and saw a tall, dark-haired man talking to an older woman. Kent was so attractive, she thought wistfully as he bent down and kissed the older woman's cheek. The woman turned and Consuelo recognized Denise Hendrix — Ford and Kent's mother. Kent said something else. Denise laughed, then walked away.

Kent started down the street. Consuelo watched him go, then started following, not sure what she was going to do if she caught up with him.

Meeting him last week had been unsettling. She'd known who he was for a while. Had seen the posters his mom had put up at the festivals and thought him attractive. But what had drawn her to him had been the kindness she'd seen in his eyes. Being close to him at CDS had been both exciting and terrifying. He'd been funny and charming and she suspected he'd never once pulled a knife on anyone. She supposed most men were like that, at least for other people. She'd always found herself in more dangerous situations.

But when he'd started talking about his work, she'd known she was in over her head. The man had gone to college. He had a degree and taught math. She'd barely passed her GED. He was educated and she was a kid from the street. A girl who had grown up in a bad part of town and gone into the army to escape. Once there, she'd been tapped for covert ops — the kind that had her doing anything necessary to ferret out secrets and then escape.

She'd had sex with men she barely knew in the name of getting the job done, and sometimes, afterward, she'd killed them. Hardly Kent's dream date.

Now, watching him, she told herself to turn away. That he could never understand and being rejected by him would hurt a whole lot more than any bullet. Yet despite knowing she was making a huge mistake, she couldn't help walking a little faster.

She caught up with him at the corner.

"Hi," she said, moving next to him.

He turned and saw her. His surprise was almost comical — or it would have been if she hadn't cared so much.

"Consuelo. I didn't see you. Are you here for the festival?"

"Yes." Despite her pounding heart, she managed a smile. "Don't I strike you as the festival type?"

"Sure, and women love this one. There's a parade later, and the Máa-zib ceremonial dance. At the end, a man gets his heart cut out."

"Are there a line of women volunteering men who have annoyed them?"

He chuckled. "Probably." His humor faded. "Can I help you with something?"

She swore silently. Obviously he'd noticed her withdrawal the last time they'd spoken. He'd probably thought she was blowing him off.

She knew how men saw her — they liked the curves and thought she was pretty. Confidence was appealing and she moved with a combination of grace and power. All the result of thousands of hours of training and ops. She'd had plenty of invitations and knew how to shut them down without a second thought.

But Kent was different. He was an ordinary man living in a regular world. If she had to guess, she would assume he figured she was telling him she wasn't interested.

"Consuelo?"

Right. Because he'd asked a question.

"Do you have a second?" she asked.

"Sure. Reese is hanging out with his friends today. I've got time. What's up?"

There was a bench around the corner on Fourth, close to the square of upscale boutiques. She led the way, thinking no one would be sitting there right now.

She was right and she settled on one end, then angled toward him. He sat down and waited.

"I'm sorry about before. How I acted when we were talking."

She drew in a breath. She'd never believed in being honest in a relationship. In her mind, telling the truth only led to more questions, and at some point, because of what she did for a living, she would be forced to lie. Only she wasn't in that line of work anymore and she was tired of having to be someone else.

She liked Kent. She'd liked him from the first moment she'd seen him, earlier that summer. She'd learned to trust her gut and it told her he was worth the effort.

"You intimidated me a little." She swallowed. "A lot," she amended. "When you talked about the kind of math you taught. Plus, the whole college thing. You're smart and educated and I'm not." She forced herself not to duck her head. "I got my GED, but that's it."

Emotions chased across his face. He was easy to read. Disbelief followed by confusion followed by what seemed like hope.

"I teach math at a high school," he told her. "I'm not a senior scientist at JPL."

She was pretty sure JPL was some jet engine–space business, maybe in Southern California. "I'm not sure why that makes a difference," she said.

"Most people don't think teaching high school math is that big a deal."

"I'm not most people."

"That's obvious."

His voice was gentle and slightly admiring, so she guessed he meant the comment as a compliment.

"I can't do algebra," she admitted.

"Yeah, and you could so kick my ass." He leaned toward her. "Seriously? I intimidate you?"

"Why is that so hard to believe?"

"Have you looked in the mirror?"

As soon as he said the words, his expression tightened. As if he regretted them.

She glanced down at the dress she'd put on. A dress! So humiliating and girlie. But she'd worn it deliberately, and she'd left her hair down after curling it. All in the hopes she would see Kent.

"I don't come from a great neighborhood," she told him. "I've spent my career in the military. I'm as good with a firearm as any sniper and I can open most combination locks in less than a minute."

His eyes widened. "Okay. That's impressive."

"Maybe from the outside, but I'm nothing like you. You have a great family and a regular job. You're a nice guy."

"Nice guy. Great." He turned away.

She touched his arm. "No. Nice is good. Nice is the goal." She paused. "I thought, if you want, maybe we could get to know each other."

Relief filled his eyes. "Yeah? Sure. That

would be great." He grinned. "What do you want to know? You've already heard about my family. Ford would have told you stuff." He frowned. "Whatever he said about me when I was a kid isn't true. You have to believe me on that."

She laughed, relaxing just a little. "He hasn't said anything bad."

"I know that's not true." He leaned back on the bench and stretched out his arm along the back. His fingers were only a few inches from her shoulders. Were he anyone else, she would assume he was trying to touch her or make a move. She had a feeling Kent didn't operate that way.

"What do you think about Fool's Gold?" he asked.

"I like it a lot. I wasn't sure at first. I've never been anywhere like this."

"It's not Afghanistan."

"How did you know I'd been to Afghanistan?" she asked.

"I didn't. I thought I was making a joke. Why, were you there?"

She shook her head. "I can't say."

He studied her for a second. "Okay. Let's talk about this town. Festivals, tourists. Not very exciting."

"I like that. I'm ready for calm and quiet." She tilted her head. "Ford mentioned you'd recently moved back yourself."

"A couple of years ago. I'd been divorced awhile and wanted a change."

"Why a math teacher?"

His smile was self-deprecating. "I'm a nerd. I can't help it. I like math and science, but I wasn't brilliant enough for anything theoretical. I thought about engineering, but after a couple of classes, I knew it wasn't my thing." He shrugged. "I like being around kids. I like the look on their faces when they figure out something difficult."

"You're the teacher they're going to remember twenty years from now," she said.

"I hope so. You know anything about dogs?"

She smiled. "I know what they are, but I've never had one."

"Carter, Reese's friend, got a German shepherd puppy. Now Reese wants one. I'm not sure we're ready for a puppy. We already have a dog — Fluffy." He held up his hand. "I didn't name her."

Her smile broadened. "Fluffy?"

"My sister is responsible for that. Fluffy was in training to be a therapy dog, but she flunked out. We took her, but she was close to a year when we got her. Now Reese thinks it would be cool to have a puppy. I'm less sure."

"I know Felicia is taking their puppy into the office, but it's not a school. She has more flexibility."

"Felicia is Carter's stepmom, right?"

Consuelo nodded. The sky was bright blue, the air warm. Kent wore a T-shirt over jeans. Sunlight brought out hints of brown in his dark hair.

She liked the way he smiled and the shape of his mouth. She liked how he seemed to relax as they talked and the way he kept his gaze on her eyes. Okay, every now and then he checked her out, but she was okay with that. Mostly she liked that she didn't have to try to be something other than who she was.

She wondered what would happen if she kissed him. Just leaned over and —

She drew back. What was she thinking? In Middle America, women didn't go around kissing men they'd barely met. It didn't work like that. There were supposed to be dates first, and the guy did the asking. She had a feeling Kent was way more traditional than she was used to and she doubted he would appreciate her taking charge.

She couldn't do this. Couldn't be like everyone else. She didn't know how, didn't understand the rules.

She found herself wanting to hit something. An hour with a heavy bag would go a long way to making her feel better. Or maybe she could run a quick ten miles.

Not wanting to have to apologize for questionable behavior a second time, she reminded herself to smile pleasantly as she rose.

"This has been really fun," she said, hoping she sounded genuine. "I need to, uh, go meet a friend. Enjoy the festival."

Kent looked confused, but he stood when she did and didn't try to stop her. "Sure. It was nice to see you."

She walked away as quickly as she could. Her eyes burned, but she told herself it was just allergies. There was no way she was getting emotional over a man. Not now, not ever.

"You're being critical," Charlie complained as she picked up a French fry.

"I'm not," Patience told her. "I'm just saying last year was more emotional." She turned to the rest of the table. "Last year after the parade, Annabelle was doing the special horse dance and then she was going to cut out the sacrifice's heart. She thought it was Clay, because he'd volunteered, only it was Shane and he told her he loved her

96

and proposed." She glanced back at Charlie. "You just pretended to cut out Clay's
heart."

"We kissed," Charlie grumbled. "Fine.
Hers was better."

Isabel laughed along with everyone else.
She'd missed much of the festival. Saturdays
were busy at the bridal shop. She'd managed to spend a little time there on Sunday
but had also wanted to catch up on the
store's books.

Noelle looked at her. "You okay? You're
quiet."

"I'm thinking," she admitted. Mostly
about Ford. The man made her insane with
his suggestions. But even more annoying,
now she felt guilty for telling him no.

She realized everyone was looking at her.

"About what?" Felicia asked, then bit her
lower lip. "Am I not supposed to inquire? Is
this one of those times when as a woman I
should wait for my friend to offer the
information or a time when I'm supposed
to prod her into telling?"

"Wait," Charlie said.

"Prod her," Noelle, Consuelo and Patience said at the same time.

Felicia nodded at Charlie. "You're outvoted."

"Yes, but that doesn't make me wrong."

Isabel was both amused and frustrated by her friends. "Does anyone want to ask me my opinion?"

"Apparently not," Felicia told her. "So what's the problem? Your reluctance indicates it must be about a man. The only other topics about which people are reticent are money-related topics. Sometimes politics, but we don't usually discuss . . ." She sighed. "Sorry. Sometimes my analytical brain gets ahead of me."

Noelle was sitting next to her and hugged her. "I love you so much."

"Thank you. Your support is gratifying."

Patience looked at Isabel. "Don't think any of this has distracted me. What's up?"

"It's nothing," Isabel said. "Really, it's silly." She paused, knowing there was no way she was getting out of it. Not unless she could think of a really good lie.

"Ford wants me to be his pretend girlfriend to get his mother off his back. I told him no and now I feel guilty."

Five pairs of eyes widened.

"I didn't know you were seeing Ford," Patience said.

"I'm not. We've talked."

"She came to CDS," Consuelo offered with a grin.

"Thanks for the support," Isabel told her.

"I wanted to clear the air. He's in the apartment above the garage. I didn't want him to think I was stalking him or anything. So we talked and it was nice. We're friends now."

"Have you had sex?" Charlie asked flatly.

Isabel was glad she hadn't just taken another bite of her salad. "What? No. Of course not. We're not dating."

"Technically, dating isn't required for sex," Felicia said. "With Gideon, I . . ." She pressed her lips together. "Never mind."

Patience grinned. "That's right. You were wild with him. I was so impressed." She turned to Isabel. "No wildness from you?"

"We're just friends." The brief kiss had been nice, but even though there were tingles, she wasn't all that interested in sex. The act never lived up to the hype, and she wasn't in the mood to be disappointed yet another time by a man.

"Didn't you used to be in love with him?" Consuelo asked. "When you were younger?"

"I was fourteen, so no, it wasn't love."

"You could use him as your interim relationship," Felicia said. "There's extensive research on the value of having an interim relationship. It helps break the emotional bond with a long-term partner. In your case, your ex-husband."

"She's helpful." Charlie picked up her

99

burger. "I like that about her."

"In addition," Felicia added, "from all accounts, Ford has a reputation for being an excellent sexual partner. Over the years, several women who slept with him have expressed their approval." She paused. "Not that I have personal experience."

Isabel felt her mouth hanging open. Even Charlie looked a little shocked.

"It's true," Consuelo said with a grin. "All the ladies say he's hot."

"Did you . . ." Noelle began, then flicked her wrist. "You know."

Consuelo shook her head. "Not my type. We worked together. I'm not interested in him that way."

"There you go," Patience said with a triumphant smile. "A plan and your friends' approval."

"I'm not sleeping with Ford!" Isabel announced, her voice a little louder than she'd planned. Patrons at other tables turned to look.

She lowered her voice. "I'm not. That's not what this is about. He asked me to help him."

"Be careful," Consuelo told her. "He's charming and sexy. Not to me, of course. I find him annoying and emotional. But other women are all over him. He tells them he doesn't do relationships and they never believe him. They always think they'll be the one to change him. And then he breaks their hearts."

"I'm not interested in forever," Isabel said firmly. "I'm leaving Fool's Gold next year and moving back to New York."

"So you're fine," Patience said with a grin. "But seriously, the fake-girlfriend thing? You need to tell him you want perks. Sexual perks."

Charlie raised her eyebrows. "When did you get slutty?"

"Since I started sleeping with Justice." Patience laughed. "I can't help it. I'm so happy and he's so amazing in bed. I want everyone to have what I have. Just not with him."

Noelle sighed. "I want that, too. I'm ready for hot monkey sex, even if it doesn't involve a relationship. If you don't want Ford, tell him I'm happy to be his pretend girlfriend as long as there are perks."

Everyone laughed. Conversation turned to sexual etiquette and then somehow moved on to Felicia's trials of potty training the new puppy in her house. Apparently dog behavior wasn't as predictable as the how-to books promised.

Isabel listened but didn't participate. She

felt uncomfortable — as if there was something wrong with her.

Did everyone like sex but her? Was there a secret she didn't know? Had she been doing it wrong all this time?

With Eric, a lack of passion was understandable, but what about before? Billy had been her first time, and the back of a truck wasn't exactly romantic, so maybe it wasn't a surprise she hadn't had much fun with him. There had been only a couple of guys in between, mostly because she hadn't seen the point. The kissing was nice and the touching, but when things progressed beyond that, she lost interest.

When lunch was over, she still didn't have an answer to what about her was different. A problem for another time, she told herself.

They all walked out and started to go their separate ways. Consuelo stopped her.

"Do you have a second?" the other woman asked.

"Sure. What's up?"

"I need to ask you something."

Isabel smiled. "Honestly, I can't think of a thing I would know that you don't already, but go ahead. I'll give it my best shot."

"You grew up here. I thought you'd have insight."

Isabel nodded. "Sure. Is this a town thing?"

Consuelo shifted her weight, then glanced around as if making sure they were alone. "Not exactly."

Stranger and stranger, Isabel thought.

"I'm interested in someone," Consuelo admitted.

"I'm surprised." Isabel shook her head. "Okay, that came out wrong. I don't mean I'm surprised you like someone. I guess I'm surprised that you think you need advice."

"I know I'm attractive." Consuelo glanced down. "I work out. I have all the right parts."

"I think you're selling yourself a little short. You're stunning and sexy and you move like a panther." She didn't need a PhD in sex to understand that Consuelo had something that left other women looking as exciting as fence posts.

Maybe that was her problem, she thought. She wasn't sexy enough. If she acted sexier, maybe she'd be sexier. Something to consider later.

"The panther thing might be the problem. I want to be seen as a woman, not a predator." She made a fist, then relaxed her hand. "This is stupid. I can't change who I am. When someone annoys me, I punch him out. Who am I kidding? I'm not going to be nice and normal. It'll never work. Thanks for listening." She started to turn away.

Isabel grabbed her arm. "Hey, wait. You can't give up, just like that. I don't believe you simply punch people out. I've been annoying and you've never punched me out."

Consuelo managed a smile. "That's different. You're my friend."

"But still — you have the skills to control yourself. What's the issue with the guy?"

The real question was *who* was the guy? She couldn't imagine anyone in Fool's Gold upsetting Consuelo. The woman was always in control. Ford and Angel both jumped when she told them to. And it was pretty darned great to watch.

"We were talking and I wanted to kiss this guy," Consuelo said. "But I remembered that guys are supposed to make the first move."

"I'm not sure he'd mind you kissing him. He'd probably be happy."

"What if he's not?"

"Any—" She started to say "straight guy" only to realize that hit a little too close to home for her. "What's he like?" she asked instead.

"He's sweet," Consuelo murmured, glancing at her feet, then back at Isabel. "Smart and funny. Cute. A good guy. I like him.

But I'm not a soccer mom. I don't know how to be normal. You know, like you."

"Ordinary and boring, you mean."

"No. The kind of woman a man wants to be with for more than sex. I don't want to be a conquest. I want to be . . ."

"In a relationship?"

Consuelo nodded slowly. "He's the first guy I've liked in a long time. But he's nothing like me."

"Isn't that a good thing? Opposites attract and all that?"

Consuelo sighed. "I should just go kill something. I'll feel better."

"That's certainly one solution," Isabel said slowly, hoping her friend was kidding. "Or you could take a chance. Go out with him a couple of times. See where it leads."

"Maybe. Is the sex different?"

"Excuse me?"

"Between normal people? Without the threat of danger or death?"

Isabel opened her mouth, then closed it. "I'm so the wrong person to ask. I've never had dangerous sex."

"Right. It's mostly indoors and in a bed."

Except for those few experiences in Billy's truck, yes. "You prefer it outdoors? You can ask the guy. I'm thinking he'll be thrilled to be flexible." This was ridiculous. Talk about the blind leading the blind. "Maybe you should ask someone else about it. Someone more adventurous."

"I don't want anyone else to know. You won't say anything, will you?"

"No." First, because she'd given her word, and second, because there wasn't anything to say. She didn't know who they were talking about or what Consuelo was nervous about.

"Any guy would be lucky to have you in his life," she offered. "The next time a guy you like asks you out, say yes. If you want to kiss him, kiss him. If he reacts badly, please don't kill him."

Consuelo got an odd look on her face. "You're saying I shouldn't have sex with him and then slit his throat."

Isabel laughed. "Probably not."

But instead of chuckling in return, Consuelo shook her head. "I'm never going to get this right," she muttered, before stalking away.

Isabel stared after her, not sure what on earth had just happened.

Chapter Five

"I like the plan," Jeff Michelson said, walking with Ford through the CDS building. "The combination of challenging physical activities and classroom time is perfect."

"I'm glad you think so. The Gold Rush Resort has plenty of rooms for the weeks you're interested in, and we can extend the reservations into the weekend for anyone who wants to bring his or her family. We'll have transportation from the resort to CDS and run a shuttle into town. Car rentals are available, too."

"Great."

This was Ford's second presentation of the week, and they'd both gone well. He was going to get a contract from both. So far he was significantly above the projected sales target, but Ford figured with the company just starting, he was picking low-hanging fruit. There would be more challenges later as he had to hunt down clients.

The plan was for the companies to be so pleased they came back every year or two, which would give them repeat business. But it would take a while to kick in.

The two men went back to Ford's office. He confirmed the tentative dates, printed out the contracts and handed them over.

Jeff took the folder. "We'll make our decision this week."

"I'll hold those two weeks until Friday," Ford told him.

"You have other companies interested in them, don't you?"

Ford smiled. "We're getting busy, but don't worry about that. As soon as I hear from you, the time is yours. I'll hold the hotel block of rooms, as well."

"I saw the casino on my drive into town. Could we stay there?"

Ford leaned back in his chair. "You can, but I'll tell you, the casino offers a big distraction. Your people will stay up later gambling, so they'll be less focused the next day. If you want to offer them accommodations there, I would suggest they switch hotels Friday night and then stay the weekend."

"Good point," Jeff said.

They rose and shook hands. Ford walked the other man out. As they reached the parking lot, he saw two blonde women walking toward them and sighed heavily. Jeff noticed, as well.

He whistled softly. "They part of the team?"

"No. They're my sisters."

"Sorry, man."

"No worries. They're both married, by the way."

"Right."

Jeff nodded and got into this rental. Ford thought about ducking into the building but knew there was no point. He had no problem running from a fight when it came to his family, but Dakota and Montana would simply continue to hunt him down. Disappearing meant postponing the inevitable.

So he waited as the two women approached.

They were the same height, with the same attractive features. Brown eyes, blond hair. Montana wore hers longer. Their other triplet — Nevada — was missing, but Ford knew he would be hearing from her soon enough.

"Hey, big brother," Montana said as she reached him and leaned in for a kiss. "How are you?"

He hugged her. "Wondering how much of a pain you're going to be in my ass."

She stepped back and laughed. "Bigger than you know."

"Montana, don't," Dakota said, taking her turn for a hug. "You'll scare him off."

"I don't scare that easily." He put his hands on Dakota's shoulders, looked into her eyes and said, "No."

"I haven't asked a question yet."

"You don't have to. I know that's why you're here and that I won't like it. So no."

"It's about Mom," Montana informed him.

He dropped his arms to his sides and headed for the safety of CDS. If only there was some kind of security system so he could lock them out. There was food in the fridge — he could make do for a while. Hole up here until they forgot about him.

His sisters followed him inside. Once he reached the hallway, he couldn't decide where to go, which meant they had him trapped.

"She's really upset," Montana told him.

Dakota nodded, her gaze uncomfortably direct. "It wouldn't kill you to humor her."

"It might," he muttered.

"All she wants is for you to be happy," Montana said. "Is that so bad? She loves you. We all love you and we don't want you to go away again." Tears filled her eyes. "We missed you so much."

That low blow was followed by Dakota setting up for the kill shot. "Just one date. How bad could it be?"

"Bad."

"Ford, she's your mother," Dakota said, as if he were in danger of forgetting.

He could feel the doors of the prison closing. For maybe the thousandth time since coming home, he had the thought that life would be a hell of a lot easier if he didn't like his family. If he could ignore them or yell at them.

What they couldn't understand and he didn't know how to explain was his mother's plan was never going to work. He wasn't going to meet a nice girl and settle down because he wouldn't do that to anyone he liked. Most people wanted to fall in love and then stay in love. He didn't.

When he got involved, he had a short attention span. When things got serious, he got gone. That had been his pattern since the day he'd left Fool's Gold. He knew he wasn't still in love with Maeve, so it must be a character flaw.

He'd tried to stay involved, to emotionally commit, but no matter what he did, he got restless and wanted to leave. He couldn't summon more than passing interest. He'd liked the women he'd been with, but he'd never once been in love. Not even with Maeve.

But his family wouldn't understand. He came from a long line of happy marriages. His mother had been a widow for a decade before she'd been willing to start dating again. Except for Kent, all his siblings were blissfully married. Both sets of grandparents had successful unions that had lasted more than half a century.

"I'm seeing someone," he said, the words as unexpected to him as to them.

Montana looked pleased while Dakota's expression turned skeptical.

"How convenient," she murmured.

"It was hard to start dating a local girl before I got home," he told her.

"Uh-huh." She didn't sound convinced.

"Really?" Montana asked, always the most trusting of the three. "You're not just saying that to get us to leave you alone?"

He hated to lie, but if he managed to convince Isabel, then he wasn't technically lying to them. He was telling a pretruth.

"I'm very interested in Isabel Beebe."

"How interested?" Dakota asked.

He thought about how Isabel always made him laugh and the way she called him on his crap. The woman had mocked his car.

She was also sexy and he would like to do a lot more than kiss her.

"I saw that," Montana said, her voice delighted. "Did you see that?"

"What?" he asked.

"You got a predatory look in your eyes." Montana smiled at her sister. "He's really interested in Isabel. I guess there's something about the Beebe girls."

He opened his mouth to protest that it wasn't like that, but he remembered in time he was trying to convince them that it was.

Dakota poked him in the stomach with her index finger. "You better not be lying."

He rubbed the spot. "Is this how you act with your patients?"

She ignored the question. "Fine. We'll tell Mom what you said. But if she finds out this is all an act to get us off your back, you are in such trouble."

"I'm trembling."

She raised her eyebrows. "Not now, big brother, but you will be."

His sisters walked away. He told himself the sound of the front door closing didn't at all sound like the gates of prison. Because he had bigger problems than sibling threats. He had to figure out how to convince Isabel to play along.

■ ■ ■ ■

Isabel ignored the growing sense of concern. Her appointment that morning was with a new bride named Lauren. The twentysomething had brought along a disinterested younger sister and no friends, which was never a good sign. Lauren also had handed over pictures of her favorite dresses. While Isabel could duplicate the look, she knew that the styles wouldn't look right on Lauren's larger frame.

But she'd done as the bride requested. As her grandmother had taught her, better to let the bride figure out that the dress she wanted looked awful than tell her in advance. Only after the wrong dress had been discarded could the right one be selected.

Thinking of her grandmother relaxed her and made her smile. The older woman had loved Paper Moon. Making brides happy had been her life's work.

Despite the passage of time, the store looked very much as it had then. The basic setup hadn't changed in fifty years. There were displays in the large windows and samples on mannequins up front. A separate room housed bridesmaid and prom dresses. Mothers of the bride had their own space and separate dressing rooms.

Three beautifully carved antique armoires displayed veils, while a fourth had shelves for headpieces, including combs and tiaras.

Madeline appeared at her side. "It's not going well. She won't come out of the dressing room."

There were no mirrors in the bridal dressing rooms on purpose. The true beauty of the gown could be seen only from an array of mirrors arranged under perfect lighting. Isabel's grandmother had believed every bride was beautiful and had done all she could to make sure that happened.

"I'll get her," Isabel said, wishing Lauren had brought along a friend or another relative. The baby sister showed no interest in her sister's plight. The teen was curled up in a plush chair, texting on her phone.

Except for the technology, she could have been Isabel herself, fourteen years ago. Isabel hadn't been interested in Maeve's wedding gown, either, although the reasons had been different. She'd been in love with Ford and desperate to avoid thinking of him marrying her sister. She suspected Lauren's sister was simply bored by the process.

Maybe, in time, they would grow closer. Not that she and Maeve ever had. Perhaps there were too many years between them, or it could be because their lives were so different. Regardless, she and her sister were more like distant relatives than siblings.

Now that she was in Fool's Gold, that could be changed, she thought, telling herself to give Maeve a call in the next few days.

She knocked on one of the three large dressing rooms. "Lauren, honey, come on out so we can see how you look."

"I can't."

"Sure you can. Let's have a look."

Lauren made a small, unhappy sound, then flung open the door.

"I'm hideous," she announced as tears spilled down her cheeks. "I look ugly. I love Dave and I don't want to disappoint him."

Isabel hated to admit that Lauren was right, but it was painfully obvious that the dress she'd picked wasn't flattering on her curvy figure. The layers of ruffles only added bulk where it wasn't needed and the stark white color made her look pale and sickly. Mouse-brown hair and small eyes didn't help.

"This is the third dress I've tried on and they're all awful."

Isabel glanced toward the pictures carefully torn out of a bridal magazine. "Your choices are really lovely, but I have some different ideas. Would you mind if I picked a couple of dresses for you to try?" She smiled. "Trust me, Lauren. I know how to make your bridal dress dreams come true."

Lauren sniffed. "It doesn't matter. Dave is going to change his mind when he sees me in this dress."

"He's not, but it doesn't matter because I won't let you buy that dress. No bride is allowed to buy a dress here at Paper Moon unless she loves it and looks like a princess. My grandmother was very strict about that."

Isabel unzipped the dress, then handed her a thick terry cloth robe. "Put this on and meet me outside."

Three minutes later Lauren appeared. The robe looked as bad on her as the dress, but as she wasn't wearing it down the aisle, it wouldn't matter.

"This way," Isabel said, leading her to a small alcove to the left side of the dressing room. She guided Lauren into a chair in front of a mirror.

"Open that top drawer. You'll find mascara samples. Put some on. You get to keep the sample, by the way, so let me know if you like it. I can tell you where to buy it."

Lauren leaned toward the mirror and dried her eyes, then applied the mascara. Isabel got a brush from a drawer and ran it through the other woman's shoulder-length hair. With a few well-placed pins, she managed a fairly nice twist that added a little volume on the sides.

When that was done, she pulled up a stool and sat, then opened more drawers. She swept dark shadow along the creases of Lauren's eyelids, then added blush on her cheeks.

"No lip gloss," she said gently. "You'll get it on my dresses and then I'll have to kill you."

Lauren managed a shaky smile. "That might solve my problems."

"You won't say that when I'm done with you, young lady. Now come on. I'm going to show you a Vera Wang dress that is going to leave you breathless."

Hope filled Lauren's brown eyes. "You promise?"

"Yes. I promise. I'm very good at what I do and I refuse to let you ruin my record. Because this isn't about you — it's about me."

This time the smile was more genuine. "Thank you," Lauren whispered.

"You're welcome." Isabel squeezed her hand and started to stand. As she did, she saw movement in the mirror and realized Ford was standing in the doorway to the dressing area.

She ignored the sudden tightness in her chest and the way she felt lighter inside. As if some bubble of happiness gave her a little lift. She also ignored the broadness of his shoulders and the way his worn jeans hugged his hips and thighs.

"What are you doing here?" she asked. "There's too much estrogen in the air. If you hang out back here, you'll grow breasts."

He gave her a slow, sexy grin. "I'll risk it."

Lauren looked at him in the mirror. "Wow," she whispered.

"I know," Isabel told her. "Now let's go find you a dress."

She picked out three simple gowns made of gorgeous fabric with just enough detailing to make them elegant. Lauren looked doubtful but agreed to try them on and went back into the dressing room.

"Why are you here?" Isabel asked again, walking up to Ford. "Do not tell me it's about the fake-girlfriend thing because there are sharp objects in this store and I'm not afraid to use them."

He studied her. "You were great with her. The bride. I saw how you calmed her down."

"Thanks. I learned from a master. My

grandmother believed a beautiful bride was a happy bride."

He glanced around. "You sell a lot of stuff."

"It takes a village. And accessories. So what's up?"

"I need you to be my fake girlfriend. Hear me out," he added when she started to protest. "Two of my sisters came to see me today."

"And that is my problem how?"

"They're my sisters. They're relentless. They started going on about how Mom just wants me to be happy and that I had to go out with some of the women who had applied." His expression turned helpless. "What was I supposed to do?"

"Grow a pair and tell them no?"

"They're family."

A simple statement she completely understood. Family made life complicated.

"I said it was you," he told her.

"What?"

"I told Dakota and Montana I was dating you."

She opened her mouth, then closed it. Honestly, what was she supposed to say to that?

"Listen," he said, taking her hands in his. "I'm desperate. I'll do anything. Wash your car, paint your house. I'll give you money. Please. Just for a few weeks. Long enough to get my mom off my back."

She wasn't sure why she resisted. What did she care if people thought she and Ford were together? He was nice to look at and fun to be around. She supposed the problem was that she felt funny when she was close to him. Both intrigued and afraid. He was a sexual being and she . . . wasn't.

Her friends had urged her to indulge in a transitional relationship. Fake-dating Ford would certainly be that.

"What do you think?"

The soft question didn't come from Ford. Isabel turned and saw Lauren approaching.

The V-neck dress was perfect. The simple lines skimmed over her curves, making her look voluptuous. The sheen on the fabric added a glow to her pale skin.

Isabel pulled free of Ford's hold and walked to the veils hanging along the wall. She selected one with a simple circle of flowers and set it on Lauren's head, then helped her up to the raised platform in front of the array of mirrors.

Lauren stared at herself, her expression disbelieving. "I love it."

Ford disappeared for a second, then returned with the teen sister in tow. The girl blinked.

"You look great," she said, her voice filled with surprise. "I like the dress a lot."

"Sexy bride," Ford added.

Lauren flushed. "I don't know what to say," she admitted. "Isabel, you were right. This one is perfect."

"You need to try the others on, just to be sure," Isabel told her. "You're making a big decision."

"I'll help," the teen said, tucking her phone into her pocket. "Come on, Lauren. Show me what else you have back there."

They disappeared toward the dressing rooms.

Ford turned to her. "You really are good at this. Are you sure you don't want to buy Paper Moon and settle here?"

"Bite your tongue."

"Will that get you to say yes?"

She rolled her eyes. "You're serious about the fake-girlfriend thing."

"Didn't I make that clear?"

She thought it was kind of sweet that a big, bad SEAL was afraid of his mother and sisters.

"You make the rules," he said. "Sex, no sex, I'll make you coffee every morning, sweep up in here, you name it."

It always came back to sex, she thought.

Felicia had told her to find a rebound guy. Her friends had agreed. She didn't want a rebound guy — she wanted . . .

Magic, she thought sadly. She wanted the giddy, excited love she saw every day in her store. Women excited about marrying the man of their dreams. She'd loved Eric and had thought theirs was a relationship of equals and shared interests. She'd respected him and enjoyed his company, but there hadn't been magic. There certainly hadn't been passion, but that was probably as much about him being gay as anything else. She wondered if her first clue about Eric should have been how interested he'd been in the details of their wedding.

He took her hands in his. "Friends don't let friends get mauled by their families."

She laughed because he was funny and she liked him. She should do this, she told herself. She was going to be leaving in a few months. What could it hurt?

"I'll do it, but only if you promise to never again throw the whole 'I'll love you forever' thing in my face."

"Done." He pressed a quick kiss to her mouth. "Anything else? Want a kidney?"

"Not today."

"I have to get to work, but I'll see you later. Thanks. I owe you."

Then he was gone, which would have been fine, except there was something wrong with her lips. They were tingling in the strangest way. She had the oddest urge to call Ford back and have him kiss her again.

"I know this is really last-minute," Noelle said, twisting her hands together. "I thought I had it all together."

Isabel glanced around at all the boxes yet to be unpacked in the store. It was Wednesday and the grand opening was Friday. "You're in a boatload of trouble."

"I know."

"I had it easier," Patience said, picking her way through open cartons. "Brew-haha doesn't have that much retail inventory."

An hour ago, Isabel had gotten a frantic call from Noelle, who had realized there was no way she could get her store together by herself. Not in time.

Felicia was busy with the upcoming End of Summer Festival — aka Labor Day — but Isabel and Patience had been able to come offer help.

"We'll never get this done ourselves," Patience said. "Let me get reinforcements." She pulled her cell phone out of her pocket and pushed a button. Seconds later, she smiled. "Hi, it's me." Her smile widened.

"Uh-huh. Me, too, but that's not why I'm calling." She quickly outlined the problem.

"Tell him to bring Ford," Isabel said, assuming Patience was on with Justice, her fiancé. "Say that I asked."

Patience looked puzzled but nodded in agreement. When she hung up she told Noelle, "They'll be here in fifteen minutes."

"They?"

"Ford, Justice, Angel and Consuelo. You're going to have more help than you can handle, so let's get organized." She turned to Isabel. "So, what was up with telling Ford you were asking?"

"I'm his pretend girlfriend. He owes me."

Noelle looked surprised. "You agreed?"

"It's for a good cause."

Patience laughed. "Does the pretend girlfriend only get pretend sex?"

"We haven't discussed that part of it yet."

"Hold out for the real thing," Noelle said, "then remind me how wonderful it is." She looked at the boxes. "Okay, we need a plan, and fast."

The CDS team arrived as promised. Noelle sorted them into teams of two, assigning each a section of the store and a stack of boxes. She supervised.

"Already taking advantage of me, huh?" Ford asked as he ripped open a box of holiday teddy bears.

"As much as I can."

He handed her bears and she attached the price tags Noelle had given her. Ford then placed the bears on the shelf. They worked well together, establishing a rhythm. Her fingers brushed his on occasion, which foolishly made her remember the quick kiss from earlier that day. And thinking of the kiss reminded her of the tingling, which was just plain strange.

On the other side of the store, Angel and Consuelo set up Nativity scenes while Patience and Justice were filling bookshelves under the window.

"Need I point out you said you owe me?" she asked, trying not to smile.

"I knew that would come back to bite me in the butt."

He looked surprisingly sweet putting bears in place, making sure the tag was tucked neatly under one teddy arm. His hands were nearly the size of the decorative toys. He had big hands, she thought, then told herself not to be ridiculous. She was helping out a friend, nothing more. She wasn't *interested* in Ford. She'd let that go years ago.

"Did that girl buy the dress?" he asked. "She looked good in it."

"I told Lauren to take her time deciding.

She'll be back next weekend to try it on again. Then she'll probably order it."

"Are all brides emotional?"

"She was nothing compared to some of what I see."

He flattened the box, tossed it on a stack of other empties and opened the next one. "She was crying." He held up a stuffed reindeer the same size as the bear. "I'm getting there's a theme here."

"It's the whole holiday thing. And I don't mind tears. It's the screaming that gets to me."

"They scream?"

"Sometimes. Rarely at me, but often at whoever they bring with them."

He shuddered. "I'd rather face insurgents."

They continued to unpack inventory. After the reindeer came polar bears.

"They're just more bears," Ford complained.

"They're completely different."

"How?"

"For one thing, they're white."

He made a dismissive sound in his throat. "That's just crazy talk."

"If that's how you speak to your girlfriends, it's no wonder you're single."

"You're feeling the power, aren't you?"

She grinned. "Oh, yeah." Maybe she *would* take him up on his offer to wash her car!

By four that afternoon, all the boxes were unpacked. Noelle thanked everyone and promised big discounts when the store opened. Patience and Justice went off together to Brew-haha. Consuelo and Angel started off toward CDS at a jog, arguing about who had better form when running.

"You going back to work?" Ford asked, standing close enough for her to be aware of his height and the warmth of his body.

"Yes. Madeline's been handling things, but I have a five o'clock fitting. I'm meeting my tailor and acting as the voice of reason."

"Another screamer?"

"No, but the bride's mother can be difficult. I run interference."

His dark gaze settled on her face. "We need to talk about our debut. As a couple."

"Oh, that." Her good mood vanished. "Right. What were you thinking for timing? The festival this weekend? The store is open Saturday, but I'm free Sunday."

"Works for me. You going to be able to do this? Pretend to be interested in me?"

She found it difficult not to stare at his mouth. Kissing had always been one of her favorite things to do, and so far, Ford hadn't really kissed her. The light brush of thanks wasn't a real, touch-my-soul kind of kiss.

"We're friends," she told him. "I don't have to fake liking you."

"But this is different. It's more personal."

"Not that much more," she said. "It's not like we have to stage someone walking in on us having sex."

His gaze sharpened. "Did you want to have sex?"

"I — No! How could you ask? Sex? Us? I — It's not . . ." She pressed her lips together.

One eyebrow rose. "That's a lot of energy. I'm open to it, by the way."

She felt her face heating. "You didn't just say that."

"I kind of think I did. Don't act surprised. You're sexy and we have fun together. Don't you think it would be the same in bed?"

Not a question she was going to answer, thank you very much. Why would he admit he wanted to have sex with her? Why go there?

Before she could say that, something in his eyes shifted. It happened so quickly, if she hadn't been staring at his face, she would have missed it.

In that heartbeat, fun, charming Ford was gone and in his place was a man hungry for a woman. Even with her limited experience, she recognized the need.

Her stomach clenched as unexpected wanting ripped through her. She forgot where she was and what they were talking about. But then his charming facade slipped back into place.

He chuckled. "You don't have to decide right now." He lightly touched her face. "Think about it. My door is always open, so to speak."

"I — You —" She drew in a breath. "We're done here."

"I can tell."

There was probably more she should say. Something pithy or cutting or memorable. But her mind was blank and she was still trying to wrap her mind around the fact that he really might want her . . . *that* way.

After Eric she just couldn't be sure, but it was nice to think about. Better than nice. But also confusing. She sighed.

"I have to go," she said.

"You mentioned that."

"I'm leaving."

"Have a nice rest of your day. I'll pick you up at eleven on Sunday."

She wanted to tell him she wouldn't be there, that she'd changed her mind. Instead she simply nodded and stalked away, ignoring the sound of male laughter that trailed after her.

CHAPTER SIX

"This was not my best idea," Isabel said as she walked next to Ford. She wasn't sure which was more difficult to deal with — the feel of his fingers laced with hers, or the fact that they were in the middle of the End of Summer Festival, surrounded by pretty much everyone they knew. It was only a matter of time until someone noticed the handholding and commented on it. Worse, she couldn't help *liking* the warmth of his light touch, the way their shoulders brushed occasionally. Being around Ford made her feel good — it just wasn't enough to counteract the compelling need to vomit.

"What was your best idea?" he asked.

"What?"

"You said this wasn't your best idea. What was?"

She turned and stared at him. He wore jeans and a T-shirt and had on mirrored sunglasses. He looked good. Better than

good — he looked fit and sexy and dangerous.

"I have no idea what you're talking about,"
she said, staring at tiny images of herself
reflected in the lenses.

For her faux-relationship debut she'd gone
with a blue summer dress. Simple, but with
great lines, and the color matched her eyes.
She'd thought about curling her hair, but
that had seemed as if she was trying too
hard. They were going to be walking, so
she'd picked cute, flat sandals that matched
the skinny belt she'd added.

"Relax," he said with a smile. "You need
to look like you're having fun or everyone
will assume I'm lousy in bed."

She came to a stop by a booth selling lav-
ender everything. Lotion, lip balm, infused
honey. Normally she would have explored,
but how could she shop with that comment
hanging between them?

"What does you being good or not good
in bed have to do with anything?" she asked,
careful to keep her voice low.

He removed his sunglasses. She saw
amusement in his eyes. "This is a new
relationship. You should be riding on the
high that is the thrill of being with me."

"Seriously? This is our public debut as a
couple, so according to the world, we

haven't been together very long. Why would I have slept with you so quickly? Are you saying I'm easy?"

"No," he said and lightly brushed her lower lip with his thumb. "I'm irresistible."

She was torn between rolling her eyes and acknowledging the faint humming that had started inside her. It was more sensation than sound. As if she were anticipating something wonderful.

"You have an inflated sense of self," she told him.

"Sometimes."

There were hundreds of people milling around them, live music in the park and shrieks from kids on the rides at the end of the street. Lots of noise that seemed to fade into the background as she stared into Ford's dark eyes.

"You're really annoying," she said, but there wasn't a lot of energy in her voice.

He leaned so close his lips lightly brushed her ear. "It's not even my best quality."

She shivered slightly and not because it was cold. What *was* his best quality? she wondered. And would knowing about it make things better or worse between them?

Before she could decide, Ford slipped on his glasses again and led her toward the area with all the food stands.

"Let's get some sugar into you," he said. "You'll feel better."

"Are you being sexist? Are you saying women like sugar?"

"You're defensive this morning."

"I know. I'm sorry. I'm nervous. What am I supposed to say when your mother walks up and asks about our relationship?"

"I'm keeping an eye out for her and will do my best to make sure that doesn't happen."

"Using your million-dollar SEAL training to avoid your mother? The navy would be so proud."

He bought her a lemonade. Isabel hated to admit it, but sipping the drink did make her feel better. She could do this. She'd practically been a pretend wife to Eric. Being Ford's pretend girlfriend couldn't be more difficult than that.

He put his arm around her as they continued walking.

"How are the brides?" he asked.

"They're good. I dealt with the interfering mother, talked another bride out of a pale green gown that made her skin sallow and averted a bridesmaid mutiny. All in a day's work."

"See, you're impressive, too."

His arm made her feel secure, all tucked

in against him. He was just tall enough that she fit against him perfectly. She could feel the muscles of his body shifting, bunching, releasing as they walked. Eric had been in decent shape, but leaner than Ford. He had narrow shoulders and a much smaller chest.

Ford exuded power — both physical and mental. It wasn't that he was a brainiac so much that he was determined. Mental toughness, she supposed. Something that had never been her forte.

"You know what you're doing in the store," he said. "You've been away from it for a long time. Did it all just come back?"

"Mostly. I have my grandmother to thank for that. I spent weekends with her and she was usually in the store. I learned by watching her. She was so great with the brides. She knew exactly what to say. Or not say. Sometimes she spent the whole afternoon keeping the mother-of-the-bride occupied. She kept games and toys in a box in the office in case there were younger kids."

His hand tightened on her shoulder. "You loved her."

"I still do. It was hard when she died."

"I remember."

His words surprised her. She glanced up at him. "The letters. I mentioned her passing."

"You were sad a long time. I remember how I felt when my dad died. It was like everything changed."

"Did me talking about my grandmother remind you of that? I didn't mean it to."

"No. I understood what you were going through and I hoped it would get easier."

"How come you never answered my letters?" They walked past a display of seed-filled pillows that could be heated in the microwave and placed on sore muscles. "You probably need one of those."

He glanced over and smiled. "Or twenty. Depending on the workout."

She had a brief image of massaging him, her hands moving against his warm skin. Her fingers tightened reflexively on the cup she held as the imaginary Isabel bent down to kiss a shoulder.

What on earth? Fantasizing about Ford? Sexually? It would be one thing if she was picturing them out to dinner or walking on a beach, but touching? Maybe she'd been out in the sun too long.

She jerked her mind back to the present and retraced their conversational footsteps. But Ford got there before her.

"At first it was because you were a kid and Maeve's sister. I was over her, but pouting. I thought if I answered, you'd both think it was because I was trying to get her back."

"I would have assumed you were madly in love with me," she said with a smile. "Or at least hoped."

"You were jailbait."

"Right. Because that was the only thing keeping us apart."

"You did okay without me."

"I had some disastrous relationships."

"That first prom didn't go well, but I'm proud of how you handled yourself."

"Kicking Warren in his you-know-what? It made him throw up."

"It wasn't the kick — it was the alcohol. And he deserved it."

"It wasn't a great night," she admitted. "And Billy wasn't smart, either."

"You had a great time with Billy. You got highlights."

She stopped walking and faced him. "Seriously, you remember my hair?"

He grinned. "I didn't know what highlights were. I had to ask around. Then you sent a picture and I saw what you meant." He removed his sunglasses. "I liked the pictures. Watching you grow up."

"It was dorky to send them." She wrinkled her nose. "When you didn't answer, I nearly stopped writing. But it was almost like a diary. I figured if you wanted me to stop, you'd tell me. Or that you were throwing out the letters and what did you care if you got a couple more?"

"I didn't throw them out."

"It can't have been interesting. I was such a girl."

"The paragraphs about nail polish colors were kind of long."

She grimaced. "I feel like I have to keep apologizing."

"Don't." He shook his head. "Things happened while I was gone. I had to go to hard places and deal with tough situations. You kept me grounded. You made me laugh and sometimes you got me through very long nights. You have nothing to feel bad about, Isabel."

His voice was so gentle, she thought, swaying toward him. "Do you ever talk about it? What you did and saw, I mean?"

"No. I was debriefed. It's enough."

How could it be? "Do you have a group or something? A place where you talk?"

"Do I look like a guy who talks about his feelings?"

"You probably should. Or you could get a therapy dog. I've read about them. Oh! Your sister raises them."

He leaned his head back and laughed. A full-throated belly laugh that made her both smile and want to punch him.

"I'm being serious," she told him, when he'd stopped chuckling.

"I know." He kissed her on the tip of her nose. "I don't need a therapy dog."

"I'm just saying if you need support, you should get it."

"I already did."

She wasn't sure what that meant, but before she could ask, they were walking again.

"You really going to be able to leave all this?" he asked, motioning to everything going on around them.

"Yes, I'm sure." She drew in a breath. "Don't tell anyone, but I sort of am liking living here. I'm not staying, of course. My new business is going to be in New York. Sonia and I have plans. But this has been nice. I'd forgotten what it was like to be this integrated into a community."

"You won't be here when Lauren gets married. You won't get to see her in her dress."

"I know."

Her voice was wistful as she thought about the "memory wall" in the office. Another tradition of her grandmother's. Each bride brought back a picture. Some were of just her on her wedding day; some were the bride and groom or the whole wedding party. The photographs filled one entire wall and were now creeping onto another. She wouldn't be adding to them, nor could she be sure the new owner would continue the tradition.

"I'll make new memories in my new store. What about you? Except for your mother's desire to get you paired up, how is it being back?"

"Good. I like being around my family." He shrugged. "Mostly. My sisters can be intense. Except for Kent and me, everyone's married. Mom's with Max."

"That's right. The new guy. Have you met him?"

"A couple times. He's crazy about her and seems like a good guy. I'm glad she's happy. She's bugging me for grandchildren."

Isabel came to a stop and the cup nearly slipped from her hands. "You're not expecting us to —"

His mouth twitched. "Didn't I mention the kids?"

She shoved away his arm. "You're horrible. Don't tease about that. I lie awake nights thinking how much harder my divorce would have been if Eric and I had had a child."

He removed his glasses again and took the

cup from her. After tossing it in a trash can, he squeezed her fingers. "I'm sorry. I won't joke about having babies with you."

She was going to snap at him again, but suddenly she couldn't speak. Because the second he said "babies" she found herself enveloped in a longing so deep and profound it nearly brought tears to her eyes.

She was divorced. Not that she regretted the breakup of a marriage that had been a mistake from the beginning, but here she was. Twenty-eight and single. Starting over. While she'd never thought much about having kids, she'd always assumed they were in her future. She was traditional enough to want a husband in the picture. She'd worked hard, thought she'd done everything right, and now she was divorced, living in her parents' house, without a real job and only a few wisps of dreams to sustain her.

Ford grabbed her other hand. "What? You're having a crisis. I can see it."

"I'm fine," she said automatically. "It's not about you, so don't worry."

"You're my girlfriend. Of course I'm worried."

"*Pretend* girlfriend."

"You get worry perks. Come on. Tell me. What is it?"

She opened her mouth, then closed it.

"I'm a failure. It's been six years since I graduated from college and look at where I am. Back in my same bedroom, with nothing to show for how I've spent my time."

"Is this about missing Eric?"

"What? Of course not. He and I should never have gotten married. I mistook great friendship for love. I'd never felt passion, so I wasn't expecting it. I didn't notice the guy I was marrying was gay. How is that possible? I loved my job, but I was going nowhere. Now I'm here."

"Not for long," he told her. "You and Sonia are going to open your store and take the fashion world by storm."

Despite her sense of failure, she managed a smile. "Do you even know what the fashion world is?"

"No, but you'll do great."

He was trying. She would give him credit. "Thanks. Sorry to dump this on you. I'll be fine."

"You sure?"

She nodded. Eventually she would be. Maybe she hadn't been spending enough time on her business plan. She would call Sonia next week and touch base with her. They should talk more, she decided. Make sure everything was in order.

"I need to distract myself," she said.

"Maybe you're right about the sugar thing. We could get an elephant ear and share it."

"Or we could do this."

Without warning, he dropped her hands, which was sad, because she was liking the feel of his fingers against hers. Only instead of stepping away, he wrapped his arms around her and drew her against him.

She went because, well, she wasn't sure why. But when she got there, she found it was really nice to be pressed up against Ford. Before she could lean in against all those muscles, he lowered his head and brushed his mouth against hers.

The touch was unexpected. Hot and tender at the same time. Almost teasing as if this were a game. If so, she wanted to play, she thought as her arms settled on his shoulders and her fingers found their way to the back of his neck.

Without meaning to, without thinking, she tilted her head. His mouth settled more firmly on hers. The next logical step was for her to part her lips, so she did. He moved his tongue against her lower lip before slipping it into her mouth, where it tangled with hers.

Several things happened at once. The sensible part of her brain pointed out that not only were they in the middle of town,

143

standing on a street during a festival, but he was only doing this because he was trying to fake out his mother.

The rest of her quickly smothered the information with a flurry of impressions. The coolness of his hair against her fingers. The way her breasts flattened against his chest. The pressure of his palms rubbing against the small of her back.

A liquid sensation seemed to flow through her, stealing her strength and leaving her pliable and willing. Wanting stirred — nearly unrecognizable in its unfamiliarity. But the need to get closer, to climb into him and be completely a part of whatever it was they were doing, was inescapable.

He kissed her deeply, stirring her with every stroke. She answered in kind, wanting to arouse him as much as he aroused her. She felt heat on her cheeks, tightness in her nipples and stirring between her thighs. For the first time in her life, she was faced with burning sexual need. It both frightened and empowered her.

She felt less controlled and more driven by need. She had always regretted when the foreplay came to an end and things got serious, but not today. Today she wanted Ford's hands on her body. Every part of her body. She wanted him touching and rubbing and nipping until she . . . Okay, that part was less clear, but one thing was certain. The kissing wasn't getting it done.

This was what her friends were talking about, she thought as she hung on to him. This desire to be naked and touch and taste. She wanted to explore all of Ford, to discover where hard planes led and caress the unexpected tender valleys. She wanted to breathe in the scent of him, to have him hold her and fill her over and over again as he —

He released her.

She surfaced, blinking, out of breath and not sure what she'd been thinking. She was the one who didn't find sex satisfying. Ever. Why on earth would she be fantasizing about doing it with Ford?

"Okay, then," he said, his voice slightly strangled. "I thought that would be a little more PG-rated." He ran his hand through his hair. "Next time, give a guy some warning."

She stared at him. "Warning?"

She started to move away and he grabbed her. "Not so fast. I need a minute."

She didn't understand what he was talking about. Then her gaze dropped to his jeans and she saw a massive erection straining against his fly.

Consuelo had warned her that Ford liked all women and he obviously knew how to kiss. So the fact that he was aroused wasn't something she should take personally. Still, it was nice to know he'd been caught off guard, too.

"I know that smile," he grumbled.

"What?"

"You're feeling smug."

She grinned. "I am," she admitted. "More than a little. We should get you something cold to drink."

"Just give me a second. I'm thinking about kittens. Kittens aren't sexy."

She rested her palm on his stomach. "Anything I can do to help?"

He grabbed her by the wrist and pulled her hand away. "Don't do that. Not doing that would help."

She giggled, inspired by her newfound power. He sighed heavily, then put his arm around her.

"Why did I think you'd make this easy?" he asked.

"I have no idea. Because it's so much more fun to make it hard."

Despite the fact that it was late afternoon, the festival was going strong. Consuelo hadn't planned to come to it at all, but somehow she'd been unable to walk away from the music and crowds. She wandered over to a booth where a pretty young woman was selling handmade jewelry.

The stones were mostly uncut, and thin strands of gold and silver had been wrapped around them to hold them in place. Tiny crystals swung from shepherds' hooks and dangled from delicate chains.

Despite the fact that she was on the short side and small boned, Consuelo didn't think of herself as petite. Nothing in this booth would suit her, she thought glumly. It was all too ethereal. She was sturdy, in her soul if not in her appearance. Pragmatic, with a foolish longing for whimsy.

She touched a bracelet, and as her fingers moved on the cool metal, she realized there were two men following her.

She'd seen them several booths back, when she'd stopped to look at a display of birdhouses. Mid-twenties, out of shape, a little drunk. One wore a baseball cap and the other had on a T-shirt featuring a gun logo. Good ol' boys, she thought.

They'd noticed her then. She'd slipped away but they'd caught up with her and now they were getting closer. She was going to have to deal with them directly.

The thought of it made her tired. She

wasn't sure if she was going to eviscerate them physically or verbally. This was a family-friendly event and there were pros and cons to both plans of action.

She turned, prepared to take them on. The guy in the baseball cap walked directly toward her.

"Hey, pretty lady." His smile was more a leer, with a hint of threat at the edges. "My friend and I thought we'd go somewhere together and get to know each other better."

A man stepped between her and the guy in the cap.

"I don't think so," he said, moving next to her. "You need to leave the lady alone."

Consuelo stared up at Kent Hendrix. Was he seriously trying to protect her? She was so startled by the thought she just stood there stupidly.

T-shirt Guy grinned at Kent. "Is that so? You gonna make us?"

"If necessary," Kent said firmly. He was close but not touching her. Larger than the other two. His voice was quiet, yet there was an air of confidence about him that impressed her.

The friends looked at each other. Then, like the bullies they were, they immediately backed off when confronted. Baseball Cap

Guy dipped his head.

"No offense meant, ma'am."

"It would probably be best if you two left the festival," Kent told them.

The men turned and started walking.

Consuelo put her hands on her hips. "What was that?"

"I noticed them following you. I wanted to make sure you were okay."

Okay? Okay? *Her?* "There isn't a man in a fifty-mile radius I couldn't destroy in hand-to-hand combat, and that includes your navy SEAL brother."

Kent nodded slowly. "I have no doubt."

"Then why would you try to help?"

"It's the right thing to do."

She opened her mouth, then closed it. She started to speak, then stopped. Was he from this planet? This century? She should be annoyed as hell, yet she felt oddly touched by his idiotic gesture.

He could have been hurt, she thought. There were two of them.

He lightly touched her arm. "I know you could have taken them. I just didn't think you should have to deal with them on your own."

She'd always been on her own. Even as a kid. Her brothers had been involved in their gang, and her mother had worked desperately long hours to keep food on the table and a roof over their heads. For Consuelo, friends had come from between the pages of a book.

Once she'd joined the army, she'd been part of a team. Until she'd gone into covert ops. Her assignments put her in harm's way by herself. There was always extraction but rarely backup. After a while she'd gotten used to looking out for herself and not expecting much of anyone else.

"Thank you," she managed at last.

"You're welcome. I keep running into you."

She glanced at his hands. They were smooth, with neatly trimmed nails. No calluses, no scars. He didn't carry a gun or even a knife. She doubted he'd ever killed anyone. No doubt he talked to his mother regularly, cared about his family, paid his taxes and drove less than five miles an hour over the speed limit.

"Want to get an ice cream?" he asked. "It's homemade. This time of year, they have all the fruit flavors. Pear ice cream doesn't sound all that exciting, but trust me, it's delicious."

She faced him, torn between what she wanted and what she knew was right.

"No one has ever asked me to get ice

cream before."

She made the statement defiantly, then waited for him to call her on it. Because she was going to tell him the truth. That men asked her for sex. Sometimes they used dinner as a pretense. Or offered money or jewelry to pay for it. She'd slept with men for her country, but rarely because she wanted to. She'd killed and walked away without looking back. She'd taken down enemy combatants, because there were a thousand places a woman could go that a soldier couldn't.

"Then you're overdue."

"What?"

"For ice cream."

He held out his hand. Just like that, as if he expected her to go with him. She should tell him to get lost, she thought. Only she couldn't. Instead she placed her hand against his and prepared to leap into an unknown world.

CHAPTER SEVEN

Kent led the way to the food court. He couldn't believe she'd said yes to his invitation. Not just because she was the most beautiful woman he'd ever seen and he was just some guy, but because she seemed skittish — almost like a wild animal. She was an intriguing combination of ultracapable and vulnerable.

When he'd seen those two guys, he'd known they were watching a woman, but hadn't known who. Stepping in had been his only option. When he'd realized they were following Consuelo, he'd been just as determined to protect her. Although he knew she was tough and could no doubt figure out thirty-six ways to kill them, he'd wanted to take care of her.

Now, with her small hand in his, he was both proud and nervous. He wanted everyone to notice who was with him, and at the same time, he was terrified of messing up.

She barely came to his shoulder. Her long hair tumbled down her back and shoulders in sexy curls that caught the late-afternoon sun. He couldn't seem to stop looking at her, at her dark eyes, the sweet shape of her mouth. She was a fantasy come to life and he had no idea what she was doing with him.

"Where's Reese?" she asked.

"With Carter and the new puppy. Gideon's hoping they'll tire each other out."

She laughed. "I'll bet. Felicia's the true anchor in that family, and I'm guessing when she's away, both her men feel adrift."

"He's just getting used to having a son. That has to be tough. I got to grow into taking care of Reese."

He drew her to a stop and pointed to the rows of booths. "The choice is yours. What's your pleasure? Tacos? Pulled pork? Ribs? Or homemade ice cream?"

She thought for a second. "I am kind of hungry. Maybe a couple of tacos and then ice cream?"

"Done."

He went to get the tacos and drinks while she headed toward the ice-cream stand. When he tried to give her money for the food, she raised her eyebrows.

"Seriously? I can afford it. Two scoops, even."

"I'm not saying you can't."

Her mouth twisted. "I know. You're being a nice guy."

Words designed to make him wince. Nice. He didn't want to be nice. He wanted her to think of him as intriguing, sexy and . . .

Kent ordered the tacos and drinks. Who was he kidding? Him sexy? Not likely. She was every man's fantasy. He knew the drill. Women who looked like her liked rich guys or dangerous guys or men who flew jets. They didn't sit around dreaming about falling in love with a high school math teacher.

They met back at a table in the shade. There was a band playing just far enough away that the music was pleasant background accompaniment and they could still talk.

"Carnitas and chicken," he said, pointing to the two plates of food. Both types of tacos had come with rice and beans, along with a handful of chips. "Which would you like?"

"Both," she said easily, switching one of the tacos with the other. "Is that okay?"

"Sure."

She wore jeans and a CDS T-shirt. No jewelry, not even a watch. She didn't carry a handbag like other women. Her jeans were tight enough that he knew her cell phone was in her front left pocket and she had the best ass he'd ever seen, including the Victoria's Secret special on TV and the *Sports Illustrated* swimsuit edition.

She picked up a taco and took a bite, then put it back down and chewed. He passed out napkins and told himself to act normal.

"You want to tell me why you're staring at me?" she asked, her voice conversational.

So much for being subtle, he thought grimly. "Uh, sure. You're beautiful."

The words were out before he could stop them and he braced himself for laughter, a scathing rebuke or her simply walking away.

Consuelo put down the taco and gazed at him. "That's it?" she asked. "You can't do better than that?"

"It's the truth." He smiled. "You're out of my league and I know it, but I'm not going to waste the opportunity."

She surprised him by ducking her head. "I'm not out of your league."

"You're used to guys like my brother. Soldiers. Operatives."

She wrinkled her nose. "Not my type."

"What *is* your type?" If only she would say "Single fathers in their mid-thirties with unremarkable jobs."

"It's been a long time since I've had a type," she told him. "Am I anything like your ex?"

"No. Nothing. She was tall and blonde. Cool, if you know what I mean." *Icy* was a better word, but he rarely spoke ill of Lorraine. There were a lot of reasons. Some of them were about how he'd been raised and some were about pride. There was also that she would always be Reese's mom.

"Where'd you meet?"

"College. I was a math major. She was studying business. We ended up in the same off-campus apartment building our senior year. Her roommate liked to party. One night, just before midterms, she knocked on my door and asked if she could please study in a closet. I offered her the kitchen table."

"Of course you did." She sighed. "Because it was polite."

"I wasn't going to make her study in a closet." He wouldn't do that to anyone. "We started hanging out. One thing led to another." He paused, not sure how much to tell.

"And?" she prompted.

"She got pregnant," he admitted. "We found out right after graduation. I loved her, so proposing was easy. We got married and Reese came along." He picked up his taco, then put it down. "I don't know how she felt about me or being pregnant. I don't think she was happy. Maybe she went along because it was easier than not."

"Did you know she was going to leave?"

"I wasn't surprised. I knew she wasn't happy for a while, but I figured that was the stress of work and life and having a kid. We went through a couple of rough patches, but I thought we'd work them out. Then she was gone."

He'd been in shock. He'd come home one day and there had been only a note. For a long time he'd thought she would come back, but she never did. Not even for her son.

That was the part he couldn't understand — her total rejection of her child. What kind of person did that? At first she'd seen him occasionally, but even that had ended.

"You're not going to call her names, are you?" Consuelo asked.

"No. I don't blame her for leaving me, but she shouldn't have left Reese, too. It's been hard on him."

"He's a good kid," she told him. "You did well."

"Thanks. A couple of years ago, I realized he needed more family around. I guess I did, too. So we moved back here. It was the right decision."

She watched him intently. He couldn't tell what she was thinking, but the fact that she was asking questions seemed like a good sign.

"I'm glad we ran into each other," he said. "There's a concert later. Want to go with me?"

"I'm sorry, but no," she said quietly.

Nothing about her expression changed, so at first he didn't get what she was telling him. Then she rose, collected her plate, drink and plastic fork and threw them in the trash.

"Bye, Kent," she said, then turned and walked away.

Tuesday morning Ford wandered over to Isabel's house. He could have gone to the office, but there wasn't much point. The contracts had been signed with the new companies, and until it was time to put the actual courses together, he was at loose ends. He needed coffee. Not that he didn't have some at his place, but he was pretty sure Isabel's was better.

He went up to the back door and knocked loudly. It swung open. Unlocked, of course. This damn town, he thought as he strolled in. Sure enough, a fresh pot of coffee sat in a carafe. He took two mugs from the cupboard and poured. He didn't think he'd ever learned how Isabel took hers, so he left it black. He could add whatever she wanted later.

He carried both mugs down the hall, pausing to take a sip of his. He passed the master, a guest room, a study. At the end were two open doors. One led to a bedroom with an unmade full-sized bed. The walls were pink. There were shelves filled with books, pictures in frames and trophies. A couple of tattered stuffed animals sat on a wide window seat. The furniture was white, as was the desk with a sleek laptop on it. Several pairs of shoes had been kicked to the side of the room.

The space was an intriguing combination of Isabel as a teenager and her today. The old and the new.

On the opposite side of the hall was the half-open door to a bathroom. Isabel stood in front of a mirror. She wore a short blue robe. Her hair was up in electric curlers and she was carefully applying mascara.

He leaned against the wall to watch.

Most guys weren't that interested in the process — they wanted the result. But he'd always enjoyed watching a woman get ready. Maybe he was trying to see where the magic went. All those potions in pots and jars, he thought with a smile.

Isabel put down the mascara, glanced into

the mirror, saw him, then jumped and screamed.

She pulled the door all the way open. "What the hell are you doing? You scared the crap out of me." She pressed a hand to her chest. "I think I'm going to have a heart attack."

"Your back door was unlocked. How do you like your coffee?" He handed her a mug.

"Black. Thanks." She took the coffee and then glanced from it to him and back. "You just walked in here?"

"Sure. Like I said, the door was open."

"I forgot to lock it. I wasn't inviting you in."

He grinned. "Yet here I am, all the same."

She narrowed her gaze. "You're bored, aren't you? That's what this is about."

"I'll admit to having a slow day."

"So typical. My day isn't slow. I'm expecting several gowns to arrive. Do you know what that means?" She didn't wait for him to answer. "Unpacking and then hours of ironing. Want to learn the delicate art of ironing a wedding gown?"

"Not really. But you could thank me for the coffee."

"It's my coffee."

"I carried it."

She shook her head and turned back to

the mirror. "Someone needs to beat the crap out of you."

"I wouldn't have pegged you as a girl turned on by violence."

"I'm not . . ." She drew in a breath. "Never mind," she muttered from between clenched teeth.

She pulled out the curlers, sliding the round part back into place on rods and dropping the pins into a plastic bowl. Her blond hair fell to just below her shoulders in loose, sexy curls. The air was scented with some kind of floral body wash and maybe lotion.

He'd spent plenty of time on navy ships and could complete his shower in less than a hundred and twenty seconds. Including shaving and dressing, from the time he walked into the bathroom until he walked out, fully clothed, it was less than five minutes.

Civilian women weren't like that.

He leaned against the door frame, watching as Isabel bent over at the waist and shook her head, then finger-combed her curls. His gaze strayed to her butt, which pulled at the shiny fabric of her robe.

She was tall and curvy. He liked how she felt when he held her, liked the softness, the warmth. The way she'd kissed him? He was still in recovery. He'd expected to enjoy himself. He hadn't thought she would take him from zero to sixty in a heartbeat.

If they hadn't been out in public, he would have been hard-pressed not to try to convince her they had to make love that very second. Maybe she wasn't as off-limits as he'd first thought, he told himself. Little Isabel was all grown-up and he had to say he was a fan of how she'd turned out.

Isabel straightened and discovered that, yes, Ford was still there. Watching her with that almost smile of his. The one designed to drive her crazy.

"Step back unless you want to risk being turned into a woman," she said, picking up a spray bottle.

He did as she suggested, retreating down the hall. "I'm going to see what you have for breakfast," he yelled back.

"You do that."

She finished with her hair, then walked quickly into her bedroom. After closing and *locking* the door, she finished dressing. She tucked her blouse into her skirt, all the while telling herself she should be annoyed that Ford had simply walked into her house. Yet she couldn't seem to summon the energy. He was one of those guys women seemed to like, and she wasn't the least bit immune.

Still barefoot, she went down the hall and into the kitchen. Ford sat at one of the stools at the bar. There was a box of cereal on the counter.

"You don't have eggs," he told her. "Or bacon. What's with that?"

"I don't eat eggs or bacon in the morning."

His expression turned suspicious. "You're not one of those eggs-for-lunch people, are you? Because that's wrong."

"You are so strange. Would you also expect me to cook the eggs and bacon?"

"No, but it would be nice if you did."

"You do realize you have your own kitchen upstairs, right? You could buy your own eggs and bacon and fix them yourself."

He leaned back in the chair. "It's better here."

"I thought macho SEALs liked to be alone. That you were all so solitary."

"No. We're pack animals. Work in a team. Hang out together."

She hadn't thought of it that way, but understood what he was saying. "So now that we're fake-dating, I'm in your pack?"

He offered her that sexy smile of his. "Every woman's dream."

If he hadn't made her tremble and want for the first time in her life, she would have laughed at him. But as it was, she could only turn away and wonder if there was a polite way to ask him to repeat the kissing thing. Just so she could confirm it wasn't a fluke.

He poured them cereal, then picked up a banana and sliced half of it into each bowl. Last he added milk.

"What if I didn't like bananas?" she asked, sitting next to him.

"Then you wouldn't have bought it."

She sighed. "You have an answer for everything."

"Sure. If I don't know it, I make it up. You gotta keep moving forward. Otherwise whatever's coming up at you from behind will catch up."

She reached for her spoon. Ford had showered and shaved that morning. He'd pulled on a T-shirt over jeans, but his feet were bare. There was something a little sexy about sitting with him like this. Over breakfast.

The memory of the kiss hovered between them — an erotic specter. She was sure the moment had happened. After all, she'd been there. She'd felt tingles and zips and that all-important hunger. The sensations were new and heady and just a little scary.

She had a feeling her friends would tell her it was chemistry and that she should always embrace the quiver when she was with a guy. But what if that was all there was? What if the longing was her peak experience? She supposed, in her heart, she worried that she wasn't like everyone else.

"What are you thinking?" he asked unexpectedly.

She put down her spoon and went for a version of the truth. "Sometimes I wonder if I should have known about Eric. The gay thing."

"He wasn't admitting it to himself. Why should you have it all figured out? He said he loved you and wanted to marry you. You believed him. It's his bad, not yours."

"You make it all so simple."

"I'm a simple kind of guy."

"Your fake-girlfriend plan is more than a little complicated. How long are we doing that, by the way?"

"I don't know. Awhile. Then we can break up and I'll be crushed." He grinned, then scooped up more cereal. "You're moving to New York, so maybe we could date until then. That's a long time with my mom off my back."

It was a long time to be around Ford, she thought. There might be unexpected dangers. At least for her. She liked him and she liked being with him. Wasn't that how real relationships started?

"At some point you need to be able to tell your mother the truth."

"No, I don't."

"You can't spend the rest of your life lying to her."

She expected a snappy comeback, but instead his humor faded. "She won't believe the truth."

"Which is?"

"I'm never going to get married because I'm never going to fall in love. I can't. Or won't. I've met some great women who were in love with me. But the second they admitted their feelings, I was gone. I couldn't picture myself with them in two years, let alone fifty. I have no interest in anything long-term. Not now, not ever."

"You wanted to marry Maeve."

"I was young and figured we were supposed to get married. Don't forget how fast I got over her. That wasn't love."

"Maybe that wasn't but you're not giving yourself a chance. You haven't met the right person." She believed in love even if he didn't. One day Ford would lose his heart.

For a second, she thought about making a joke about it, only to realize she didn't like the idea of him falling for someone else. Not that she was interested in him that way, but was just . . .

She paused, unable to come up with an explanation.

"There's something missing in me," he said. "Something I don't get." He shrugged. "I like women. I like being around them, but picking one and staying with her forever? I don't see it happening."

Classes started in the morning. The information was right on the sign out front of the Fool's Gold High School. Consuelo could see it from where she stood on the sidewalk.

She hated apologizing even more than she hated being wrong. She hated being unsure and feeling stupid and a thousand other things that had nothing to do with why she was standing here.

She'd done it again. Walked away because she was afraid. Walked away from the nicest man she'd ever met because when she was around him she couldn't breathe.

She forced herself up the stairs and into the school. The polite lady in the office gave her Kent's room number and then pointed the way. Consuelo walked in that direction, still not sure what she was going to say.

She hadn't been able to sleep in two days and yesterday she'd spent an hour sparring with Angel. He'd finally collapsed on the mats, gasping for mercy, but she hadn't been done. She'd climbed ropes and finished with an eight-mile run. Even so, she'd spent much of the night staring at the ceiling.

It was all so ridiculous, she thought. The fear and her reasons for it. A man had asked her out and she'd run off like a frightened puppy.

She found the room in question. The door was open and Kent sat alone at the desk in front. She watched him for a few seconds, taking in the concentration as he looked from his computer to the screen behind him. A PowerPoint presentation flipped from slide to slide. No doubt he was preparing for when classes started.

The man wore a tie, she thought, not sure if she should laugh or whimper. A tie and rolled-up shirtsleeves, with jeans. The combination was sexy and appealing and she both wanted him and needed to head in the opposite direction equally. Before she could decide what to do, he looked up and saw her.

"Consuelo."

That was all he said. Her name. Just like

that. No hint of what he was thinking, no anger or frustration or disinterest.

She stepped into the room and walked toward him.

She'd dressed specifically for the occasion in her favorite cargo pants, an army-green tank and combat boots. She wore no makeup and had pulled her hair back into a tight ponytail. This was her at her core. She needed him to see that, mostly so he would understand she wasn't trying to be different. It, in fact, came naturally.

He rose as she approached. Of course he would. The man was polite.

"How can I help you?" he asked.

"You can't. That's what I came to tell you. I'm sorry about what happened at the festival. I *did* want to go to the concert. I wanted to a lot, but I didn't know how."

He frowned slightly. "Concerts aren't usually tough. You, uh, sit and listen to music. There's not a lot of interaction. Sometimes during the ballads you hold up your phone like a light. My mom swears that when she was a teenager, people held up lighters and lit matches. Sounds like a fire hazard to me."

Despite everything, she started to laugh; then the laugh broke off into silence and she was fighting tears.

What the fuck? She didn't cry. She mocked

the criers. She was tough. She was —

Strong arms came around her and pulled her close. She found herself held. Gently, without force. She could have broken free easily. A soft, low voice promised everything would be fine.

Large hands stroked her back, but in a comforting way. He didn't try to touch her butt or cop a feel. Instead Kent was, once again, the perfect gentleman.

She jerked free and glared at him. "I'm not like other women you've dated."

One eyebrow rose. "Which ones?"

"Anyone. Pick one. I'm not like them, those women out there." She pointed to the windows. "I'm not from here."

"Okay," he said slowly. "By 'here' I assume you mean Fool's Gold. Or the suburbs. As opposed to, say, earth."

She wiped her cheeks. "I'm not a space alien."

"Good, because I'm not a fan of interspecies dating."

"How can you want to go out with me?" she demanded. "I'm a mess. I'm doing it wrong." She remembered all the reasons men usually wanted to spend time with her. "Unless this is about getting laid."

"It's not."

She stared at him, wanting to believe.

He gave her a rueful smile. "It's not *just* about that. Because, hey, what guy wouldn't want you?"

"Do you know what I did in the military?" she asked, then kept talking because she had to tell him now while she had the courage. "I killed people. I wasn't a sniper, Kent. There were no long-range rifles. When I did it, it was personal. Up close." She felt her hands curling into fists.

"You don't need this mess," she told him quietly. "I'm sorry. That's what I wanted to say. I'm sorry. You must know that it's a good idea for you to stay away from me."

His dark gaze never strayed from her face. "Have you talked to anyone?" he asked gently. "A counselor?"

Her chin shot up. "You think there's something wrong with me?"

"I think you're in a lot of pain."

Words she'd heard before in the safe confines of a therapist's office. "I see someone," she said. "Once a week, in Sacramento." She managed a slight smile. "I'm getting better. Imagine if we'd met six months ago."

"I still would have asked you to that concert."

"I probably would have gutted you like a fish."

171

"Police Chief Alice Barns doesn't take kindly to that sort of thing."

"I'm more afraid of you."

Words she hadn't meant to say, but it was too late to call them back now.

"I don't scare anyone."

"You do me. You're nice."

He winced. "Great."

"No, I mean it. You're kind and funny and a good dad. Jeez, Kent, why are you bothering with me?"

"You have attitude. Reese likes you and he's a good judge of character. You frighten my brother." One corner of his mouth turned up. "And yes, you're the most beautiful woman I've ever seen in my life. Guys are visual — I'm sorry."

"Don't be sorry." She liked that he found her attractive. At least that was something. "I'd really like to go to a concert with you."

"Sorry, but the band is gone. Would you settle for dinner?"

She nodded.

"At my house," he continued. "Reese will be there. It's not a date. It's me inviting my son's martial arts instructor over. We'll never be alone. How does that sound?"

"Nice," she said.

He grimaced. "I'm cursed."

"Don't say that. You're the dream."

He chuckled. "Yeah, right."

He didn't believe her, which was okay. She knew it was true.

CHAPTER EIGHT

As Isabel unpacked dresses and hung them, she thought about what Ford had claimed. That he'd never been in love. The idea seemed impossible. He was so charming and fun — women must have fallen for him. Which was what he'd said. But he'd never reciprocated their feelings.

Not to fall in love. How sad, she thought, only she wasn't sure she was any different. Look at her disaster of a marriage. Was that romantic love? Certainly not on Eric's side and she was having doubts about her own feelings.

Isabel shook off the thoughts and finished unpacking the dresses. There were six in all. Two samples and four orders. She would let the dresses hang out overnight, then start pressing them in the morning.

As she worked, she glanced at the phone. She'd left two messages for Sonia and had yet to hear from her.

Isabel threw out the packing material and flattened the boxes for the recycling bin, then returned to the front of the store. A few minutes after one, a woman walked in, carrying a garment bag.

"Hi," the twentysomething said with a smile. "I don't know if you remember me, Isabel. We were in school together years ago."

Isabel stared at the brown-eyed brunette. She was about five-five, with pretty features. Memories flashed through her brain as she remembered a girl with two younger sisters whose parents had died in a car crash.

"Dellina?"

Dellina's smile broadened. "That's me. I wasn't sure you'd remember."

"Of course I do. How are you?"

Dellina put down the garment bag and they hugged.

"I'm good," the other woman said. "Busy. My sisters are doing well."

Isabel remembered that Dellina had younger sisters. Twins, she thought.

"I've spent the past few years getting them settled," Dellina said. "They're doing great now and I'm focusing on my business. I'm doing party planning and decorating in town."

Isabel nodded slowly. "I heard about that.

You were in charge of Charlie and Clay's wedding a couple of months ago. It was great. The luau was so much fun and everyone was surprised."

"Thanks. Charlie had to be sold on that idea, but it turned out well."

"Come on," Isabel said, motioning for her to follow her. "Let's grab a seat and catch up."

They sat in the plush chairs by the mirrors the brides used. Isabel was able to see if anyone walked in the store while she chatted with her friend.

"You've been in New York," Dellina said. "Impressive."

"Less impressive than you'd think," Isabel admitted. She briefly explained about her divorce. "So this is a bit of a change."

"It would be. I keep telling myself I have to pick. Either party planning or interior decorating. In a way, they're both about staging, which I like. But I can't decide and there's not enough business in town for me to give up one. So for now, it's both." She grinned. "And possibly a third challenge. Let me show you what I've brought."

She picked up the garment bag, then unzipped the sides. Two dresses hung from hangers. The first was black and royal-blue, with a scoop neck. The sleeves and sides were black, while the center of the dress was blue. Gathers pulled in the garment around the waist.

Isabel saw right away how the style would create the illusion of being smaller than you were in any size. The fabric was substantial without being heavy, and the dress itself was ageless. It could be accessorized to go from day to night easily.

The other dress was just as intriguing. There was also a jacket with a pair of black pants.

"I love them," she admitted, seeing possibilities for both using them in a display and wearing them herself. She mentally ran through her shoe collection and found at least three pairs that would work with each outfit.

"A friend of mine designs them," Dellina told her. "She's too shy to sell them herself and I couldn't stand to see them just hanging in her spare room, so I took them. These are samples of her work. I thought maybe you could display them here."

How could she? Paper Moon sold wedding gowns and dresses for bridesmaids and mothers of the bride. Not clothes a woman could wear to work.

She started to say no, only she couldn't seem to form the word. Her gaze drifted to the display window on the north side of the store. It was too small for a wedding gown, so they'd always used it for prom dresses or accessories.

If she pulled out the fabric background, the walls were stark white. Usually too harsh for her purposes, but the plain backdrop would highlight the clothes.

"Over here," she said impulsively. "In this window."

Dellina draped the clothes over a chair and followed her.

They quickly removed the shoes and veils. Isabel unhooked the pale pink, fabric-covered board that covered the back of the display window and the two of them wrestled it out into the storeroom.

"I have two spare mannequins," Isabel said, then pointed. There was a slim brass coatrack in the corner. "We could hang the third dress from that."

"It's perfect." Dellina studied the two mannequins. "Can we take their heads off? The look would be cleaner."

"And slightly creepier," Isabel said with a laugh. But she saw what the other woman meant. "Let's try it."

She reached for the mannequin, then stopped. "Wait a minute. I can't do this. I'm not staying."

Dellina stared at her. "I don't understand. Am I keeping you from an appointment? I can come back."

"No. It's the store. We're selling it. After the first of the year."

Dellina's eyes widened with shock. "You're selling Paper Moon? But it's been in Fool's Gold forever."

Not the first time Isabel had heard that statement, she thought grimly.

"What are these?" Madeline asked, walking into the back room. "Did you go shopping? Where did you get the jacket? I love it. And this dress."

She held up the purple one.

"Dellina's friend designed them," Isabel said. "Do you two know each other?"

"Sure," Dellina said. "Those are Margo's designs."

Madeline sighed. "You said she was great, but I've only heard about the designs." Her expression brightened. "Are you going to carry them here at the store? Will you offer an employee discount?"

"I was telling her about the family selling Paper Moon after the first of the year," Isabel said.

Madeline shook her head. "Don't talk about that. I finally found a job I love."

"I'm sure the new owners will want to

keep you on," Isabel told her, determined to put in a good word for her employee. "Besides, that's months away."

She looked from the clothes Madeline held, back to the window. "I'm not going to worry about the fate of the store right now. Dellina, if you want to put your friend's clothes in the window, you can. If someone wants to buy them, we'll figure out what we're doing then."

Dellina grinned. "I agree."

She and Madeline started dressing the two mannequins. Isabel left them to it and went to the front of the store. When they were ready, she would go out and check the display from the sidewalk.

This was good experience, she told herself. For when she and Sonia opened their own business. Retail was a different world, and selling original designs was even more specialized than wedding gowns.

Isabel picked up the price sheet Dellina had brought with her. It listed the inventory Margo had in her house and how long it would take to make a dress in a size other than what she had on hand. She could —

The front door to Paper Moon opened. Isabel looked up and smiled automatically. It was only when she recognized the other woman that her smile became a little forced and her throat got dry and tight.

Denise Hendrix looked around the store, spotted her and headed directly over.

Ford's mother didn't bother with a lot of chitchat, but instead went right to the heart of the matter.

"Are you really dating my son?"

Ford opened the refrigerator, then handed Isabel a diet soda. She took the can but didn't open it.

"You don't understand," she repeated, glaring at him. "I had to lie to your mother."

"I know. You've told me." More than once. "You knew what we were doing when you agreed."

She slapped his upper arm. "Knowing and experiencing are two different things. She was there, in my store, looking at me. I had to stare into her trusting eyes and lie. Do you know what that was like?"

"Yes," he admitted, ignoring the sensation of his collar getting tight. After all, he was in a T-shirt. He didn't have a collar.

Isabel shook her head. "It was so horrible. The way she watched me. It's like she knew I was lying."

"She didn't know. My mom raised six kids. She does guilt the way other people breathe." He put his arm around her.

"Come on. We'll talk this out and you'll feel better."

She stepped out of his embrace. "Being charming isn't going to help."

"It might." He was good at charm. "Look, Isabel, I'm doing the best I can. You think I like this? I agree — everything would be a whole lot simpler if I could just fall in love. But I can't."

She didn't look convinced. "Have you tried?"

"Yes. I come from a long line of happy marriages. I don't have any serious emotional trauma in my past. I like women. I don't know what's wrong with me and I'm sorry for putting you in this position."

Her gaze held his for a long time before she nodded. "Fine," she said with a sigh and popped the top on her can of soda. "I know you're not torturing me on purpose. It was just icky."

"I know. I owe you."

"More than you know. Your mother invited us over to a big family dinner."

"I'll delay as long as I can."

"You'd better." Her mouth twisted.

Oddly, her discomfort made him like her more. She was an honest person and it troubled her to be deceptive. This situation was his fault.

"I'll make it up to you," he promised.

"Yeah? I'm thinking the only way that's going to happen is if you learn how to iron a wedding gown."

"Why do I feel guilty?" Noelle asked, glancing uneasily over her shoulder.

"Because Jo has us all trained." Charlie squared her shoulders, as if determined not to give in to the pressure. "We aren't *required* to go to her bar for lunch every time. It's good to support all the businesses in Fool's Gold."

Isabel grinned. "Keep saying that, and maybe it will be true one day."

They were all in line by a gleaming silver trailer that had been converted to a rolling kitchen. Delicious smells wafted from the windows, and the chalkboard hanging by the open front door offered many tempting choices.

Ana Raquel, Dellina's younger sister, ran the "street cart," as it was known. She planned the menus and did all the cooking in her small trailer. Today she'd parked by Pyrite Park, opened all the windows and the door and fired up her stove. The amazing smells had drawn a crowd of hungry customers.

"You're helping a friend," Dellina said

183

firmly. "My sister needs the support. If Jo asks, that's what you tell her."

"If you say so," Noelle murmured, still sounding doubtful.

Isabel was less afraid of Jo than the others. Maybe because her time in Fool's Gold was temporary and she didn't have to worry about being cut off from one of the town's best locales. She looked at the hand-printed lettering on the chalkboard and felt her mouth starting to water.

There were sandwiches and burgers, but with ingredients like fresh basil and goat cheese, or watermelon-and-jalapeno puree. The red wine with summer vegetables risotto had a star by it, indicating a more "special" special. Caprese Pasta Salad with Balsamic Chicken. And the dessert of the day was Picnic S'Mores Bars and Fun Apple Fritters with Caramel Dipping Sauce.

"I'm gaining five pounds just looking at the menu," Patience said. "I can't decide between the grilled cheese, pear-and-prosciutto sandwich and the fajita quesadilla."

"I'm getting a burger and the S'Mores Bars," Charlie said flatly. "Don't try to talk me out of it and don't expect to share."

Felicia glanced at her. "Possessiveness about food is an unusual characteristic for you," she observed. "Do you think it's caused by your cycle or some other hormonal imbalance?"

Charlie turned slowly and glared at her. "You did not just ask about my period."

Felicia held her ground. "Was that inappropriate? I wasn't trying to pry."

Charlie relented with a sigh. "I know. Sorry. I just have a thing for S'Mores. I don't want to talk about it."

"I understand," Felicia told her kindly. "Many of our unhealthy obsessions with food can be traced back to early childhood."

Isabel grabbed Felicia and pulled her away from Charlie. "Time to change the subject," she murmured.

Felicia gave her a quick smile. "I can't help it. I love bugging Charlie."

"You were doing it on purpose?"

"Maybe a little."

Isabel chuckled. She had to say that one of the best parts of coming home was the friends she'd made. While she'd enjoyed herself in New York and had had several girlfriends, it wasn't the same. Here getting together happened more often, because of close proximity. It was easy to grab lunch or a drink after work. She always ran into people she knew at the festivals or the grocery store or Morgan's Books.

They both placed orders, then paid and collected their lunch. Dellina and Charlie both had blankets in their cars. Those were spread out and everyone took a seat.

Except for Charlie's burger, the food was evenly split between quesadillas and sandwiches, and there were three servings of S'Mores Bars and two orders of the apple fritters in the center of the blanket. Isabel noticed Charlie kept eyeing the S'More Bar closest to her, as if prepared to pounce on anyone who tried to take it.

"Great idea," Patience said when she'd chewed and swallowed her first bite. "I love the food and getting outdoors. What's Ana Raquel's plan for her trailer?"

"She's going to be in different spots on different days. The menu is seasonal."

"I'm glad she came back," Patience said.

Isabel nodded in agreement, doing her best not to moan as she ate her sandwich. The cheese was creamy, the pears barely crisp, the flavors a perfect blend.

Ana Raquel had spent the early part of the summer in San Francisco. Her "street food" had been very successful. But she'd missed home and had returned a couple of weeks ago. Based on this experience, Isabel was ready for her to stay.

"Fayrene has her own business, too,"

Charlie said. "She's a great temp. We had her at the fire station for a couple of weeks. I tried to get her to take the job permanently, but she wasn't interested."

"Fayrene's into change," Dellina said.

Noelle leaned close to Isabel. "So Dellina and her sisters aren't new to town?"

"No, they were all born here. Ana Raquel and Fayrene are twins and a few years younger. Their parents were killed while Dellina was still in school. Dellina has taken care of them since she turned eighteen."

Noelle's eyes widened. "That's a lot of responsibility."

"It is and they've done great. You can taste how talented Ana Raquel is. Fayrene has her own business, too, and so does Dellina. She plans parties and does interior design." Isabel mentioned the clothes she'd brought into the store.

"All I did was open a Christmas store," Noelle said with a sigh. "I feel like a slacker."

"We love your store."

"I do, too, but wow."

Charlie pushed her fries toward the middle of the blankets. "You guys can have some if you want."

Dellina grinned. "Right. Just don't touch the S'Mores. We got it."

Charlie's eyes narrowed. "Really? You, too?"

Felicia chuckled. "Charlie, we love you. That's why it's fun to tease you."

"Yeah, yeah. Where's Webster?"

"Safely sleeping in my office. If I brought him here, he would be attacking all of you. He's still in the chew, eat, sleep, poop stage of puppy life." Her gaze softened. "But he's wonderful and I love him. Once he's a little more mature, I'm going to talk to Gideon about us having a baby."

Isabel felt her mouth drop open. "Just like that?" she asked.

"Of course." Felicia looked surprised. "I love Gideon and he loves me. Why wouldn't I talk about what I want? I would expect him to do the same. We're very supportive of our dreams and goals, and the happiness of the primary couple ensures the happiness of the family unit."

"I think the startling part is how mature you're being," Dellina said. "I have trouble asking for what I want, especially when it comes to men."

"If you don't ask for what you want, how do you get it?" Felicia asked. "If you're relying on him guessing, you're sabotaging your own happiness."

"Which probably explains my single state,"

Dellina admitted. "You're brave and take-charge. It's impressive."

Felicia smiled. "Thank you for the compliment. I'm also too direct and socially awkward. Thanks to my friends in town, I'm better than I was."

"We love you," Patience said, then turned to Charlie. "You would fall under the category of saying what you want."

"Pretty much. I'm better at saying what I don't want, though. Clay's really good at picking up cues."

"I'm not brave," Patience admitted.

"Me, either," Isabel said.

Noelle smiled sympathetically. "Yeah, I'm not good at talking around what's bothering me. But I'm very good at ignoring it."

"You're our leader," Patience told Felicia.

"At least she'll get us where we need to go," Noelle joked. "Using GPS, a compass, the stars and astral projection."

"I've never been successful at astral projection," Felicia said. "I suspect it requires a level of faith I can't accommodate. It's difficult to turn my brain off and simply believe."

Isabel did her best not to stare. "But you've tried it?"

"Of course. Haven't you?"

"Not recently. The closest I've come to an

out-of-body experience was facing down Ford's mother when she flat-out asked me if I was dating him."

Charlie winced. "I love Denise, but she can be fierce when it comes to her kids. What happened?"

"I lied and said yes. It was horrible. I don't know if she believed me or not. Either way I had to agree to a family dinner."

"Ford seriously owes you," Noelle said.

"That's what I told him." Isabel put down her plate of risotto.

"I'm sure the sex will be worth it," Patience said, her expression serene.

Isabel nearly scrambled to her feet. "What? We haven't had sex."

"But you're going to."

It wasn't a question, but Isabel still considered the words. "I don't know," she admitted. "We've kissed and that was hot, but . . ."

She hesitated, not sure how to explain her confusion on the subject of sex. A week ago she would have said thanks, but no, thanks. Why bother? But after that kiss, she couldn't help wondering if the rest of it would be just as good.

"Things with Eric were complicated," she said at last.

"Are you worried you're still in love with him?" Noelle asked.

"Not exactly." Isabel drew in a breath. "We were friends more than anything else. Good friends. I . . . He . . ." What the hell? If she didn't trust these women, who could she trust?

"Eric and I split up because he realized he was gay."

Her friends stared at her with identical expressions of shock. She braced herself for what was to follow — pity and an uncomfortable silence. Maybe some recrimination for not confessing sooner. Instead Noelle gave her a hug and Charlie grunted in disgust.

"He couldn't have had his moment of inner clarity *before* the wedding ceremony?" she demanded.

"That was really selfish," Patience added. "He must have hurt you. You know you're not responsible, right?"

Felicia nodded. "There is more and more scientific evidence that gender preference is determined long before birth. There were some fascinating studies done in Britain after the Second World War. One theory is that the stress of the blitz in London . . ." She cleared her throat. "A discussion for another time."

"I wanted to say something earlier," Isabel began.

"No," Noelle said firmly. "Don't apologize. That's huge and there are things a person needs to keep to herself until she's ready for everyone to know."

She spoke with emphasis, which made Isabel wonder what secrets Noelle was hiding. But as her friend had just said — she would tell them when she was ready.

"Thanks, everyone," she told them. "For listening and for being my friends."

"You're welcome," Patience told her.

Felicia reached out for one of the S'Mores. Apparently it was the wrong one. Charlie grabbed it away from her and glared. "Don't even think about it."

CHAPTER NINE

Consuelo parked in front of the one-story ranch house not all that far from the rental she and Angel shared. The roof was new and there was a pretty garden in front. A bike leaned against the front porch. Reese's, she thought.

She picked up the bottle of wine she'd brought, along with a plate of cookies she'd purchased at the bakery. She walked toward the front door and told herself there was no reason to be nervous. She'd been in much more dangerous situations than this one. No one was going to try to kill her, and national security secrets weren't on the line. She could relax.

A statement easier to say than live.

The front door opened before she could ring the bell. Reese Hendrix grinned up at her.

"Hi," he said. "Please tell my dad I need a puppy."

His easygoing grin relaxed her. He was a good kid and she liked having him in class. She would think about that instead of his father, she told herself. Or the fact that she hadn't been on a date since she was seventeen. Her boyfriend had gone to jail her senior year. Then she'd been accepted into the army. It had seemed foolish to date anyone she worked with. After a while, her covert assignments had made the idea of dating impossible.

But all that was behind her, she reminded herself. She was just a regular woman, living in a small town, joining a friend and his son for dinner.

Just then a large Lab-golden mix nosed past Reese to launch herself at Consuelo. The dog was all wagging tail and kisses. Consuelo grabbed her collar and told her to sit. The dog did as she said.

"You want a puppy when you already have all this dog energy in the house?"

Reese was wide-eyed. "Whoa, she doesn't normally obey people like that."

"You have to be firm without being mean," she said.

She stepped into the house and handed Reese the cookies. They were in a large living room done in neutral shades. Even the big sectional sofa was brown. Fluffy leaned against her boy.

"You don't think she needs someone to play with?" he asked, rubbing her head.

"She has you."

He grinned. "We're having steaks tonight. My dad's grilling them. Usually we only have hamburgers, so this is special."

"There you go, spilling all our secrets."

Consuelo turned toward the sound of the voice. She saw Kent walking toward her. He wore jeans and a light blue long-sleeved shirt. He'd rolled the sleeves up to his elbows, which wasn't any big deal but seemed really sexy.

Her gaze skittered around the room, as if unsure where to settle. That matched the fluttering she felt in her fingers and the uneasiness in her chest. Running was an excellent idea, she thought, even as she knew she had to stick it out. Not only because it was polite, but because in her heart she wanted to.

"Dad, it's okay people know we don't eat steak very much," Reese said. He held out the plate of cookies. "Look at what Consuelo brought."

"My favorite," Kent said, never taking his gaze from her face.

"You don't know what they are," his son said.

Kent smiled. "I know."

Consuelo felt herself flush, which hadn't happened to her in a decade. "Thanks for having me over," she said, the words barely making their way past her suddenly dry mouth. "I brought wine."

"Thank you," he said. "Come on back and I'll open it."

She followed him into a large, modern kitchen. There were plenty of cabinets and the countertops were granite. Reese looked from the grill on the patio to his father.

"Can I go play computer games until it's time to cook the steaks?" he asked.

"Sure. I'll call you when I'm ready."

Reese grinned at her. "Because I'm in charge of the steaks tonight."

"A man who cooks," she teased. "Impressive."

Reese took off down the hall, Fluffy at his heels.

"I'll supervise," Kent admitted when his son had disappeared. "But I've been teaching him to use the grill this summer and he's catching on really well."

"Better than your brother," she said. "Ford is a horrible cook. When we first moved here, he and Angel had a bet. Ford lost and had to cook dinner. It was supposed to be for a month, but the food was so horrible I made him stop after a couple of days."

Kent went to a kitchen drawer and got out a corkscrew. "You lived with Ford?"

"Yes. He moved out because he and Angel compete too much. It became too dangerous for the furniture to have them wrestling all the time."

Kent glanced at her. "Now you live with Angel?"

It took her a second to understand the implication of the question. "He's a co-worker. We're friends. We've shared a house before."

"Ever dated?"

Kent asked the question casually, as if the answer didn't matter. She wanted to believe it did, although she wasn't sure.

She took the glass of wine he offered. "If the real question is have I ever slept with him, then the answer is no. Like I said, we're friends. Angel lost his wife and son a few years ago. Single-car accident during a storm. He went through a rough patch. I knew him before they died and I liked Marie a lot. Even if I hadn't known her, Angel isn't for me. I don't want a guy in the business. It's not like the movies. What we did together wasn't romantic. Trust me."

He pretended disappointment. "Don't tell

me action movies aren't based in reality. Reese and I will be crushed."

"You watch them a lot?"

"I'm the single dad of a thirteen-year-old boy. Some days action movies are all we have in common."

"I like a good action movie. Except most of them get the fighting wrong and that's annoying."

"Kind of like being a doctor and trying to watch a medical drama?" he asked.

"Just like that."

He gave her a wry smile. "Not too many shows about math teachers, so I'm an easy audience."

"They don't know what they're missing. I'll bet half your female students have a crush on you."

Kent shook his head. "No way. I've cultivated an asexual demeanor in the classroom. Most of my students are shocked to find out I have a kid. A few have even come up and asked if I adopted. I'm their math teacher, not a man. I prefer it that way."

An attitude she could respect, she thought grimly. Why was it every time she turned around, Kent was even more perfect?

"What?" he demanded.

She looked up at him.

He put down his wineglass and moved

toward her. "You have it again. That look. As if you're thinking of running away."

Again. He didn't say that last word, but it hung between them all the same.

"Sorry," she murmured. "Maybe it would help if you listed your flaws."

"I don't understand. Why do you want to know my flaws?"

"To even the playing field."

Kent stared at her. "You're kidding, right? If anyone needs a level playing field, it's me."

"Why? You're successful and smart. Responsible, good-looking and really nice." She held up a hand. "I know you don't like the *nice* part, but it sure works for me. Do you know where you live?"

He nodded slowly. "I'm clear on my address. So far I'm not exhibiting any signs of dementia. Do you find memory loss a turn-on?"

She managed a strangled laugh. "No. I mean look at the town you live in. Your house. It's so normal."

"Isn't your house normal? Are you and Angel nailing the furniture to the ceiling?"

"I've never lived in a house before. I've never had a front yard or a backyard or a mailbox by the curb. I've never lived in the suburbs. People I don't know wave at me here."

"Do you wave back at them? It's what's expected. Because hitting them or shooting them is really frowned on."

He moved toward her as he spoke. She found herself having to tilt her head slightly so she could meet his gaze.

"You're not taking me seriously," she complained.

"I am. I understand that this is different for you. I'm not sure of all the ways, but I respect that you're trying to fit in. I really like that your past has given you an inflated sense of my appeal and I hope that you never correct your opinion."

She found herself feeling slightly trapped by his body. Trapped in a good way. Because getting away from him would be a snap. Only she didn't want to go anywhere. Scared as she was, she wanted to be right here — with Kent close and getting closer.

She put her wine on the counter, then found she didn't know what to do with her hands. She started to tuck them behind her back, only that made her feel vulnerable. Then she twisted her fingers together. She felt herself getting uncomfortable and knew that anger was only a heartbeat away.

But before she could settle into her go-to

emotion, Kent took her hands in his.

"You okay?" he asked.

"I'm not sure."

"A woman who tells the truth. That's a new one."

She smiled, liking the faint scent of soap and man. He was tall and broad, without being overly muscled. She found herself wanting to find out what men in the regular world did on a date. She wanted to listen to Kent talk about almost anything. She wanted to snuggle close and, for the first time in as long as she could remember, feel that someone might want to take care of her.

"Do you think disparaging women is really a smart move?"

"When I'm around you, I can't think, let alone be smart," he admitted. "I've accepted that. And the fact that you could crush my windpipe."

She lowered her gaze from his dark eyes to his throat. "It's not an efficient way to kill, but yes, I could."

"I guess that means I'm taking my life in my hands if I do this."

He drew her hands to his sides and then behind him. When her fingers touched his back, he released them and put his on her waist. Then he lowered his head and kissed her.

His mouth was light and soft and more gentle than the brush of a butterfly wing. He didn't grind or take or pull her against him. There was space between them. Too much space.

This was what she wanted, she thought. A kind man who respected women. A man who took only what was offered and would stop if she asked him to. A man who would never make her feel dirty or afraid.

He drew back and looked at her. His expression was concerned. "You okay?"

She pressed her lips together and nodded. "I wasn't ready."

He stiffened and straightened, even as he took a step back. "I'm sorry. I thought —"

She read the emotions flashing through his dark eyes. Horror and shame were the dominant ones. There were others and each of them made her long for him more than she had before.

"No," she said, grabbing his arm before he could say anything else. "I wanted you to kiss me. I wasn't ready for how it made me feel." She smiled. "I liked the kiss."

He relaxed a little but didn't move toward her.

She grabbed the front of his shirt and

pulled. He didn't move. Of course, she could have forced him to do anything she wanted, but that didn't seem like the best way to begin their first official date.

She released him and sighed. "It sucks to be short. Could you please just lean over and kiss me again?"

The corner of his mouth twitched. "You're not going to threaten me with violence?"

"I want to, but I told myself it was wrong, what with this being a date and all."

"I'm impressed by your self-control. Impressed and relieved." The seriousness returned. "You're sure?"

"Yes. Very. Please kiss me."

He moved toward her. "I love it when women beg."

She laughed as he wrapped his arms around her. Then they were touching everywhere and suddenly the situation wasn't humorous.

She liked how he held her, as if he never wanted to let go. His body was warm and strong. Safe, she thought, letting her eyes drift shut. Perfect.

He touched his mouth to hers. There was more pressure this time. A hint of wanting. Gentleness still ruled, but she felt the potential of what there could be between them.

He didn't try to deepen the kiss and he pulled back before she was ready. But instead of releasing her, he continued to hold her close. One of his hands lightly stroked her hair.

"Thanks for coming to dinner," he murmured.

She let herself lean against him. "Thanks for asking me."

"Anytime."

She relaxed, feeling her defenses start to crumble. She might not understand how to do whatever it was they were doing, but with Kent there to guide her, she knew she could find her way.

"So, the back of Billy's truck, huh?" Ford asked.

Isabel had just licked her ice-cream cone. She forced herself to swallow. "Excuse me?"

He winked. "Your first time. It was Billy, right?"

She glanced around. They were out on a sunny Saturday afternoon. The morning had been cool, but the afternoon had warmed up. Plenty of other people crowded the sidewalks as if everyone had suddenly noticed the changing of the leaves and realized there wasn't much summer left.

"We are not discussing this," she told him.

"Not where anyone might hear."

"You're saying it's the problem of being overheard, not the subject matter."

"Mostly, although I'm not sure I want to talk about my first time with you."

"Too late," he said triumphantly. "You told me all about it in your letters."

"You're the most annoying man."

"No way. You love spending time with me. I'm funny and nice to look at."

She held in a smile. "Actually, what I most adore is your lack of ego. You're so unaware of your charms."

He bumped her shoulder with his. "My flaws keep me human."

She licked her cone. "Then you're one of the most grounded people I know. What made you think of Billy?"

He pointed.

She turned and saw a young couple making out by a pickup truck. They were probably still in high school.

"If either parent catches them, I guess there's going to be some big-time explaining to do," she said, turning back to him.

"Was it like that?" he asked.

"I don't know. It wasn't planned. He'd been surfing and I came down to the beach. It was dark and one thing led to another."

Ford chuckled. "It wasn't spontaneous."

"How do you know?"

"He's a guy. You were a beautiful young girl who was crazy about him. Trust me, Billy had been planning it for weeks."

"You think so? He never said anything."

"What's he going to say? 'I'm going to do my best to get into your pants, moving as fast as you'll let me'?"

"That's not very romantic."

"Which is my point."

She told herself not to dwell on the "beautiful young girl" part of his statement. He was generalizing. As in all teenagers were attractive by virtue of their youth and vitality.

"That would have been a good letter to skip," she said instead. "I can't believe I went into detail." She paused. "Did I?"

"I lived it in real time."

"You should have answered me. Then we would have had an actual correspondence."

"I liked being your diary." He finished his cone and dropped his napkin into a trash can. "You sent me a very detailed letter about the birth of Maeve's first baby, then a second one telling me not to read it."

"I was afraid you'd be hurt."

"I was well over her by then."

She tossed away the rest of her cone and wiped her hands. "Something I would have known if you'd ever answered."

He put his arm around her shoulders. "Never gonna happen."

"Obviously, what with you being out of the military and here now."

"You could still write me if you wanted."

"For what reason?"

"The thrill of entertaining me."

"Thank you, no."

She'd never been one to walk with a guy's arm around her shoulders before. Eric hadn't been tall enough, so they'd mostly held hands or just walked side by side. She was nestled close to him and there was plenty of body brushing and rubbing and bumping. It made her think about the kiss Ford hadn't bothered to repeat. Which was just like a man.

Why wasn't he kissing her? Did he not want to or did he think it wasn't appropriate? She saw now that she should have gotten a detailed list of the fake-girlfriend perks.

"I've got a corporate guy coming into town next week," Ford said. "We're close to signing a deal with him."

Isabel nodded and waited, not sure why he was sharing.

"He's bringing his wife."

"It's too bad they missed the End of Summer Festival over Labor Day. There isn't another one until the Fall Festival in two weeks. Are they staying that long?"

"No. They're here overnight. I thought the four of us could go to dinner."

She shrugged out of his arm and faced him. "Dinner? With your clients?"

"You're my girlfriend. Who else would I take?"

"Why can't you go alone?" She glanced around and lowered her voice. "This is only about faking out your mother."

"And the town."

"I don't want to think about that."

They'd paused by the park, where it was quiet. Across the street, tourists went in and out of Brew-haha. She would guess Noelle was getting plenty of business in her store, as well.

"Come on," he said gently. "A nice dinner with some nice people. It'll be fun."

She wasn't concerned that she wouldn't have a good time. Ford was so easy to be with. He knew when to be funny and when to be serious. They had an easy rhythm together. It was just . . .

Her gaze settled on his mouth. It was like the kissing, she thought. She wanted to know where things stood.

"Sure," she told him. "But in return, you

have to go to an estate sale with me."

His hands came up in a gesture of protection, even as he took a step back. "An estate sale? But I'm not a woman."

She said nothing and waited.

His hands dropped to his sides. "That's playing dirty."

"It's my deal. Take it or leave it."

He actually ground the toe of his athletic shoe into the sidewalk, just as if he were eight.

"All right," he grumbled. "I'll go to the estate sale with you if you'll do my corporate dinner."

She linked arms with him. "Now, was that so hard?"

"Ask me after the estate sale."

Ford pushed the lawn mower to the sidewalk and then turned to make the return trip. The afternoon was sunny and warm, but already the leaves were starting to turn. In a few weeks, Isabel was going to have to get the sprinklers blown out so they wouldn't freeze over the winter.

A blue Prius pulled into the driveway and Isabel got out. She wore black pants and a blue blouse that matched her eyes. Her hair was curled on the ends and she had on makeup. Her usual work look.

"Hey," he called and stopped the lawn mower. "Sell any dresses today?"

She walked toward him. "What are you doing?"

"You've never seen a lawn mower before?"

She rolled her eyes. "Of course I have. So why are you mowing my lawn?"

"We're dating. Boyfriends do that sort of thing." He pointed to the bags stacked by the front of the garage door. "I'm going to feed your lawn later. Give it a last boost before it gets cold."

"Thank you," she told him. "This is really nice and you don't have to do it."

"I can't help it. I'm a nice guy. A nice guy who shouldn't have to go to an estate sale."

"Sorry," she told him. "A deal's a deal." She started toward the house. "Get back to work."

He grinned and started the lawn mower.

After finishing the last few passes, he emptied the clippings into the yard-waste bin, then put the lawn mower away. Later in the week he was going to take it to the local hardware store for an end-of-season cleaning and blade sharpening.

He got out the mechanical spreader and dumped the organic fertilizer into it, then began to make his passes across the lawn. He did the front first, then moved to the backyard. By the time he was done, he was hot and sweaty. He was about to take the spreader to the garage when Isabel appeared on the back porch.

She'd changed into jeans and a T-shirt. Her feet were bare. She had two beers in one hand and a plate with chips and salsa in the other. He joined her on the patio.

"Exactly what I needed," he said, reaching for one of the beers.

"The least I can do," she told him and headed for the house. "I'll be right back."

She returned with a bowl of bean dip. "Be careful. It's spicy."

"I like spicy."

They sat at the table under the awning. A cool breeze tickled the back of his neck.

This was what he'd come home for, he thought as he took a drink of the beer. Yard work, spicy bean dip and a beautiful woman. Maybe not in that order.

"Why are you smiling?" she asked, reaching for a chip.

"Maybe it's the company."

She laughed. "Maybe you're full of crap."

"You don't think you're good company?"

"I think I'm great company, but I don't think that's a reason to smile the way you were."

"Then you don't know me." He motioned

to the yard. "This is a top-ten moment."

She leaned back in her chair and grinned. "Why do I know you have more than ten of them?"

"You should have a top-ten moment every day."

Her T-shirt was old, her jeans worn. She'd washed off her makeup and brushed out the curls. The more casual look suited her as much as the other had. She was a beautiful woman, with pretty features and a ready smile.

He supposed what he liked best about Isabel was how well he knew her. As they'd joked about over the weekend, he'd watched her grow up. He knew her character. He'd listened to her pour her heart out to him. She'd confessed things to the page that she would never have said in person, and in that, she had revealed her true self.

She was good to the bone. Oh, sure, she had faults, but she was a decent, caring person. Affectionate and giving. There were so many days he'd faced desperate situations and barely survived. There had been injuries and death and times when he'd stared down the barrel of his rifle and wondered why he had to kill yet another person.

But he'd done it all, and at the end of the

day, her loopy writing and easy conversation had pulled him back from the edge.

"Lauren came in and bought the dress today," she said.

"Good for her. She'll be a beautiful bride."

"She will. I'm really happy for her."

"It must be nice to be a part of that. Someone's wedding. You'll always have a piece of that memory."

"I hope so," she admitted. "My grandmother told me it's about the right dress, not the sale. She sent more than one bride to another store, because none of the dresses we had were right. It's an interesting business."

"You'll miss it when you leave."

"Maybe a little." She picked up her beer. "I told you about those clothes Dellina brought in, right?"

"Yes, you have headless mannequins in your windows and everyone is talking."

She giggled. "No one is talking."

"How do you know?"

"I just do. Anyway, everything sold and Dellina is bringing in more. We're going to raise prices a little and see what happens. I figure this is good practice for when I go into business with Sonia."

His gaze lingered on her blond hair. He liked the way the light hit it. She didn't have much of a tan, but he still wondered about where she might be a little paler than her arms and neck. From there it was a quick journey to her naked and him exploring.

His bed? Her bed? He was comfortable with either. Of course, he was pretty hot and sweaty after his yard work. He should clean up first. Or they could take a shower together.

"You're not listening to me," she complained.

He met her gaze. "That would be true."

"What were you thinking?"

He took a swallow of the beer. "You don't want to know."

She shifted in her seat. "I can't decide if I believe you or not."

"I'll never lie to you."

"Wow. There's a statement. So, what were you thinking?"

"That I need to go take a shower and that you could join me."

Isabel's cheeks darkened with color and she looked away. "You weren't thinking that."

"Sure I was. Want details?"

Her gaze returned to his. "Something else I'm not sure I should ask."

He put his beer on the table and slowly stood. For a woman who'd been married a few years, she was surprisingly naive about what went on in a man's mind. He supposed that most of the reason was that her ex was gay. He doubted Eric had thought all that differently, only that the object of his interest must have been someone else.

He circled around the table and pulled her to her feet.

"Never doubt," he told her right before he kissed her.

Isabel remembered the last time with Ford. The passion had built slowly, catching her off guard and making it difficult for her to understand what was happening. This time, that wasn't the problem. Her body recognized the upcoming kiss and apparently approved. Even before his mouth settled on hers, her nerve endings were buzzing in anticipation.

His lips claimed hers with a combination of heat and passion. Her eyes closed, allowing her to concentrate on the feel of his hands gently cupping her face. She rested her fingertips on his shoulders.

He was strong, she thought absently. Strong and powerful and very male.

Their mouths brushed once, twice before she parted for him. *Just like that — kiss me more,* she thought, a little shocked by her reaction. He obliged and slipped his tongue inside.

Her body came alive at the first stroke. Heat exploded low in her belly and spiraled out, capturing every part of her. Her breasts, which had never been that interesting to her, began to feel heavy and ache. She knew her nipples were tight.

She kissed him back, moving her tongue against his, wanting more of the heat and need. The hunger itself was pleasure. Anticipation was like a nip followed by a kiss. Slightly uncomfortable but ultimately pleasing.

She leaned into him, wanting to feel her breasts crushed against his hard chest. Only not like this, she thought, running her hands up and down his back. Not with so many layers of clothing between them. She wanted skin on skin. She wanted him touching her and licking and —

The clarity of the image was as startling as her imagining it and she pulled back, unable to believe what was happening. She stood on her back porch confused, breathing hard and with a strong need to rip off her shirt and bra and have Ford put his hands on her breasts. Not just his hands. His mouth. And not just her breasts.

She tried to catch her breath. What was

happening? This so wasn't her.

"You okay?" Ford asked with a grin.

She nodded. "Confused."

"I do that to women. You're overwhelmed with desire. I should have warned you."

Which would have been funny if it wasn't true.

His smile faded. "Seriously, Isabel, are you all right?"

"I'm fine. It's just kissing you is different."

"Is it the fangs? Not everyone finds them a turn-on."

She managed a laugh. He pulled her close again and lightly kissed the tip of her nose.

"Not like with Eric?" he asked.

"Or Billy. Or the unnamed hordes in between."

"You had hordes?"

"I had one other guy. Maybe two. It wasn't impressive."

His dark gaze met hers. "So it's the passion that has you nervous?"

"I guess. I like what I feel, but it's so strange."

His mouth twisted. "Well, damn. Now I can't take advantage of you."

"Did you plan to?"

"I was hoping."

She took a deep breath and then placed

her palm on his chest. She looked into his eyes and murmured, "Maybe next time."

Now it was his turn to suck in a breath. "Just say the word."

CHAPTER TEN

Consuelo watched her class walk into the gym. The thirteen-year-old boys were at that awkward stage. Some were tall and lanky, while others had yet to start their puberty-induced growth spurt. Reese and Carter walked in together, as they always did. Reese had been in town awhile because of his dad, but Carter had shown up only a couple of months ago. His mother had died and Carter had come looking for his father — Gideon, a man who'd never known about his son. After a few missteps, the two had connected. With Felicia as the glue in their relationship, they'd formed a family.

Now Carter crossed the room and stopped in front of her.

"You went on a date." His voice was accusing.

Consuelo nodded slowly. "I know." She wasn't going to apologize. Carter's declaration of everlasting love was sweet, but hardly real.

"You're not going to wait for me, are you?" he asked with a sigh. "Even though I'll be eighteen in five years?"

"I'm too old for you. But there will be other women in your life."

"It won't be the same."

She held in a smile. "I know and I'll have to live with that."

Reese came up and rolled his eyes. "You gotta let it go, bro."

"I will. There are some cute girls at school."

"See?" Consuelo told him. "Your heart is already healing."

"But if you ever change your mind," he began.

"You'll be the first to know."

Reese shook his head. "Crazy talk," he said, then lowered his voice. "My dad said to say thank you for coming to dinner the other night." He shrugged. "I thought it was fun, too, even if you didn't tell him to give me a puppy."

"Not getting in the middle of that discussion."

"But you could convince him if you tried."

She thought briefly about the tender kiss that had left her shaken to her very soul.

"You overestimate my powers."

"I don't think so. My dad thinks you're hot."

She raised her eyebrows. "That's a lead into a very awkward conversation. You sure you want to have it?"

"Probably not. He's happier around you. I'm glad he's dating. Do you cook?"

"Some," she said cautiously. "So you're only in it for the meals?"

Reese grinned. "A man's gotta do what a man's gotta do."

"I'm starting to see that." She glanced at the clock. "Go get in line. We're starting."

Reese waved and headed for the far side of the gym, where her students were waiting. She walked toward them. For a second she allowed herself to believe it was all possible. That her date with Kent could lead to something special. That he could see past the pretty face to who she really was and like her anyway.

What was that old saying? If wishes were horses . . .

"I'm not sure I have the body to pull this off," Isabel said as she turned back and forth in front of the half circle of mirrors in her store. "I need shape-wear."

Madeline raced into the other room and

221

returned with a body shaper that went from boobs to midthigh.

"Here you go. But honestly, I don't think you need it."

Isabel laughed. "And you're a woman who deserves a raise." She unzipped the dress and let it fall to the floor, then stepped into the shape-wear and began the arduous process of pulling it into place. Madeline joined her on the raised platform and tugged along.

Three minutes later Isabel could barely breathe, but all her curves were as they should be and the bulgy places were suitably squished. Madeline reached for the sample Dellina had brought by earlier that morning.

The dress was silk, in a wrap style with a draped bodice. The style made her waist appear smaller, her legs longer. The color seemed purple in some light and blue in others. Long sleeves were deceptively demure. While they went down to her wrists, there was a slit from shoulder to cuff, and as she moved, she bared her arms.

"What about shoes?" Madeline asked.

"I have some ridiculously high nude pumps," Isabel told her. "They'll be perfect." She fastened the side hook, securing the dress in place, then faced herself in the mirror.

"You look great," Madeline breathed. "You really have to buy that dress."

"It works," Isabel said. "It would work better if I lost ten pounds, but I'll accept being unable to breathe."

"Can you eat? Aren't you going to a dinner?"

"Details." Isabel flicked away the concern.

In New York, she'd dressed in the city's traditional black. Here, she was aware that while she had to look professional, she never wanted to outshine the bride. She channeled her fashion interest into shoes and other accessories. But every now and then it was good to cut loose and indulge herself with a perfectly fabulous dress.

This one had the advantage of being appropriate and hot enough to make him look twice. At least, that was the plan. After their last kiss, she was hoping to leave him a little off balance. It might help to put them on more even footing.

"You want a smoky eye with that for sure," Madeline said firmly. "Great earrings."

"I can borrow a pair from my mom." Isabel pulled her hair up in a twist. "Up or down?"

Madeline grinned. "You're going up to the

resort. Definitely up."

"I'll need to add an hour to my prep time."

"It'll be worth it," the other woman promised.

Ford walked in through the back door. "It's me," he called as he entered Isabel's kitchen. "You need to think about keeping your door locked."

"Then how would you get in?"

Her voice drifted down the hall.

"I can pick the lock. I was thinking about you keeping out other people." He started to walk out of the kitchen, then paused. "Are you going to make an entrance? Should I wait here?"

"You tell me."

She appeared in the doorway. She wore a blue dress and had her hair up. A simple description that did nothing to describe the reality of a beautiful woman in a flowy fabric that hugged every sexy curve.

Earrings dangled, making him follow the line of her neck to the open V of her dress. There was enough cleavage to get his attention. Three-inch heels put her close to eye level, and all he could think about was kissing her and then getting her naked.

"You're in a suit," she said, walking toward him. "You look good."

"You look better. Wow."

She smiled. *"Wow* works. Too many men underestimate the power of *wow."*

"I won't. Ever. I promise."

She did a full turn. "So this is okay? It's corporate, but it's Fool's Gold. I wasn't sure."

"I'm sure."

She smiled and moved close enough to adjust his tie. She smelled like flowers and vanilla.

"Better or worse than dress whites?" she asked.

"About the same. Only in a dark suit, it's safer to spill."

She laughed. The sweet sound kicked him in the gut. Or maybe a little lower. How was he supposed to think about business with Isabel next to him all night? Not that he wanted her to be anywhere else.

"You're messing with my head," he complained.

"I'm not doing anything."

"Then God help me if you start to try."

The Gold Rush Ski Lodge and Resort was nestled in the mountains above Fool's Gold. The location offered stellar views and luxury lodgings. In the winter, the lodge was filled with skiers and snowboarders.

Spring and summer were wedding season. The fall was usually a hodgepodge of seminars and retreats.

"When I was growing up, this was the fanciest place we ever went as a family," Isabel told Ford as he drove onto the property. "It was only for special occasions. Graduations and my parents' twenty-fifth wedding anniversary."

"The clients are staying here for a couple of nights."

"Then they'll be impressed." She watched the valet stare at the Jeep. "Oh, look. He's afraid."

"He's not afraid. My Jeep's a classic."

"Then you should treat it with the respect it deserves. You really need to think about painting it. At least get rid of the flames."

"The flames are the best part."

They pulled up to the valet.

"Thanks," Isabel murmured as her door was opened. She was careful as she stepped to the ground. Heels and a long drop to earth were not a good mix — especially when wearing a wrap dress. But she managed without flashing anyone.

As they walked toward the entrance, Ford put his hand on the small of her back. She liked the warm pressure of his fingers against her body — even with the firm layer of Lycra between his skin and hers.

Once inside, Ford motioned to the bar. "They're meeting us there."

She hesitated. "I'm oddly nervous."

"It's not your fault you're the most beautiful woman in the room."

The unexpected compliment caused her to burst out laughing. She knew she cleaned up pretty well and could comfortably call herself average-plus, but the most beautiful woman in the room? Not on this planet.

Ford's eyes narrowed. "You're not supposed to laugh."

"Then stop being funny." She slipped her arm through the crook of his elbow. "Lead on, faux boyfriend."

"You're still giggling."

"I'll do my best to stop."

"Ford!"

They turned and saw a couple in their late thirties walking toward them. He was a few inches shy of six feet and she came to his shoulders. They were both dark haired. The woman was obviously pregnant.

"Clyde," Ford said, stepping forward and offering his hand. He turned to the woman. "You must be Linda. Nice to meet you."

"You, too," Linda said with a pretty smile that lit up her face.

"This is Isabel."

There was more handshaking.

"At the risk of stating the obvious," Clyde said, putting a possessive hand on his wife's waist, "it's probably best we skip the bar and head into dinner."

Isabel nodded and Ford agreed. They walked toward Henri's on the west side of the resort.

Linda fell into step with her. "I love this town," she said. "It's adorable. Clyde was telling me that there are festivals nearly every weekend."

"We do like to celebrate."

"So you're from here?"

"Born and raised. I've spent the past six years in New York, though."

"But you came back." Linda sounded delighted. "We're in Phoenix and it's nothing like this. For one thing, the heat in the summer is brutal. We also don't have the trees. Everything is so green."

"Wait until the fog rolls in and frizzes your hair," Isabel said lightly. "It's almost heaven on earth here, but Phoenix has its appeal, too."

Linda laughed.

Ford gave his name to the hostess, who showed them to a table by the windows. They had a view of much of the town and the valley beyond.

"Are those vineyards?" Clyde asked.

"Yes," Ford said. "We have a few wineries in the area. They have tastings every weekend."

"Something for next time," Linda said, resting her hand on her belly. She sighed. "Let's just say number three is a surprise. We have two children already, a boy and a girl. We were done. Or so I thought."

Clyde nodded. "Jack's our youngest and he's nearly seven."

"I couldn't believe it." She leaned toward Isabel. "Clyde's been in for the surgery now, but it's too little too late." She sighed. "Not that I'm not excited about the baby, but was he unexpected!"

"You're having a boy?" Isabel asked.

"Clyde Junior," Clyde said.

Linda looked at her husband. "You are not saddling a tiny infant with that name."

"Why not? You can call him CJ," Isabel said.

Linda looked at her. "That's certainly better."

Their server appeared with menus and explained about the specials. She took their drink orders and left.

Linda put down her menu. "So, what do you do? I'm a stay-at-home mom. I was just getting my résumé polished to get back in the workforce when I turned up pregnant with this one." Her smile turned wry. "Not that I don't love my kids. I do. But there are days I want to put on office clothes and go talk to adults."

"My sister has four kids and another on the way. I'm sure she shares your feelings."

The mention of Maeve reminded Isabel to go see her sister. They'd talked by phone a few times, but it was silly that they were in the same town and rarely saw each other. It wasn't as if Isabel was staying in Fool's Gold forever. After the first of the year, she would be heading back to New York, and she wasn't sure how long it would be until she returned.

"Do you have kids?" Linda asked.

"No. I'm divorced and we never quite got to that stage."

"I'm sorry." Linda's brown eyes filled with sympathy. "That's hard. But Ford's very handsome." She smiled and leaned in conspiratorially. "In a sexy, muscled, tall kind of way. If you like the type."

Isabel grinned. "I'm finding I like the type very much."

"What are you two whispering about?" Ford asked.

"Nothing you want to know."

He studied her for a second. "I'm going

to take your word on that."

"Smart man."

Although imagining the look on his face if he found out that very-pregnant Linda thought he was sexy would be kind of funny.

"You never said what you did," Linda mentioned a few minutes later.

"My family owns a bridal shop in town. Paper Moon. As I said, I've been living in New York. After the divorce, I wanted to get away, so I came back to run the business for a few months."

Linda sighed. "Oh, that must be fun. All those happy brides. You get to help them find the perfect dress. Is there drama?"

"All the time. Emotions are running high and there are often mother-daughter conflicts. One wants traditional, the other wants anything else."

"Sounds exciting. Clyde's in auto parts. His dad left him a struggling business and he's turned it into a multistate distributorship. We have over twelve hundred employees."

"That's impressive," Isabel told her, thinking she and Sonia had talked about hiring one other person as they started their business. Twelve hundred was unimaginable.

"He wants to bring the sales team to the retreat," Linda continued. "To help them relate to each other a little better. Sales can be competitive and Clyde's worried their sense of unity is getting lost."

"Clyde sounds like a smart guy."

"He is." Linda smiled at her husband, then turned back to Isabel. "Except when it comes to naming our baby."

The server returned with drinks and took their order.

Clyde passed the basket of warm rolls to his wife, then looked at Ford. "How did you two meet?"

"I used to date her sister."

Linda raised her eyebrows. "Really? And she doesn't mind you two are together now?"

Isabel held up both hands. "There has been a lot of space and time," she said. "Ford and my sister were engaged fourteen years ago. I was desperately in love with him, but he didn't bother to notice."

"My mistake," Ford said lightly. "Maeve and I were way too young. A few weeks before the wedding, she realized her mistake. Because I was still a kid, I pouted. I left town in a huff, joined the navy. I got out a few months ago, returned home and we opened CDS."

Isabel realized he'd given all the facts, yet kept many of the details private. She liked how he didn't tell Clyde and Linda about Maeve cheating with Leonard.

He leaned toward her and grinned. "Isabel wrote me. A lot."

She laughed. "Like I said, I was fourteen and had a mad crush on him. I wrote and wrote."

"That's so romantic," Linda told her.

"Not really. He never wrote back."

"Not once?" Clyde asked.

Ford shrugged. "There were a lot of reasons. But I enjoyed getting her letters." His smile faded. "I was a SEAL. We had some tough missions. Reading about Isabel being a normal teenager in high school helped. She was a little wild in college, though."

She pushed him. "Don't spill all my secrets the first night."

He grabbed her hand and lightly kissed her knuckles. "I would never do that."

"Then what happened?" Linda asked eagerly. "You came back, took one look at her and realized she'd been the one all along?"

"Something like that," Ford admitted.

Just words, Isabel told herself. It wasn't true, but it sounded good for company. Still, she found herself wishing he was telling the truth. That he *had* taken one look at her and had known they belonged together.

Foolishness, she thought. She and Ford were only pretend-dating. None of this was real. She was passing through town and he was a guy who didn't know how to be in love. They didn't belong together.

Sure, the kisses had been great and she was looking forward to more. She liked his company and enjoyed seeing him. They shared a sense of humor, and she had the sense that if she needed him, he would be there, but that was different. They were friends and their relationship was something they'd created to fake out the world.

"You did great tonight," Ford said as he drove through the quiet streets of town.

Isabel leaned against the door and drew in a breath of cool air. She'd had just enough wine to give herself a slight buzz. She wasn't going to start singing anytime soon, but if she started giggling, she might have trouble stopping.

"I had a good time. I thought you and Clyde would talk a lot of business, but you didn't. They're a fun couple."

"I agree." He glanced at her. "You're a fun girlfriend."

"Thank you. Except for this car, you're a really good boyfriend."

He pulled into her driveway and parked. "I love my Jeep. Do not mention the flames."

She opened her door and stepped out. "Admit it. They're starting to embarrass you just a little."

He came around and put his hand on the small of her back. "Never. They represent my lost youth."

"If these flames are your lost youth, you need to go out and find it."

They reached her back door. Ford turned the door handle and sighed. "When are you going to start locking your door?"

"This is Fool's Gold. Nothing bad is going to happen."

"It could."

"Oh, please." She brushed off his comment. "You want to come in?"

"I am in."

"Okay." She kicked off her shoes and walked barefoot across the hardwood entryway. "That's always the best part of the evening. Even the heels that start out comfortable usually end up hurting by the end of the night. There's math involved. An inverse relationship between how gorgeous the shoes are and how much they hurt my feet."

She dropped her purse on a small table in

the hall and started toward the living room. Halfway there, she paused.

"Where are we going?" she asked.

Ford shrugged out of his suit jacket and hung it on the coatrack by the door. His tie followed. He toed out of his shoes and then walked toward her with an air of determination that made her tummy get all fluttery.

"You have this strange look in your eye," she murmured. "It's predatory."

"That's how I'm feeling."

She swallowed against her suddenly dry throat. She wasn't nervous, not exactly. If she had to define the tingle in her body, she would say it was anticipation.

He reached for her and she sidestepped him. "We have to talk first," she said.

One eyebrow rose. "I'm not that interested in conversation."

"Still, it's necessary. Before we do, you know, the sex thing."

His mouth twitched. "The sex thing?"

"Uh-huh. Because that's where this is going."

He shifted so he was leaning against the wall. "Good to know. What do we have to talk about?"

This was not the best time for her head to be fuzzy, she thought, sure she had a comprehensive list memorized but unable to recall it that second.

"I'm on the pill," she began. "I like having my periods regulated, and my doctor said it was safe for me to stay on it after my divorce."

"I brought condoms. We'll still use them."

"You *planned* this?"

"I was optimistic. Besides, I'm a SEAL. It's my job to be prepared."

Her eyes narrowed. "I thought that was the Boy Scouts."

"Them, too. What else?"

"I don't think I'm doing it right," she admitted. "The sex thing. If I was good in bed, Eric wouldn't be gay."

"You don't have that much power."

"It wasn't very good with Billy, either."

"Or the hordes?"

She sighed. "Right. Him, too. I think it's me. That I'm not —" She waved a hand up and down the front of her body. "Maybe there are parts missing or something."

He straightened. "Is that it?"

"Don't you want to talk about the parts?"

His gaze drifted over her body. "I would love to, but not in the way you mean." He took a step toward her. "Because if that's all, I'd like to get started."

She scurried back a couple of steps. "No, that's not all. You can't undress me."

"Is this an Amish thing?"

"Amish? What do the Amish have to do with anything?"

"I don't know. Why can't I undress you?"

She felt herself flushing. "What do you know about SPANX?"

Now it was his turn to look startled. "You want me to spank you?"

"No! Of course not. Jeez. Not spanking. SPANX. It's . . ." She sucked in a breath. "It's shape-wear. You can't take it off me. It's not sexy and you'll probably hurt your back. I'm not this skinny naturally. I have to take it off myself or you won't want to have sex with me."

Was he being stupid on purpose or was this a guy thing?

"Just go in the bedroom and wait," she told him. "I'll take care of this myself and join you."

"No way. You're not taking care of anything yourself. Besides, if we're talking underwear, I want to watch."

CHAPTER ELEVEN

Isabel had not planned to relive the granny-panty scene from *Bridget Jones's Diary* ever, but here she was, having her own humiliating moment.

"But I could be almost naked," she told Ford. "With almost no work on your part. Isn't that nice to think about?"

"I like the work." He both looked and sounded confused. "Isabel, I've been with my share of women. There's not very much I haven't seen."

"Yeah, well, you haven't seen this!"

Before she could come to her senses, she undid the hooks holding the wrap dress in place and let the silky garment fall to the floor. She stood in front of him wearing her beige shape-wear that went from the scoop-neck top to midthigh.

"It's a slip," he said.

She put her hands on her hips and momentarily enjoyed how narrow and firm they felt. Of course, all that was going to change when she wrestled her way out of the SPANX.

"It's more than a slip. It's practically magic. But that's not the point. There's no way you can get this off me. So I'm going to go into the bathroom and take it off —"

She wasn't aware of him moving, but one second she was talking and the next she was in his arms and he was kissing her.

It was a good kiss. All lips and tongue. Her determination melted along with the rest of her. She wrapped her arms around him and hung on. He touched her hair, her jaw, then dropped to run his fingers along her spine.

He straightened and looked her up and down.

"Just let me go to the bathroom and I'll —"

Ford reached for the straps over her shoulders. He pulled them down her arms. The garment peeled away, over her breasts, her waist, her hips and ended up in a rolled circle at her feet. She stepped out of it.

"Problem solved," he announced, his voice filled with satisfaction. "Anything else?"

Aside from the fact that he was fully dressed while she was standing there in a bra and very brief panties?

"Uh, not really."

"Good."

He nudged her toward the hall. She started walking, aware that he was unbuttoning his shirt as he went. His pants were lost in the doorway, and by the time they reached the bed and she turned around, he was naked. Completely naked.

Isabel stared at the broad shoulders, smooth chest and narrow waist. He was all muscle, with chiseled planes and sculpted lines.

"I welcome comparisons," he told her.

She laughed. "Fine. Eric was much thinner and shorter than you. Billy had a similar build, but wasn't as muscled."

"And the horde?"

"I don't really remember."

"Hordes usually make a bigger impression," he said, reaching for her and drawing her close.

She knew there was some funny reply, but what with being pressed against his naked body, she couldn't think of it. Not when she didn't know where to put her hands. There was so much bare skin. And his erect *penis* was pressing against her belly in a very suggestive manner.

"Relax," he murmured, pressing his mouth

241

to her jaw and then moving it down her neck.

"Relaxing isn't my strong suit. Not during . . . you know."

He raised his head. " 'You know'? That's your euphemism?"

"Do you have a better one?"

He nipped her earlobe. "About a dozen. Why are you nervous?"

She found it difficult to think with him kissing her like that. Everywhere he touched, she felt both heat and little sparks. They moved through her, settling in her breasts before heading south. She wanted to squirm — not to get away but to get closer.

He moved his hands up and down her back. With each pass, his fingers dipped lower. She found herself anticipating him touching her butt, which was strange, but she was going to go with it.

"Isabel?"

"Hmm?"

"Why are you nervous?"

"We're going to have sex. I'm not very good at it."

The words came out involuntarily and she winced. Ford raised his head and looked at her.

"You mentioned that and I don't believe it."

242

"Nice of you to say, but you have no actual proof. I don't think it was good with Billy."

"Your first time and not your fault."

"And it wasn't very fun with Eric."

His dark gaze never wavered. "The being-gay thing could have something to do with that."

"I don't like it that much."

He put his hands on her shoulders. "Let's find out why."

Before she could figure out what he had in mind, he'd basically removed her bra and was sliding her panties down her legs. The man worked quickly. She didn't even have time to get embarrassed.

When she was as naked as him, he moved her to the bed and had her lie down. He settled next to her. He leaned over and lightly kissed her.

"You like the kissing," he said.

"Yes."

"Then we'll do that." He shifted closer and settled his mouth on hers. He kissed her slowly, moving his lips against hers before slipping his tongue inside.

Uncertainty faded and she wrapped her arms around him. As their tongues tangled and her blood moved a little faster, she moved her hands up and down his back.

She could feel his muscles moving underneath his skin. He was so wide through his shoulders, she thought. Then his back narrowed as she got closer to his waist.

He broke off the kiss to trail his mouth down her throat to her collarbone. He placed one of his hands on her belly, which made her tense. But then he kept it there, just moving in a slow circle. She could handle that, she told herself.

His mouth eased closer and closer to her breasts. She found herself thinking about him kissing her there. A little jolt zipped from her breasts down her middle to between her thighs. A jolt that caused her breath to quicken.

His mouth settled over her nipple and he drew on it. The jolt returned, stronger this time, creating a direct line from her breast to that place between her legs. The place that had, honestly, never been all that special.

He raised his head. "Yes? No?"

"It's nice."

He chuckled. "You're not easy. I like doing this. Do you mind if I keep at it for a while?"

"No."

He moved from breast to breast. Licking, sucking. She felt trapped in her own skin, kind of hot and cold at the same time. She raised her hands to his head and ran her fingers through his hair. Her legs moved against the cool sheets.

The hand on her belly moved. Slowly, he shifted it across her stomach until his fingers dipped between her thighs. She parted her legs instinctively, knowing what would happen next. He would rub her there a few minutes, then assume the position. Once he was inside, she would make those noises guys seemed to like and then he'd come and then it would be over.

She turned her head, trying to see the clock. If it didn't take too long, she could still watch a movie on pay-per-view.

He explored her gently, sliding over her clitoris before easing a finger inside her.

"You're wet," he murmured.

Not surprising, she thought. It wasn't that she didn't *like* what he was doing. It was just . . . so what? Yes, it felt nice for a while, but then she wanted it to be over. Why did it have to take so long?

He began to rub her center. As he did that, he shifted so they were kissing again. She was aroused, she thought, frustrated. She usually got aroused. But then it went nowhere. He continued to kiss her as his fingers moved against her center. She liked what he was doing — liked the warmth flowing through her, the tension. She wanted to push or strain, and as need built inside her, she started to feel uncomfortable. Not physically. She wasn't sure how. Maybe in her head?

She just wasn't that woman, she thought grimly. The one who threw herself on the bed and breathed, "Take me now!" Sex was fine. This was better than it had ever been, but still, she didn't understand what —

"I can hear you thinking from here," Ford said, shifting so he rested his head on his hand, his weight supported on his elbow as he faced her.

"My brain doesn't turn off."

"I can tell." He lightly traced her breast, his finger slipping over her tight nipple.

A shiver rippled through her.

He did it again and she shivered again.

"Count backward from a thousand," he told her. "In threes."

"What?"

"I want your mind busy so it can't freak you out."

"I'm not freaked out. I'm totally calm." She reached over and put her hand on his hip. His erection strained toward her. He was going to fill her completely and that would feel nice.

"It's your turn," she murmured. "Let's do that."

"I don't think so." He rolled onto his hands and knees, then slipped between her thighs. Although he loomed over her, he didn't try to enter her. "A thousand, nine hundred ninety-seven . . ."

"Fine. It's a stupid idea. Nine hundred and ninety-four."

"Close your eyes and count."

She did as he instructed. She didn't know why he was making such a big deal of this. Not everyone felt the earth move every time. Or ever. She was okay with that.

"You counting?"

"Yes," she lied and turned her attention to the numbers.

Ford leaned down and took her nipple in his mouth. He'd done that before and it was still nice. She liked the way his tongue swirled and teased. When he lightly bit down, her breath caught and she lost her place. Nine hundred and forty-something, she thought. Seven. Forty-seven. Only seven wasn't divisible by three, so that wasn't right.

He kissed his way down her belly. She giggled as his breath tickled, then caught her breath as he circled her belly button. Two, she told herself. Nine hundred and forty-two. Nine hundred and thirty-nine. Nine —

He went lower and lower, until his fingers lightly parted her and he pressed his tongue against the very center of her.

Her eyes flew open as he moved against her core. Moved in a way that made it impossible to count. It wasn't so much the pressure, she thought as her eyes slowly closed. Or the speed. It was the combination. Over and over that single swollen knot of nerves. Around and over. Her skin got hot and felt a little tight. The bottoms of her feet burned. She ached in the strangest places, and when she tried to figure out if she was breathing, she realized she was almost panting.

He didn't go faster or slower. Instead he kept moving his tongue against her. She was caught in the sensations flowing out from that single point. The world completely faded and she wanted to beg him not to stop, only she couldn't speak.

There was something just out of her reach. She could feel it getting closer, but she didn't know what to look for, what to feel, what to —

He slipped a finger deep inside her. Instantly her muscles clamped around him. He withdrew and pushed in two, then curled them slightly, stroking her from the other side. Rhythm matched rhythm. She could almost see it. Could almost.

Pure liquid pleasure rushed through her. It claimed her, every cell, every thought. She no longer existed except through the shuddering sensations rocking all of her. She got the falling reference and the wave one. Either worked. She lost herself in the amazing response of her body, letting herself become little more than a floating entity.

Ford continued to touch her, slowing the contact until the last ounce of her release faded. Isabel lay there on the bed, both thrilled and embarrassed.

How on earth had she missed that for the past twenty-eight years? Or even ten? What on earth had she been doing wrong? And when could she have her next orgasm?

She opened her eyes and saw Ford smiling down at her. He looked like a man who had taken on the biggest supervillain ever and won.

"Yeah, yeah," she said, unable to keep from smiling. "You're amazing and you can be as smug as you like."

He grinned. "So you came."

"Yes."

"For the first time ever."

She laughed. "Yes."

"Because of me."

"Because of you."

Then he wasn't grinning. He touched her cheek. "I'm glad."

"Me, too." She raised herself on her elbows. "Do you think I can come with you inside?"

"Let's find out."

He had to get up and go find his pants. She enjoyed the view of his muscled body first from the back, then from the front. He slipped on the condom and knelt between her thighs. But instead of pushing inside, he took her hand in his.

"Do this," he said, settling her fingers on that still-swollen center.

She pulled her hand away. "I can't touch myself."

"Why not?"

"Because it's . . . People don't."

He raised his eyebrows. "Seriously? 'People don't'? That's your reason?"

"*I* don't."

"I got that. It might be part of your problem." He put her hand back in place. "Just give me five minutes. If you don't like it, you can stop."

She stared into his face and tried to guess what he was thinking. So far everything he'd done had been designed to make her feel at ease and sexually satisfy her. Did she really want to start complaining now?

"Five minutes," she agreed, putting her fingers back where he'd placed them.

"Slow circles. Steady pressure."

She blinked at him. "You're telling me how to do this?"

"Someone has to."

She didn't know if she should laugh, hit him or accept the criticism in the spirit in which it was meant. She picked the latter and collapsed back on the bed.

Her fingers were smaller than his, so she used three instead of two. She moved slowly, not sure how to duplicate what he'd done. But with each circle, she got immediate feedback and was able to adjust the speed to one that was —

"Damn, that's hot," he said.

She opened her eyes and saw him watching her. She pulled her hand away immediately. Heat burned on her cheeks. "You're not supposed to stare at me."

"You have a lot of rules." He shifted so she felt his thickness pushing into her. "But as soon as you're comfortable with us making love, I'm going to have you do that all the way."

"You want me to touch myself and have an orgasm while you watch?"

"Sure."

She opened her mouth, then closed it. Repeating "people don't do that" seemed silly. "Would you do that, too? With me watching?"

"Sure."

The idea of him touching himself with her right there was oddly exciting. What else did couples do in bed that she didn't know about? She had a feeling Ford would be happy to tell her all about it.

He tapped the back of her hand. "Back to business, young lady."

She did as he requested. With the first stroke, she felt the familiar tension return. Then he eased into her.

Ford was both long and thick. He stretched her, pushing in until her legs fell open more. Nerve endings cooed in delight at the friction. He withdrew and pushed in again.

There was no counting this time, no need to busy her mind. Her body understood what was happening and hurried toward the path. She touched herself as he'd taught her, keeping time with him. They both moved faster and faster. She started to lose control as pressure built up inside her.

Without thinking, she dropped her hand and held on to him. She wrapped her legs around his hips and drew him in closer. He surged harder, thrust deeper and the first ripple of her release washed over her.

He quickly followed, opening his eyes to stare into hers as they both surrendered to the pleasure they shared.

Isabel stood in her shower the following morning and did her best not to break into spontaneous song. Because she so could. She could sing and dance, and she wouldn't be the least surprised if little woodland creatures were waiting in her bedroom to help her dress.

Because it was that kind of morning. The sun was shining, the earth rotating, and she had spent the night having orgasm after orgasm.

Maybe that made her a shallow person, but she could live with the judgment. The things Ford had done to her had been spectacular. She hadn't known her body was capable of such pleasure. She wasn't sure why she hadn't figured it all out before. Of course, she and Billy had both been young and the horde had been a one-night kind of thing that had left her feeling icky. With Eric, well, she'd already dissected those problems.

She turned off the water and got out of

the shower. After drying off, she wrapped herself in her robe and opened the bathroom door. And screamed.

Ford was standing right there.

"Are you trying to give me a heart attack?" she asked, pressing a hand to her chest. Her heart pounded hard against her rib cage.

"I brought you coffee."

She took the offered mug, then glanced down and realized he was not only naked but erect. Anticipation sent heat rushing all through her.

She turned, set down the coffee, dropped her robe on the floor and stepped into his arms. He was kissing her and moving her back at the same time.

After he shoved the coffee to the back of the vanity, he lifted her up to the counter and spread her legs. She reached between them and guided him inside.

He filled her in a single stroke.

She wrapped her legs around his hips and nibbled at his jaw. "Hard," she instructed, already halfway to her release. "Don't hold back."

"You're my kind of girl."

She brought his hands to her breasts and arched her head back. As he pumped in and out, he squeezed her nipples. Less than a minute later, she was flying, crying out her release. He followed quickly.

When they were done, they stayed where they were, trying to catch their breath.

"You're going to kill me," he told her.

"Is that a complaint?"

He grinned and kissed her. "No. It's a challenge."

Ford spun slowly in his seat. Justice looked up from his notes.

"Are we keeping you from something?"

"Nope," Ford said easily, doing his best not to grin. Mostly because he didn't want questions, but if ever there was a morning to be a happy guy, this was it.

Isabel had been a revelation. Sweet and sexy. When she'd come apart in his arms . . . He shook his head. There weren't any words. He just knew it was the best feeling ever.

Consuelo looked at him. "Stop it."

"Stop what?"

"You're too happy. It's annoying."

Angel grunted. "You were supposed to have dinner with Clyde and his wife last night. He's a potential client."

"More than potential now," Ford told him. "He's coming in later to sign on the dotted line."

He reached for a sheet of paper, crumpled

255

it up and tossed it into the trash can. "Score one for me."

"That was your handout for the meeting," Justice told him.

"I'll share with someone else."

Consuelo continued to glare at him. "I'm going to hurt you later."

As they had a workout planned at three that afternoon, there was every chance she was telling the truth. Not that he cared. He could still please Isabel with a broken leg or arm.

Once she'd figured out the whole point of sex, she hadn't been able to get enough. They'd reached for each other again and again in the night. And that morning — talk about hot.

What he couldn't believe was that no one had bothered to take the time to figure out how to please her. She wasn't especially difficult; she was just inexperienced. He supposed Eric had something of an excuse, but what about the other guys?

Idiots, he told himself.

He should go online and find her some toys. Nothing that would freak her out, but a few fun things. He had a feeling she would enjoy playing, as would he.

Angel crumpled up his notes and made a basket into the trash can. Justice snapped his laptop shut.

"What about the meeting?" Consuelo asked.

"There's an assembly at Lillie's school. I'd rather be there than dealing with these two." He motioned to Ford and Angel.

"So I'm in charge?" Consuelo asked, sounding pleased.

"No blood, no dead bodies, no broken bones."

"You're limiting my fun."

"We're still business partners. If you kill them, it's more work for you." Justice walked out of the conference room.

Ford heard footsteps in the hallway; then Justice said, "He's back in there."

Was Isabel looking for him? He got up and hurried out the door, only to find Leonard walking toward him.

"Hey," he said, nodding at his friend. "What's up?"

"Is there a place we can talk?"

"Sure." He motioned to his office, two doors down. "Everything okay?"

"Fine."

Leonard followed him inside, then shut the door. He pushed up his glasses and cleared his throat. "I want to start working out."

Ford leaned against his desk. "Sure. That's

easy. Have you joined a gym?"

"I'm going to, but I thought maybe you could give me some lessons or something. Tell me what I need to be doing." Leonard's face crumpled. "Maeve mentioned that you looked good. When I pressed her, she made a comment about . . ." He swallowed. "Your butt."

Ford raised his eyebrows and held up his hands. "Look, there's absolutely nothing going on between Maeve and me. I haven't seen her since you were in the hospital."

"I know that," his friend told him. "I'm not saying there is. But look at you. You're a SEAL and I'm an accountant. I want her to talk about my butt."

Ford saw the combination of love and worry in Leonard's eyes. "Easy enough. You don't look like you need to lose any weight."

Leonard slapped his stomach. "I could lose ten. Maybe fifteen, but what I mostly need is to put on some muscle. Can you help with that?"

Ford walked over and patted him on the back. "I sure can. We'll make a schedule and I'll get you started. Just remember, it's not a good workout if you don't puke."

Leonard's eyes widened slightly. "You're kidding, right?"

"You're going to have to wait and see."

CHAPTER TWELVE

"You have to let go of the door handle," Ford said.

"Technically, I don't."

Isabel hung on to the Jeep with both hands. If she stayed where she was, she didn't have to go into the house. She didn't have to see anyone and she didn't have to lie. If she let go, Ford was going to make her walk into the family dinner. And then what? Denise would take one look at them and know they'd had sex.

Ford stood in front of her. "What's the problem? You know everyone in the family. We're all friendly. They like you."

"I glow."

He smiled slowly, looking more than a little self-satisfied.

"Stop it!" She glared at him. "Denise is your mother."

"She thinks we're together, so why is your glowing a bad thing?"

"It's tacky. And I don't want to talk about it."

He moved close, crowding her. "That's not what you said this morning."

Isabel kept her chin up and refused to blush. It wasn't as though she was exaggerating. Now that she'd discovered what all the fuss was really about, she couldn't seem to stop wanting Ford. While he hadn't moved in or anything, he was spending every night in her bed.

"What I said this morning has nothing to do with your family. Especially your mother." She drew in a breath. "Fine. I can do this. Just don't look at me that way."

His gaze turned predatory.

"That way. You know you're doing it. Just stop."

He chuckled and pulled her hands free of the handle, then lightly kissed her knuckles. "Just know that in three hours we'll be able to leave. We'll head home and you can be on top."

The image of what happened when she was on top quickened her breathing. "Don't do that!" she pleaded.

"Kittens," he told her. "Think about kittens. It really helps."

They walked up to the front of the house. The door opened before they got there.

"You made it," Denise said with a smile. "Welcome, Isabel."

"Thanks for inviting me," Isabel said as Denise pulled her son close and hugged him. Then she was hugged as well, and they all went into the house.

The spacious living room was empty and quiet, but plenty of noise spilled out from down the hall.

"Brace yourself," Ford murmured as they followed his mother. "It's going to be chaos."

He wasn't kidding. They stepped into the huge family room and found themselves surrounded by people. Ford was one of six kids. Four of his siblings were married and every one of them had at least one child. Some more. Which meant there were thirteen adults and eight kids, a number of dogs and more noise than a rock concert.

"Ford!" Montana called when she saw her brother. She rushed toward him. His other sisters followed suit.

Isabel stayed close and greeted everyone. As Ford had promised, the family was friendly and welcoming. But as the minutes passed and Ford was hugged and patted on the back and attacked by toddlers who thought he was cool, she felt a subtle tension invading him.

She studied him closely, wondering at the cause. He was still smiling and joking. But she saw the tightness of the muscles in his jaw and the way he kept glancing toward the exit. She felt the extra beat before he responded to questions about settling into town.

She didn't know if it was the press of people or the fact that he was dealing with his family at close range and all at once, but she realized the situation was difficult for him.

Not sure what to do, she moved next to him and took his hand. "Can we get something to drink?"

Her request caused a flurry of activity. While the family was distracted, she squeezed his fingers. She raised herself on tiptoe.

"Three hours, big guy. Then I get to be on top."

He flashed her a smile and she felt him relax.

By the time the bottles of wine had been opened, the guys had gone back to watching the game and the women were collecting in the kitchen. The older kids disappeared into the game room, while the babies were passed around.

"Can I help with anything?" Isabel asked Denise.

"I've got it under control," Ford's mother said, then sighed. "It's so nice to have the whole family here."

Montana joined them. "Kent's by himself."

"You say that like you're surprised," Denise said.

"I am. He's seeing someone. I thought he'd bring her."

Denise turned around and stared at her middle son. "Kent is dating?" She raised her voice to be heard across the room and over the game. "Kent, you're dating?"

Kent looked at her, then stared at Montana. "Really?" he asked. "You couldn't give me a couple of weeks of privacy?"

Montana winced. "Sorry. It just slipped out."

Simon, Montana's husband, was instantly at her side, as if to protect her. "Is everything all right?" he asked.

Montana smiled at him. "I'm fine. If I need you to slice up my brother into tiny pieces, I'll let you know."

Simon kissed her. "I would appreciate that."

He returned to the game.

"Who's Kent seeing?" Denise asked,

lowering her voice. "One of the women I suggested?"

"I don't think she was on the list."

Over Fourth of July, Denise had set up a booth at the festival — looking for a wife for Kent and for Ford. She'd had baby pictures of her boys so interested women could get an idea of what their children might look like, and she'd taken applications.

"Do you know Consuelo Ly?" Montana asked.

Denise frowned. "Why is that name familiar?"

"She teaches at the bodyguard academy," Isabel said, wondering why her friend hadn't mentioned dating Kent. "Have they been seeing each other long?"

"No," Montana said. "I don't think so."

Isabel figured Montana had been talking to Carter — Reese's friend. Reese was Kent's son and would be the person to know if his dad was seeing anyone.

Ah, the thrill of small-town living.

"He's a flirt," Dakota said with a sigh. "I don't want to think about what he's going to be like when he's in high school."

"It'll start before high school," Nevada said with a grin. "Look at those dimples."

"Speaking of dimples and babies," Denise said, passing around the sliced roast. "Are you and Tucker ready to have another baby?"

Nevada grimaced. "Mom, get off me. It hasn't even been six months."

"I know, but you waited awhile to get started. Grandbabies, people. I can't have too many."

"Denise," Max said gently from the far end of the table. "Don't torture your children."

She smiled at him. "You're right."

Dakota leaned toward Isabel. "Max is the voice of reason. He keeps Mom in check and for that we're grateful."

Isabel knew that Denise had been seeing Max for a few years, but so far they hadn't decided to marry. He was a great guy, very calm and centered.

The Hendrix family had produced a lot of kids, Isabel thought, feeling a twinge of longing. She and Eric hadn't discussed having children very often. She'd thought they had plenty of time and he . . . Well, she didn't know what he'd been thinking. Either way, it was good they hadn't started a family, what with the divorce and all. But she'd always seen herself as a mother. Being single was going to complicate that situation.

More food was passed around the table. Isabel watched Ford take small portions of everything, but he didn't seem to be eating. She put her hand on his thigh and felt the tension in his muscles.

He looked as though he was having a good time, but she could tell the evening was wearing on him.

"How are things going at work?" Denise asked him.

Isabel squeezed her fingers against his thigh. "He's so busy," she said with a smile. "Have you seen the facility? It's amazing. Angel's building an outdoor course that is incredibly challenging." Information Consuelo had told her. "I couldn't do it, but those of you who are more athletic should try it."

"That would be fun," Montana said. "Not that I'd go. I'm not very coordinated. Max, do you think we should have an obstacle course to train the dogs?"

And just like that, the attention was off Ford.

He put his hand on top of hers and then smiled at her. She smiled back.

Ford was always so funny and charming, she thought. Joking with everyone and acting as if he was just one of the guys. It was easy to forget that he'd been gone so long,

serving his country in difficult and dangerous places.

He wasn't the kind of man to brood, but
that didn't mean he didn't have ghosts of
his own. She ate her dinner and talked to
people, but stayed alert to any conversation
shift that might upset him.

Later, when they were driving home, she
wondered if she should say anything. Or ask
questions. In the end, she decided to let him
speak or not.

When they arrived back at their place, she
climbed out of his Jeep and started for the
house. Ford stopped her and pulled her into
his arms. He didn't kiss her; instead he held
on tight.

She rested her head on his shoulder and
breathed in the quiet of the night.

She wondered what had happened. Was it
his family? The close quarters? The questions? Just that some days he had to deal
with his past and some days he didn't?

But she didn't ask and he didn't offer.
Instead he shifted so his arm was around
her and led her toward the house.

"I'm thinking ice cream and then sex," he
said as she pulled her keys out of her purse.
"What about you?"

She fumbled with the key and he took it
from her. As he opened the door, she knew

that she wanted this. What they had to-gether. The fun and the conversation. The sex and the friendship. She wanted to be his buffer and have him take care of the yard and be manly with the barbecue. She liked the rhythm of their life together.

It wasn't love, she told herself firmly. But it was still special and something she wanted to hang on to for as long as she could.

"Ice cream and sex sound great," she told him.

He grinned. "You're the best girlfriend ever."

"I bet you say that to all your women."

"Maybe," he admitted. "But this time I mean it."

"You ready for this?" Consuelo asked.

"Sure," Kent said, even though he wasn't.

Somehow he'd agreed to work out with her. It wasn't his idea of a date, so he wasn't sure how it had happened, but here he was, in the CDS gym. Any confidence he'd arrived with had been destroyed by the sight of Ford helping his friend Leonard to his car. Leonard had been shuffling, as if his legs hurt too much to walk regularly, and he'd held an ice pack to one shoulder.

Ford's comment "Not a good place for civilians" hadn't helped.

Now he faced a petite fireball who was very likely going to kick his ass. To make matters worse, she was dressed in formfitting workout clothes that left nothing to the imagination. He was in baggy sweats and a T-shirt, but even so, if he got an erection, the world was going to know.

Basically, he had a three-part plan. Don't get injured, don't make a fool of himself and keep his eyes off Consuelo's ass.

"What do you want to do?" she asked, tilting her head so her ponytail swung toward the ground.

"You tell me." Which was a better answer than the real one, which went along the lines of "I want to have sex with you. Anywhere, anytime, again and again." He had a feeling she wouldn't respond well to that line of conversation and that if he pursued it, he would end up with something broken.

"We have a basic workout we give recruits to assess them," she told him. "How about that?"

"You don't have a basic math-teacher assessment instead? Because I'd be good at that one."

"You can take pi to eight digits?" she asked, her voice teasing.

"And beyond."

"Impressive." She grinned. "Okay, let's start with jump-squats."

She demonstrated by squatting down, then jumping high in the air before landing and then repeating the procedure.

"Ready?" she asked.

He nodded and they did them together. By the tenth, he was feeling it in his thighs. By fifteen, he was breathing hard. By number twenty, he had a vision of himself limping like Leonard.

They moved on to other exercises, each more challenging than the one before. Consuelo gave instructions as she worked along with him, barely breaking a sweat. He was thinking that he needed to up his game when it came to his four-days-a-week run. And maybe add a little weight lifting to his regimen.

"How about the ropes?" she asked, pointing to the ropes hanging from a crossbar.

"Sure." Something he could do better, he thought. Men had more upper body strength than women. At least, he hoped they did.

They jogged across the gym. She reached for a rope as he did, then started to shimmy up. She reached the crossbar before he'd climbed more than four feet. He dropped back to the mats and started to laugh.

She joined him. "What?" she asked.

"You're incredible."

"I do this for a living."

"Still, you're in great shape. I'm completely intimidated."

She got them each a bottle of water from a refrigerator in the corner. "You're not. If you were you wouldn't have wanted to work out with me. You knew I'd be good."

"True, but I underestimated your ability." He took a long drink of water and studied her. "Men do that a lot, don't they?"

She shrugged. "Sometimes."

"All the time. Because of your face and your body, they assume you're a piece of ass and don't bother to get to know you. They don't take the time to understand you and they don't offer you respect."

The reality of what he'd just said struck him. He stared at her, horrified. "I'm sorry. I shouldn't have said that."

"It's the truth."

"It was rude."

She drank more, her dark gaze never leaving his face. Her expression was unreadable. "You didn't call me a piece of ass. You said others do."

"I'm sorry."

"Like I said, it's the truth. Very few men take the time to find out who I am."

He wanted to say he was willing, but was afraid he would sound like even more of a jerk.

"If nothing else, you now have proof that I haven't dated much since my divorce," he offered.

"You think I'm mad," she said.

"Aren't you?"

She lowered the bottle and smiled. "No."

He waited, but that was all.

They finished their water and completed a few more exercises. He had a feeling he was going to be crippled in the morning. Something his students would find amusing.

"Are you limping?" she asked when he staggered to his feet after a rousing round of push-ups. She'd done more than him.

"No." He straightened, ignoring the fiery pain searing his thighs and biceps. "How about a flashy finish?"

She put her hands on her hips. "Are you challenging me?"

"Sure."

He knew he was going to regret the cocky attitude, but figured the low point of the workout had been the "piece of ass" comment.

She walked over to him and took his left arm in both her hands. Before he knew what was happening, she'd jerked him forward and then he was facing the ceiling and the floor came up very, very quickly.

He'd fallen out of a tree back when he'd been a kid. This was a lot like that, only without the broken arm. All the air rushed out of his body, and for a split second, he couldn't draw it in.

Consuelo was on her knees at his side. "I'm sorry," she said quickly, touching his face, then his arms. "Are you okay? That was so stupid of me. I was showing off. I shouldn't have done it."

Worry darkened her brown eyes. Her ponytail lightly brushed his cheek as she fussed over him. He opened his mouth and pretended to be unable to speak.

"What?" she demanded. "Are you hurt?"

He motioned her closer. "I can't breathe," he fake-gasped. "I think I need mouth-to-mouth."

She sat back on her heels and shook her head. "You are such a guy."

He sat up. "Is that a problem?"

"Not for me."

He figured she would scramble to her feet, then pull him to his. Or laugh at him. Or walk away. Instead she leaned in and kissed him.

The touch of her mouth against his was

light and brief, but the heat burned all the way down to his cock. He wanted to pull her close and let things get interesting. But they were at her place of work and she wouldn't appreciate that.

She drew back. "I really am sorry about throwing you like that."

"I'm not." He grinned. "The kiss was worth it."

"You're easy."

"As long as you consider that a good thing, I can live with that." He gently touched her cheek. "Dinner? Just us?"

She glanced around and then leaned in again. This time her mouth lingered. "Dinner," she whispered.

Isabel paused on the porch to check her phone. Still no return call from Sonia. She wondered what was going on with her friend. She'd left a message on Sonia's Facebook page, where her friend had regular updates. But the lack of direct communication was troubling.

"Auntie Is, Auntie Is!"

Isabel grinned and dropped to her knees so Brandon, Maeve's six-year-old, could run into her arms.

"Look at you," she said, squeezing him as he laughed. "You're so big."

He hugged her back, then broke free and hurried back through the front door. "I can read, Auntie Is. I have a book."

Isabel watched him bolt into the house, then followed. While she appreciated the happy greeting, she wondered how much of his enthusiasm came from his memories and how much was inspired by his older siblings. Isabel knew she'd had more to do with them than the younger ones. Mostly due to time and distance, but still.

Maeve waited at the front door. "You're going to have to listen to one of his 'Bob' books now," she said by way of greeting. "It's the first level of reading. 'Bob can walk. Bob can jump.' "

"Sounds like a bestseller."

They hugged. Isabel patted her sister's stomach.

"You seem to have something in there. You knew that, right?"

"Very funny."

They settled in the family room. In addition to a huge sectional sofa, there were several chairs, a large, square coffee table with padded corners and toys everywhere.

Maeve burrowed onto a cushion and sighed. "I tried to pick up before you got here, but I'm at the tired stage of my pregnancy. In the next few weeks, I'll get my energy back and then watch out."

"You would know," Isabel said, thinking Maeve had plenty of practice.

Maeve and Leonard had waited a year before getting married, just to make sure their love was the real thing. By then Leonard had graduated from college and passed the CPA exam. He got a job with the biggest accounting firm in town. Two years later, Maeve had gotten pregnant. The kids had kept on coming. Now she had four, all under the age of nine, with a fifth on the way.

"Is this the last one?" Isabel asked.

"I think so." She smiled. "Leonard says yes, for sure. But we love having kids. We've talked about maybe stopping having our own, but adopting a few. Not babies. There are plenty of people who want an infant. We're thinking maybe older kids who would benefit from a stable home and life in a town like this one."

"Impressive," Isabel murmured. "Now I officially feel shallow."

Her sister's blue eyes were concerned. "Why would you say that? You're a successful businesswoman. That's impressive. All I do is stay home with a bunch of kids." She smiled. "Not that what I do isn't important and I love it, but I haven't ever seriously worked in the world. When Leonard and I were first married, I knew my job was to save for our house down payment. I didn't want a career. When the youngest is in school, I may get something part-time, but I can't imagine doing what you do."

"Right now I'm working at Paper Moon. Which isn't that notable."

"But you'll start your own business."

"That's the plan."

Maeve leaned her head against the sofa. "You always loved that store. You and Grandma were there together every weekend. You knew all the styles of dresses by the time you were five, and by ten, you could have ordered the inventory."

Isabel nodded. "She was wonderful."

"She liked you best."

Isabel wrinkled her nose. "She liked that I loved the store."

"Same thing. Paper Moon was her life. I never got the point. I guess retail isn't my thing." Her sister looked at her. "You'll take that with you when you open your own place."

"I hope so. It's going to be different. Back to New York for me."

"I wish you could stay around." Maeve raised one hand. "I know, I know. New York is a fashion capital and all that. Fool's Gold isn't going to be a star on anyone's trendy map. Still. Mom's been getting regular reports from our local gossips, and everyone says you're doing great. Just so you know, the parents are secretly hoping you'll change your mind and stay."

Isabel sighed. "I know. She mentioned it the last time we talked."

"You tempted?"

"I have a goal and it doesn't include staying here." Not that being home was as horrible as she'd thought it might be. In fact, parts of her return were quite excellent. Her friends, for one, and Ford. Ford was an unexpected gift.

"Do you and the folks have a timetable?" Maeve asked.

"They're due back from their trip before Thanksgiving. Then we'll go over my plan for refurbishing the store. It should all be done by the holidays, and then we'll put the store up for sale after the first of the year."

"That makes me sad," Maeve admitted. "Paper Moon should stay in the family. But you have your dreams and I have no interest in running it."

"I know what you mean," Isabel told her. "I feel badly about it, too. Sometimes I wonder if I could stay, but I don't want to deal with crazy brides all day. I want to do more. And I have my business partner."

"That's right. Sonia. Let me guess. She's one of those East Coast people who assumes the continent simply ends when you hit the Mississippi."

"Pretty much."

Conversation shifted to how Leonard's business was doing and then talk about the kids. Brandon came back downstairs with two toys and one of his books that he read to both of them. Two hours flew by. When Isabel realized the time, she stood.

"I've left Madeline alone for too long. She gets nervous if there are too many things going on."

"Does she like the work?" Maeve asked, struggling to her feet.

"A lot and she's good at it. I'm hoping whoever we sell to will keep her on."

The sisters hugged.

"I'm sorry I haven't come by sooner," Isabel said. "I won't wait so long next time."

"I'd like that," her sister told her. "You could be wild and come on a Saturday morning when everyone's home. It's loud then, but it's fun."

"I will," Isabel promised.

"Good. Because you're always welcome here, sis. I want you to know that."

CHAPTER THIRTEEN

"I'd like to speak to you about a dress."

Isabel glanced up at the woman who had just walked into Paper Moon and wanted to ask what was wrong with this picture. The potential customer was tall and elegantly dressed in a dark gray tailored suit. Long black hair hung straight down her back. Her eyes were a nearly violet color of blue, and she had on killer red pumps with at least four-inch heels. She looked capable of ruling the world and still having time left over to organize international banking. She exuded confidence and determination. If Isabel had to guess an age, she would say close to mid-thirties. And while she was familiar, Isabel didn't know where she'd seen her before.

"A wedding gown?" Isabel asked.

The woman shuddered. "God, no. I meant the purple dress in the window. It's gorgeous. I want to buy it."

Isabel grinned. "You might want to try it on first."

"Right. I always get hung up on the details. Let's start there."

"Sure." Isabel walked through the store and opened the door to the display window. "You said the purple one?"

"Uh-huh."

Rather than wrestle the mannequin out of the window, she undid the zipper and pulled off the dress. She stepped back into the store.

"Here you go. There are dressing rooms through this way." Isabel paused. "I feel like we've met, but I can't place your name."

"Taryn Crawford." The woman held out her hand. "I'm moving here to town, I'm sad to say."

"You don't want to move to Fool's Gold?"

"No. It's small. I like the big city. Los Angeles is more my speed. I like the fact that everyone is shallow. It's refreshing. There's no pretense of empathy. You know what you're getting. From what I can tell, Fool's Gold is one giant beating heart of caring. All those festivals. People talk to me while I'm waiting in line for coffee." She shuddered. "Happy families everywhere. It's not natural."

Isabel laughed. "You're not big on families?"

"Not for me. Families are a wonderful thing for other people. I like children . . . mostly from a distance." She sighed. "This all makes me sound horrible and I'm not. I'm very nice. Not as nice as the people in this town, though."

Isabel opened a dressing room door, then stepped back to let Taryn enter. The woman thanked her, then closed the door.

What an interesting person, Isabel thought. Talk about honest to a fault.

A minute or so later, Taryn walked out in the purple dress.

It was fitted, with long sleeves and a conservative hemline. But in the back, a deep, teardrop-shaped cutout turned ordinary into sexy.

Taryn stepped up onto the low platform in front of the mirrors and studied herself.

"The dress is really well made," she said. "You're not charging enough. The quality workmanship is only exceeded by the fabric. This is excellent. I love the fit."

"It looks great," Isabel said, trying not to feel bitter that the other woman was about two inches taller than her and yet a good five sizes smaller. Isabel had never minded being curvy, but every now and then she wondered if she should cut back on the cookies, or maybe go to the gym.

Without having much of a plan, Isabel walked to the accessory armoire and started opening doors and drawers. She discarded three belts before finding the right one. She also had a scarf, she thought, digging through piles of discarded props for various weddings.

When she found the scarf, she brought it and the belt to Taryn. "Try these."

Taryn piled her hair on top of her head and turned to looked at the cutout. She released her hair and fastened the belt. "Fabulous," she breathed as she reached for the scarf. "Is this your design?"

"No. Someone I know represents the designer. Dellina, my friend, is in town. She organizes parties and does some decorating. She asked me to carry a few pieces. They've been selling really well."

"I'll take it," Taryn said, letting her hair fall. "But seriously, Dellina needs to tell her friend to raise her prices." She stepped off the platform and walked barefoot toward Isabel. "I'm going to need Dellina's number."

"Okay, um, why?"

"As I mentioned, my business is moving here. We're going to be buying new offices in the next few months and remodeling them. I'm guessing we'll make the physical move in February or March of next year. At that point, I'll need a decorator."

"What's the business?"

"Score. It's a PR firm." Taryn rolled her eyes. "My partners are former football players. They're the ones who found Fool's Gold. A friend of theirs had a pro-am golf tournament here and they played in it. Apparently it was love at first sight. We had a vote and I lost." She flashed an unexpected smile. "Not to worry. I'll figure out some way to punish them. But in the meantime, we're relocating our headquarters."

Former football players in Fool's Gold? Isabel started to tell Taryn that good-looking men were always welcome, but decided the other woman might not appreciate the news.

"It's a great place to live," Isabel offered.

"How long have you been here?" Taryn asked.

"I grew up here, then moved to New York. I'm only back for a few months . . ." Her voice trailed off.

Taryn nodded. "You're proving my point. All the good ones escape."

Isabel laughed. "If you're going to be around for a while, maybe you'd like to have lunch with me and my friends. It might help you feel more excited about the move. You know, if you meet a few people."

Taryn stared at her. "Please don't take this wrong, but is everyone nice? Because I find that to be a problem."

"No. They're fun and great people, and they can be snarky. Especially Charlie. In fact, I think the two of you could be very good friends."

"Then count me in."

The old house was about an hour outside Sacramento. The large trees on the property had started changing colors, and orange and red leaves drifted across the ground. In the distance, a couple of horses ran together, as if they, too, felt the perfection of the cool fall day.

Forty or fifty cars were parked beside an old red barn with fading and peeling paint. A second barn stood a couple of dozen feet away.

"You've stopped pouting," Isabel teased as she got out of the Jeep.

Ford shrugged into his beat-up leather jacket. "I wasn't pouting."

"Sure you were. There was heavy sighing and a few moans."

"I didn't moan."

She laughed. In truth, Ford had come

through on his promise to take her to an estate sale. They'd picked this one together. Although it was a fair drive from Fool's Gold, Isabel had thought he would enjoy the variety of items being sold.

"The farmhouse has been in the family over a hundred and fifty years," she said. "Look at it. All that attic space and out-buildings. We could find something really special today."

"Hey, maybe I can get a tractor."

She sighed. "Are you going to be difficult? Because if you are, can you wait in the car?"

He laughed and took her hand in his. "I'm not going to be difficult. Come on. Let's go find some treasures."

They moved toward the house.

A teenaged girl handed them a flyer. "Furniture in the house," she said, pointing. "Smaller items in the two barns. Cash only. We'll hold the furniture a week, if you need us to, but you have to pay a deposit."

"Thanks." Isabel took the flyer and turned away from the house.

"They're organized," Ford said. "I figured it would be like a garage sale, but they have way more stuff."

"Most aren't like this. At least, not the ones I go to. I guess they've been planning the sale for a while."

They walked toward the first barn. A steady crowd flowed in and out. She saw that someone had set up an awning, and there were three cash registers on tables. Several teenaged boys helped carry purchases to vehicles.

"What are they going to do here?" he asked. "With the land?"

"I heard it was going to be a subdivision. Which makes me sad. A family owned this land for years."

"For some people, this is progress." He glanced at her. "You're not going to say you want to buy it, are you?"

"No. I'm moving to New York. But still, that was a great house, back in the day. There were probably a lot of kids running around. You had that."

"Yup. It was loud."

She liked the feel of his hand in hers and the way he walked next to her. He was fun to be with, she thought. Conversation was easy.

"Want to talk about being at your mom's the other night?"

She thought he might say no or pretend not to understand what she was asking. Instead he squeezed her hand and spoke.

"It's family," he said. "They make it easier and harder. I'm one of the lucky ones. I don't have flashbacks. I don't have night-mares. But every now and then, the social situations get to be too much." He shifted in front of her so she had to come to a stop and look up at him. "You ran interference."

She stared at the center of his chest and shrugged. "I tried to help."

"You did. Thanks for that."

She raised her chin and smiled. "And now I'm going to introduce you to the delights of an estate sale. Yet another reason you should treasure me."

He groaned. "I'd nearly forgotten. All right. Let's get this over with."

They went into the first barn. Isabel liked how they'd set out everything by category and on large folding tables pushed together in long rows.

"We can ignore the clothes," she said. "I'm not into vintage. Unless you want something circa 1950."

"No, thanks. Hey, look. They have old records."

"Do you have a record player?"

"No, but Gideon loves them. Let's see what they have."

They started sorting through LPs and 45s. There were a couple of old jazz records from the late 1940s, along with plenty of stuff from the '50s.

She saw that he was going to look in earnest, so she wandered away to check out the stacks of books. She found several older children's books she remembered from when she was a kid and thought Maeve might like them for her kids. In the kitchen section, she found a cute pitcher with a cracked handle. She carried it over to Ford.

"Could you fix this?" she asked.

He glanced at the pitcher. "No. I'm good in bed. Anything else, we're going to have to hire out."

A reasonable trade, she thought, then glanced at the stack of records he'd accumulated. "You're buying all those?"

"Yup. They're cheap enough. Gideon can give away the ones he doesn't want or already has."

They paid for the records and took them to the Jeep, then returned to the second barn. There Ford was excited to find a couple of tables overflowing with vintage Harley memorabilia.

"For Angel?" she guessed.

"Just a couple of things." He tucked them into an empty box from the stack against the walls. "Let's go look at toys. I've got nieces and nephews born what feels like every other month."

By noon, they'd nearly filled the back of

the Jeep. Isabel had fallen in love with an old handmade quilt. She'd also bought two antique wedding veils. She might not be into all things vintage, but some of her clients were.

They walked around the barn to an open, grassy area. There, tables and a grill were set up. Ford ordered two burgers while she grabbed canned soda and chips. When their food was ready, they sat at one of the picnic tables.

"Okay," he said, smearing mustard on his burger. "You were right. This was better than I thought it would be."

"They aren't all like this," she pointed out, "but I'm glad you had a good estate-sale experience."

"You're gloating," he said with a grin. "Admit it."

She laughed. "Okay, yes. I love to be right. Doesn't everyone?"

"Not me. I'm a consensus builder."

"Oh, sure. That's why you're always betting with Angel about races and workouts."

"I have no idea what you're talking about." He took a bite of his burger and chewed. When he'd swallowed, he said, "He and I haven't been doing that as much. I guess because I don't live with him anymore." His gaze settled on her face. "Not that I'm complaining about my living arrangements now."

She sipped her soda but didn't speak. Ford had pretty much moved into the house. He spent every night in her bed and hogged the shower in the morning. The good news was, he was only in it for about fifteen seconds. Apparently the navy taught a seaman how to shower quickly. No doubt it was about the whole being-on-a-boat thing.

"You're saying I'm more fun than Angel?" she asked.

"You're a different kind of fun."

"Thanks." She picked up her burger. "What about when you were on missions or whatever? Did you have girlfriends there?"

"A girl in every port?" he asked as she took a bite and chewed.

She nodded.

"No. We would go in, do what had to be done and leave."

"Were you ever stationed in another country?"

"Lots of times. A few years ago, I was invited to be part of a task force. We pooled skills."

"Any women?"

He raised his eyebrows. "What do you want to know?"

"I'm not sure. Nothing specific. Were you like James Bond, with a woman waiting around every corner, or more like in those war movies where the only women are waitresses?"

"Not a lot of women where I went," he said. "No women on the team. Consuelo worked with some special forces units, but we never had an assignment together."

"Then how did you meet?"

He grinned. "She'd been flown in for a secret assignment. My team was there for a different op. Quarters were tight and she had to bunk somewhere. I offered my room."

Isabel put down her burger. "You slept with her?"

She tried to keep her voice calm, but it was difficult. Knowing Ford loved all women but committed to none was one thing. Thinking about him with beautiful, sexy, dangerous Consuelo was something else.

"Sleep with her?" He shook his head. "No way. Not only did she threaten to cut off my balls if I tried anything, she reminded me of my sisters. That wasn't very appealing." He shrugged. "We became friends. She wasn't with me and Angel when we rescued Gideon, but she was waiting in the village.

She's the one who found Gideon the place in Bali."

His dark eyes widened. "You're not worried that I had a thing with her, are you?"

"Not anymore."

"She's not my type." He put his hand on top of hers. "Hey, I'm faithful. I might not marry the girl, but I don't cheat on her."

"I appreciate that."

"Do you believe it?"

She nodded.

They went back to their lunch. Isabel knew that she had to keep her heart safe when it came to Ford. That what had started out as something fun but meaningless had turned into something more. Not just because he'd helped her figure out what it really meant to be physically intimate with a man, but because she liked him. From the flames painted on his Jeep to the records he'd bought for his friend, to how he brought her coffee every morning, she liked him. But he was committed to staying and she was committed to leaving, so anything other than what they already had wasn't possible.

She would be strong, she told herself. She would hold her heart separate and not let him touch her emotions. It was safer that way.

After lunch, they made a quick pass through the house, but didn't see any furniture they had to have.

"Just as well," Ford said. "We don't have the room."

"They said they'd hold it. We could have made a second trip."

"I don't go backward," he said. "Move forward or die."

"That's a cheerful philosophy."

He held open the passenger door for her. She started to climb into her seat, only to find a small box there.

"Did you want to put this in the back?" she asked, holding it out to him.

"No. It's for you." He shrugged. "It made me think of you, so I got it."

She opened the box and saw a dragonfly pendant on a delicate gold chain. The dragonfly was made up of different-colored stones. Sapphires and amethysts, garnets and topaz. The small pendant was both beautiful and whimsical.

"I love it," she whispered, then looked at him. "Thank you."

"I know pretend-dating me has been hard on you." One corner of his mouth turned up. "Not the sex. We both know I'm a god in bed. But dealing with my mom and family stuff. You've been great and I appreciate it. This is to say thank you."

She took the necklace out of the box and handed it to him. After turning so her back was to him, she moved her hair out of the way.

He fastened the necklace around her neck and she released her hair.

"What do you think?" she asked.

"Beautiful," he murmured. "Just like you."

He lightly kissed her, before stepping back and closing the door.

She touched the small pendant, then reached for her seat belt. Ford got in next to her and started the engine. They discussed the best way back to Fool's Gold, but her heart wasn't in the conversation. It was, she realized, shifting loyalty. Her plan of keep it, and her, safe had a flaw she hadn't noticed before. That flaw was Ford himself. A man it might be impossible not to love.

Ford looked at the empty plate on the table. He and Angel had already eaten nearly a dozen cookies between them. Getting more would mean a harder run later. But the price might be worth it. The planning meeting was tough to get through. Sugar and another coffee might help.

"Don't even think about it," Angel said

with a growl. "Keep your ass in the chair."

"Are you talking to me, old man?"

Angel looked up from his pad of paper. "We have to get this done today. Justice has to present the obstacle course to the client."

"And that would be your job," Ford reminded him. "I'm the sales guy."

"You're bringing in too many customers," Angel mumbled.

Ford leaned back in his chair. "Sorry, what? I didn't catch that."

"I should kill you where you sit," his friend grumbled.

Ford looked around the brightly lit interior of Brew-haha. "And ruin Patience's store? The one she's worked so hard on? Justice wouldn't like that. Plus, with me dead, you can kiss your successful business goodbye."

"We'd find another sales guy."

"Not like me."

Angel tossed down his pencil. "If you're so damned special, you fix it."

Ford took the pad and studied the design. "Who's this for again?"

His friend swore. "Seriously? We've been talking about these customers for an hour and you don't know who they are?"

"I was thinking about something else."

Angel's expression darkened. Ford recognized he might be hitting the breaking point.

"Corporate, right?" he asked hastily. "So we need to assume some of the team are out of shape." He looked back at the course Angel had come up with. "Walk-arounds."

The other man's eyes brightened. "Walk-arounds. We get to build a challenging course and no one gets dead."

"Or seriously injured."

Angel took back the pad and started making notes. "You think they expect that? There has to be some blood. If there isn't, how will they know they've had a good time?"

"Civilians don't think like that, my friend."

A walk-around would mean anyone could simply walk around whatever the challenge was. A rope bridge, a chin-up bar, anything they couldn't physically do. But they'd stay with the group and enjoy the collective experience.

"Is rappelling too much?" Ford asked. "It's hard but satisfying. It would give them something to talk about on Monday morning, when they're back at the office."

He paused, but there wasn't an answer. He returned his attention to Angel to find his friend staring at a woman getting coffee.

"You know her?" he asked.

Angel didn't speak. As far as Ford could tell, the man wasn't breathing. Slowly, his expression tightened from interested to predatory.

Ford looked back at the woman. She was tall, with long dark hair that hung straight down her back. She had on a suit, so she worked in some kind of business, and she wore those really high pumps that he'd always thought were a good way to break a leg. Although he had to admit she wore them well.

She was attractive enough, he supposed. Nowhere near as pretty as Isabel, but few women were.

The woman paid for her latte, got her drink and left without once glancing at Angel.

"Who is she?" Ford asked.

"Hell if I know."

"You're going to find out?"

Angel gave him a slow, determined smile. "If it's the last thing I do."

CHAPTER FOURTEEN

"Should we say something?" Patience asked as she and Isabel walked into Jo's Bar for lunch. "Do you think she saw us?"

"I don't think we should worry," Isabel said. "We've had lunch at other restaurants before."

"But not right in front of me," Jo said, appearing out of nowhere and staring at both of them. "Really? Street food? Is that what it's come to? Have I been wasting my money on things like tables and chairs?"

Isabel couldn't tell if the other woman was kidding or not, and based on her silence, Patience wasn't sure, either. Felicia walked in and moved toward them.

"Jo's upset," Patience murmured.

"Don't be ridiculous. She has no reason to be upset. There's no way to avoid competition, especially in a town this small. Maybe Ana Raquel shouldn't park directly in front of Jo's place, but other than that, she's within her rights. Besides, the street food will be less appealing when it gets cold, and Jo's customers will return. She hardly wants to chase them away by pretending anger." She paused. "I could be wrong about all of that, too."

"Nope," Jo said, handing them menus and pointing to a table by the back wall. "I heard you were expecting a big crowd today, so I saved that space."

"She was messing with us," Patience said. "I don't know how I feel about that."

"I'd go with it," Isabel told her. "We love coming here."

They took seats at the table. Charlie and Noelle arrived next. Consuelo followed. Heidi and Annabelle Stryker took chairs and said how happy they were to join them for once. Taryn Crawford arrived last.

As the tall, gorgeous brunette walked up to the table, everyone went silent. Isabel motioned to the seat she'd been saving next to herself and rose.

"Everyone, this is Taryn. She's new to town. Her business is moving here."

"Officially after the first of the year, but I came early to get things ready." She raised her eyebrows. "I was promised you weren't especially nice and I'm hoping that's true."

Charlie chuckled. "Next time sit by me."

"Sure," Taryn said as she sank into her chair.

"I'm going to go around the table and introduce everyone," Isabel said. "Then you're on your own."

"Great suit," Heidi said when Taryn had been introduced to them all. "I never get to dress like that. It wouldn't be practical."

"What do you do?"

"Raise goats. I make cheese and soap."

Taryn blinked. "Seriously?"

"Sure. I sell goat milk and manure, too."

"Do we have to shake hands?" Taryn asked.

Heidi grinned.

"You are really beautiful," Patience said. "That's trouble. We've barely gotten used to Felicia."

"My attractiveness is offset by social awkwardness," Felicia reminded them.

"She's really smart," Consuelo added. "It's a weird combination. But she's fun. I, on the other hand, am only a pain in the ass."

"That's not true," Annabelle told her. "You were seen with a certain someone recently. Going out to dinner with Kent. There was no report of kissing, but rumors are flying anyway."

"So it's true?" Isabel said. "You're really

dating him? His sisters said something at the family dinner, but I wasn't sure."

"*Dating* is a strong word," Consuelo mumbled. "We're seeing each other. It's early."

Isabel turned to Taryn. "Kent is part of the Hendrix family. They're one of the town's founding families. There are six kids, including Kent. Three boys and triplet girls. They're all married now. Except for Kent and Ford."

"Tell her how you're fake-dating Ford," Charlie called from across the table.

Isabel winced. "Don't say that so loud. This is Fool's Gold. What if someone reports back to Denise?"

Taryn's eyes glazed over. "Fake-dating?"

"It's complicated," Isabel said, glaring at Charlie. "And a long story."

"She's sleeping with him, too," Charlie added with a grin.

"What's the point of fake-dating if you aren't getting laid?" Taryn murmured.

Jo came up in time to hear the last comment. "Nice," she said. "I'm going to like this one. What'll you have, ladies?"

There were orders for diet soda and iced tea. Chips, salsa and guacamole were ordered for the table.

"I have specials," Jo told them and explained what they were, then left.

"So what is your company?" Annabelle asked.

"PR and marketing," Taryn said. "We handle a lot of sports-based companies, not surprising considering the boys. We have a couple of microbrewery accounts, but I swear it's just so they can go off and taste samples."

"The boys?" Patience asked. "They can't be your sons?"

"Oh, sorry. I get so used to calling them that. Not boys in age, although a case could be made in emotional maturity. My business partners. I work with three former football players."

"Anyone we would have heard of?" Charlie asked.

Taryn sighed. "Jack McGarry, Sam Ridge and Kenny Scott."

Even Isabel had heard of Jack McGarry. "Wasn't he some famous quarterback?"

"Unfortunately."

Consuelo laughed. "Why unfortunately?"

"Because it goes to his head. Jack is very much the guy walking around thinking, 'But hey, it's *me.*' Sam was a kicker and one of the best. Kenny's a receiver. Good hands and he runs like the wind." She smiled. "They are good-looking, handsome and single. Women are everywhere. One of the reasons I agreed to move here is because I thought it would be quieter. Fewer fans to interfere with work."

"They're all single?" Heidi asked. "What about you? Not interested? I mean, if they're all you say . . ."

"They're all that," Taryn told her. "They're also spoiled, petulant and disgustingly good at their jobs. Sam handles the money. I want to complain, but I can't. Jack and Kenny are the rainmakers. There's not a client alive they can't charm into signing."

"Which makes you what?" Charlie asked.

"The one who holds it all together. They bring me the client, I do the presentation. We have an in-house graphics team and account reps who are assigned various clients. That's why I'm here. To find us office space that doesn't include a basketball court or isn't across the street from a strip club."

"I don't think we have a strip club in town," Annabelle said.

"That's a blessing."

"CDS — the company where I work — remodeled an old warehouse," Consuelo told her. "You might want to look by us. There are other old warehouses available. They have plenty of room and aren't too expensive. You're going to have to remodel anyway."

"That's an idea. If we're not in the center of town, they can be as loud as they want."

"They're loud?" Patience asked.

Taryn shrugged. "They're good guys, but think about it. They were football players who made it to the NFL. No one ever tells them no. If they can't win it, they can buy it. But they're sweet. Jack and Kenny especially. Sam's a bit more reserved. But these are not men comfortable with losing at anything. Ever. It's exhausting."

"And you haven't —" Heidi began.

"Slept with them," Charlie interrupted. "She's asking if you slept with them."

"I didn't say that," Heidi said primly. "I was going to hint strongly."

"No," Taryn said. "Well, except when Jack and I were married."

Isabel felt her eyes widen. "You were married to your business partner?"

"A long story for another day. Preferably over martinis," she said as Jo arrived with the drinks and the chips.

"Now we all have to see them," Annabelle said. "To check out what you've said. If they're as hot as you say."

"They're hot. Great bodies and they look good naked." Taryn sipped her soda.

"I thought you'd only slept with Jack,"

Consuelo said.

"I have, but these are guys who have been in locker rooms all their lives. They don't care about things like being naked. Plus, they're proud as hell of their bodies. If I had a nickel for every meeting I had to attend in some damn steam room . . ."

"I know that one," Consuelo admitted. "I work with a bunch of former military guys. They're always walking around naked. It gets old."

She and Taryn touched glasses in solidarity.

Isabel looked at Patience. "This is news to me. Is it news to you?"

"Oh, yeah," Patience said, her expression determined. "Justice is going to have some explaining to do."

Conversation shifted to other topics. Nearly two hours later, lunch was done and everyone left to head back to work or goats. When they were standing outside Jo's, Taryn hugged Isabel.

"Thanks for inviting me. That was fun and it helps to know some people around here. After I pick the office, I'm going to be gone for a few weeks. At least until escrow closes. I'd like to call when I get back. Maybe we can hang out."

"I'd like that."

The tall, well-dressed woman walked away.

"She makes me feel short and casual," Consuelo said. "But she's hot."

Isabel laughed. "Me, too, and I'm about her height."

They started walking together.

"So, how's the fake-dating going?" Consuelo asked.

"Good. It's fun. We went to an estate sale." Isabel touched the dragonfly pendant she wore.

"It's not fake for you, is it?" her friend asked, her voice uncharacteristically gentle.

"I don't think so. Not anymore. I like him."

"Liking can be dangerous."

"Feeling a little nervous yourself?" Isabel asked.

"Yeah. Kent's a great guy and I like his son a lot. But who am I kidding? I'm not going to fit into their world."

"Why not? You're single, he's single. You'd be terrific with Reese. Is it the small town? Are you still adjusting to living here?"

"Some. I just worry about my past." She glanced over her shoulder. "Look, I need to go."

Isabel wanted to ask her more. About her experiences and what she should know about Ford's. But her friend was already walking away. Isabel wondered if she really had an appointment or if she was just trying to escape the conversation.

Ford walked into Jo's Bar and nodded at Jo. Because she ran the kind of bar that was easy to be in, she didn't ask a lot of questions designed to make him want to bang his head against the wall. Instead her only word was "Beer" and that was in the form of a question.

"Great," he told her and started for the back room.

Here the space was smaller, darker, and there weren't any fashion shows on the damn TV. Baseball played, along with a car auction. Ethan stood at the pool table, racking the balls.

"Hey," he said when he saw his brother.

"Hey."

Kent walked in carrying three beers. "Jo gave me these."

"Good woman," Ethan said, taking one.

Ford grunted in agreement.

They stood in a loose circle and proceeded to use rock-paper-scissors to determine which of them would play first. Ethan lost and stepped away from the table. Ford and Kent both grabbed a pool cue.

"So, how's it going?" Ethan asked.

"Good," Kent said, taking his place to break.

"Same." Ford sipped his beer, then glanced at Ethan. "You?"

"Great."

Kent broke and the balls went speeding around the table. Two and three dropped into pockets.

"Nice," Ford said.

Kent grinned. "Reese and I have been practicing."

"So you want stripes?"

"Right," Kent said, ignoring him. "Seven in the left front pocket." He angled his cue and gave a sharp shove. The maroon ball sailed into the pocket without touching the sides of the table.

Ethan put down his bottle. "You bring cash?" he asked Ford.

"Yeah, but maybe not enough."

Kent chuckled. "It's your first time since you're back, baby brother. I'm going easy on you."

"Good to know."

On the TV the Red Sox player hit what seemed to be a home run. The three of them stopped to watch the ball sail over the outfield and drop into the stands.

"Hell of a hit," Ethan said.

"Great player." Kent lined up his next shot.

Ethan walked over to Ford. "Things okay?"

"Sure."

He turned to Kent. "You?"

"Fine. At your house?"

"All good."

"Four in the corner," Kent said, leaning over the table.

And with that, Ford thought, they were done. Emotional temperatures gauged, problems discussed, the world righted. Something the women in his life would never understand.

Ford dragged the rake across the grass. Fall had definitely come to Fool's Gold. The days were notably shorter; the leaves were turning and falling. Up on the mountain, scarlets and yellows created a quilt of bright colors. Here in town, all those colors meant leaf cleanup.

Isabel collected the yard-waste bin and eyed the growing pile. "There's not going to be enough room," she said. "The trees are serious about shedding."

"You have yard-waste bags in the garage," he told her. "On the shelf above the lawn mower. They'll take the extras."

She put her hands on her hips. "You're spending way too much time over here if you know where stuff like that is."

He grinned. "I happened to see them last time I mowed. I'm not taking inventory."

He wore an old Los Angeles Stallions sweatshirt and jeans. Battered boots and no jacket. His hair was mussed and he hadn't shaved that morning. He looked better than a hot-fudge sundae. Looking at him practically made her stomach growl.

Their fake relationship was starting to confuse her. Mostly because it was so easy. He was here every night. They had dinner together, did chores. She'd joined him on that work dinner, and he occasionally popped into Paper Moon.

Lately, the thought of leaving wasn't as thrilling as it had been. Sure, the dream of her own store was still a draw, but what about Ford?

Whenever those questions arose, she reminded herself that this wasn't real. That while she was emotionally engaged, he wasn't, and that if she stayed, he would break her heart. Wouldn't it be easier to be on the other side of the country instead of having the risk of seeing him around every corner?

She heard the phone ring in the house.

311

"I'll go get that," she said.

"I know you're calling yourself on your cell," he yelled after her. "To get out of work."

She was still laughing when she picked up the phone. "Hello?"

"Hi, Isabel, it's Denise Hendrix. How are you?"

The laughter faded in her throat. "Fine, thank you. And you?"

"I'm doing great. I was thinking we didn't get much time to talk when you and Ford were over for dinner. The family is such a crowd. I think we should spend some quality time together, so I thought we could go out for tea. The lodge has one every month, on Saturday afternoon. I'd invite the triplets, so it would just be us girls. How does that sound?"

Isabel opened her mouth, then closed it. Tea with his mother and sisters? Lying to them directly for a couple of hours?

"I'm sorry, Denise, but Saturdays are really difficult for me," she said. "It's our busiest day at the store. I usually have fittings and showings. I only have Madeline helping me, so I can't really leave her alone on a Saturday."

"Hmm, I hadn't thought of that. All right. I'll come up with something else. Your store is closed on Monday, isn't it?"

"Yes," Isabel said weakly.

"Good. I'll be in touch."

Trapped, she thought grimly. She was completely trapped.

She dragged herself back to the front porch and collapsed on the steps. Ford frowned at her, then dropped the rake and walked over. Even the sight of him, all masculine and sexy, didn't make her feel better.

"What?" he asked when he was in front of her.

"Your mother wants me to have tea with her and your sisters. But the lodge only does tea on Saturday afternoons and I can't leave the store then."

"Problem solved."

"Not exactly. She confirmed I have Mondays off and is going to come up with something else. Something I won't be able to get out of."

He tugged her to her feet and wrapped his arms around her. "I'm sorry," he said, staring into her eyes. "How can I make this up to you?"

He smelled good. Clean with a hint of leaves. The air was crisp, but he was warm, and as she settled into his embrace, she wondered what it would be like to never let

313

go. Dangerous thoughts, she reminded herself. Also pointless. But the question remained.

"You don't have to," she told him. "I just want to pout."

"You're an adorable pouter. Cutest ever."

That made her smile.

Then his mouth was on hers, and he was nudging her back toward the front door.

"What are you doing?" she asked, not doing very much to avoid his hot, arousing kisses.

"Making it up to you."

"You're not all that," she told him.

He grinned. "Yes, I am."

Yes, he was, she thought, giving herself over to the feel of his mouth against hers and his tongue slipping past her lips. She hung on as he kicked the front door closed, then moved his hands under her sweater.

Her body already anticipated the pleasure that would follow. The slow, steady road to arousal, of how he would touch and lick and tease every inch of her. She trembled slightly as she thought about the laughing argument they would have about who got to be on top and the way their rapid breathing synchronized as they got closer and closer. How he held off until he was sure she'd fallen over the edge of the world and then how he followed her.

Once they were in the living room, she pulled off her sweater. He took it from her and dropped it onto a chair. While she pulled off her shoes and socks, he did the same. She unfastened his jeans and he ripped off his sweatshirt. Her jeans and thong followed, because for them, the fun didn't start until they were both naked.

"Me," she breathed, moving behind him.

"Me" meaning she got to be in charge. She got to say when and how.

He growled his complaint but didn't protest.

As she stopped directly behind him, she noticed all the perfection that was his body. Not that there weren't cuts and bruises. You couldn't do what he did in a day and not have physical evidence. There were also scars — a couple she thought might be bullet wounds. Not that he would tell her. Ford simply didn't talk about what he'd done in the military.

But he knew how to work out so every inch of him was honed muscle. Now she placed her hands in the center of his back and slid out and down, over his narrow hips, before grabbing his butt and squeezing.

She got close and pressed the front of her body against the back of his. She cupped her breasts in her hands and lightly dragged her tight nipples against his back. He sucked in his breath.

After she dropped back to his hips, she eased her hand around to his front. She leaned her cheek against his back and closed her eyes, then explored as much as she could reach. His chest, his rib cage. She danced her fingers against his nipples before sliding down his belly to his erection.

Her eyes still closed, her face still pressed against his back, she began to move the way he'd taught her. The way she'd watched him please himself one evening after they'd shared a bath. He'd stretched out on the bed, with her sitting next to him, not touching him, just watching as he took himself over the edge.

She'd been too shy to return the favor, despite how turned on she'd been, so he'd gone down on her, bringing her to orgasm in about thirty seconds. But a few days later, she'd managed to put on her own show, at halftime with a football game on TV. Ford had told her it had been by far the best play of the game.

Now she moved up and down, steadily increasing the speed, focusing on the tension she felt building in his body and the increase in his breathing.

Heat moved through her, making her want to squirm closer and rub against him. Blood hummed as her excitement grew. She was swelling — she could feel it. Getting ready for him. The thought of him pushing inside her, filling her, made her own breath catch.

He grabbed her wrist and pulled her hand away, then spun toward her. Before she knew what he had planned, he was lifting her onto the sofa table and spreading her legs.

He filled her with one long, powerful thrust. She groaned as she arched back, taking all of him into her. When they were pressed together, groin to groin, she wrapped her legs around his hips and held him close.

"Now you'll never get away," she said with a smile.

He cupped her breasts in his hands and rubbed his thumbs against her nipples. "Why would I want to?"

He kissed her then, deeply, his tongue moving against hers. She ran her fingers along his shoulder and the back of his neck. Suddenly he wrapped his arms around her and held her tight. There was almost a fierceness to his embrace. Not from aggression, she thought, hugging him back, but from some need he would never name.

He was still hard, still inside her, but the moment had shifted. They weren't having sex. This was about connecting, and it shook her far more than any orgasm.

She clung to him, feeling the warmth of his body, listening to the sound of his steady heartbeat. She wasn't sure how long they stayed like that. Not speaking. Completely still. Then he began to move again.

He withdrew and filled her over and over. He shifted his hands so he was cupping her face.

"Look at me," he breathed.

She opened her eyes and stared into his. Emotions chased across his face, but they changed too fast for her to read them. She still hung on to him, feeling her body begin the journey to pleasure.

"Isabel."

Her breath caught as he pushed in deeper still and then she lost control, shuddering in her release. He kept his cadence steady as she shattered, then still gazing into her eyes, came himself. Deep pleasure shared and a moment when she was sure she could at last see all of him.

CHAPTER FIFTEEN

Isabel, Consuelo and Felicia settled at a table at Brew-haha. Patience was in the back with an early delivery and the store was quiet.

"No puppy?" Isabel asked.

"Webster's sleeping in my office," Felicia told her. "He gets enough attention during the day. Plus, I don't think Patience would appreciate having an animal in her establishment. Ignoring the various health codes, some people find dogs off-putting." She smiled. "I'll admit I was concerned when Gideon wanted to get Carter a dog, but I find him to be an excellent companion. He's friendly and helps establish a rapport with people I don't know."

"We're talking about the dog and not Gideon, right?" Isabel asked.

Felicia smiled. "Yes, the dog."

"You're not as weird as you think," Consuelo told Felicia. "Being in Fool's Gold has changed you. You're much more open and relaxed."

"The town has helped," Felicia said. "And having a family."

"And the sex," Isabel teased.

Felicia nodded solemnly. "The combination of physical pleasure and emotional bonding is very satisfying."

Felicia was strange, Isabel thought, but in a good way. The woman was some kind of genius and had an interesting past that included working for the military on secret missions. That was how she'd come to Fool's Gold in the first place — through Ford and his company. But she fit in perfectly.

Isabel supposed that was because the town was especially welcoming to those who weren't exactly like everyone else.

Felicia looked at Consuelo and picked up her latte. "After years of you taking care of me, I finally get to ask what's going on with you. Something is different."

Isabel expected the pint-sized commando to threaten Felicia with bodily harm, but instead Consuelo dropped her head to her hands.

"My life's a mess."

"Empirically or emotionally?" Felicia asked.

"Emotionally." Consuelo turned to Isabel. "You can't say a word. Seriously."

"I swear." Isabel put down her latte and made an X over her heart.

Consuelo sighed. "It's Kent. I'm still seeing him."

"I thought you liked him," Isabel said. "He's a really great guy."

"I know. That's the problem. He's so normal. Nice and smart. Reese is a great kid, and Kent is a great dad. It's like stumbling into some perfect sitcom. I don't belong."

Isabel didn't understand. "Have you looked in the mirror? You're every guy's fantasy. Plus, you have the tough thing going on, which is fun, but you're secretly caring."

Consuelo glared at her. "What did you say?"

Felicia shook her head. "We're not supposed to notice she cares. It makes her feel vulnerable."

Isabel wondered if she should back slowly out of the room. "Sorry."

"No, it's fine." Consuelo touched her arm. "My bad. Automatic response. Which is why I'm totally wrong for Kent. Have you met his family?"

"Yes," Isabel said glumly, thinking about

the tea she was going to have to share with his mother and sisters. "Many times."

"I haven't and I'm going to have to. They're going to ask about my family. What am I supposed to say? That my father took off when my youngest brother was born and no one's seen him since? Mom's dead, as is one of my brothers. The other's in jail. There's a happy conversation."

Isabel hadn't known the details of Consuelo's past. "That's a lot to overcome," she said quietly.

"I didn't overcome it. I left. I took off and never looked back. I thought —" She shook her head. "Hell, what does it matter? It can't work. He and I are too different."

"You're looking for trouble," Felicia said, then smiled, as if pleased to have found the right cliché. "Your past has made you who you are today. Yes, you and Kent come from different places, but you have a lot in common. You're both good with children. He's a teacher and you teach your classes. Your students are very fond of you. You both have a strong sense of right and wrong."

"Blah, blah, blah," Consuelo muttered.

"Is it because you were a soldier?" Isabel asked, suddenly wondering if Consuelo was simply verbalizing what Ford wouldn't talk about. "Because of what you've seen or done? Is the inability to connect more about a fear of opening a door? That if the two worlds collide, something bad will happen?"

Consuelo stared at her with an expression Isabel couldn't read.

"Don't hurt me," she said quickly.

"I won't," Consuelo told her. "How did you know?"

"I didn't. I've been thinking about it because of Ford. There are times when I have no idea what he's thinking. I can only guess and wonder if he'll ever talk about what happened."

"Not with you," Consuelo said flatly. "He won't want you to see it through him."

Which made Isabel wonder what Consuelo kept hidden. "So, who do you talk to?"

"Some people don't talk to anyone. They let it fester inside. Or eventually it works itself out." She hesitated. "I see a counselor."

"I'm glad," Felicia said quietly, touching her friend's arm.

"I don't know if it helps," Consuelo admitted. "Sometimes I feel as if I'm fine and other times . . . There's a reason they call it the 'ragged edge.' " She looked at Isabel. "No one can go through what Ford did and remain unaffected. War leaves scars. Some are on the inside and some are on the outside, but we all have them. Ford's basically a good guy, but he's still dealing."

"Like how?" Isabel asked.

"Moments when he isn't sure where he is. Or why he made it when others didn't."

She hadn't seen any signs of that, Isabel thought. Every now and then he got quiet, but that was it. Like the last time they'd made love. When he'd held on to her. If she had to guess, she would say she'd been the only steady object in a rapidly spinning world.

"Are the scars the reason you worry about being with Kent?" Felicia asked.

"I don't know. Maybe. I'm just not like him."

"You keep saying that," Isabel pointed out. "But he's obviously interested in you and you in him."

"Because he doesn't know me."

"Of course," Felicia said. "The root of all fears. Not being accepted by those we care about. Being rejected and isolated. It's a primal fear. As a species, we are meant to be part of a group. A community. We mistrust loners because we don't understand them. With the exception of our romanticizing the loner in movies and novels, of course."

Consuelo stared at her. "What the hell are you talking about?"

"You're terrified Kent is going to reject you, so you withhold yourself from him. He will sense that there are secrets he will never know and parts of you he can't touch, which will in turn make him feel rejected." Her voice gentled. "You're already planning your exit."

"I'm not!" Consuelo said loudly, then sighed. "Okay, maybe. But . . ." She pressed her lips together. "Damn it, Felicia."

Felicia's smile was just a little bit smug.

"You're good," Isabel said.

"With others. I'm less insightful with myself."

"While you're being brilliant, what about Ford? He claims he can't fall in love. That he's tried but it simply hasn't happened for him."

"What are your thoughts?" Felicia asked.

"He was pretty young when he was engaged to my sister. So getting over Maeve quickly isn't a statement on his character. Since then, he's been in different war zones and on secret assignments. I know he was in a task force, but I don't know any details."

She picked up her latte, then put it down. "He didn't work around many women, and I don't think his leaves were long enough for him to really get involved with someone. So he made the decision to keep things casual. He likes women and they like him. But is that all he has in him? Did he skate on the surface because it was how he kept himself safe, only now that's all he knows and anything else is too scary to try?"

"Possibly," Felicia said.

Isabel laughed. "I was hoping for more."

"Why? Your analysis is sound. If Ford has never had the opportunity for a significant relationship — either through circumstance or preference or both — then he's unlikely to be willing to try now without motivation. Are you giving him that?"

The question was unexpected. "No. I'm leaving for New York in a few months. We're only fake-dating."

At least, she hoped they were. Isabel thought about how she'd felt holding him. How she looked forward to seeing him and how she avoided thinking about what it would be like when she was gone.

"I refuse to fall in love with him," she said flatly. But as she spoke, she was touching the dragonfly necklace Ford had bought for her. The one she didn't take off, except to shower.

"Good luck with that plan," Consuelo told her, looking sympathetic.

Patience came out from behind the counter. "Sorry," she said as she approached the table. "My refrigerated goodies are all put away. Now, what did I miss?"

Isabel leaned forward and adjusted the toe separator on her right foot. She'd decided that a spectacular sex life deserved painted toenails and had dug out some polish, a nail file and the toe separators. Now her left toes were a deep violet.

The bathroom door opened without warning and she shrieked. "What are you doing?"

Ford stood by the sink, his expression wounded. "You locked the back door."

"Yes," she told him. "On purpose. I wanted privacy."

He glanced around the bathroom. "Why? What could you be doing that I couldn't watch? It's not like you're waxing or something."

She shoved the brush back in the bottle. "It's not like you asked before you burst in."

"Good point. So, what are you doing?"

She waved the bottle of nail polish. "I would think it was obvious."

He glanced at her toes. "I could do that."

"Paint my toes? I don't think so."

"Why not? I'm good with my hands."

"This is different and the polish on my

left foot is still wet. So go away."

He flashed her a grin. "Right. Because telling me that always works."

He moved closer. She tried to duck away, but there was nowhere to go. He reached down, picked her up. She yelped.

"Inside voice," he told her as he carried her into the kitchen, where he put her on a chair.

He pulled up a second chair and sat down, then grabbed her unpolished foot and set it on his hard thigh.

"Bottle," he said, holding out his hand.

"Fine." She sighed. "Don't use a lot of polish. I do a second coat."

"Then topcoat?"

She stared at him. "You know about topcoat?"

"I have three sisters. I know everything."

"You are a constant surprise," she murmured.

"One of my best qualities."

He painted her nails with slow precision. She watched his steady hand and realized that she was in more trouble than she'd first thought. Walking away from Ford could very well break her heart.

When he was done, he applied the topcoat, then screwed both bottles shut. She leaned back in her chair, both her feet on his thighs, thinking that this was one of the best views in town. She would remember this should her heart end up smashed.

"Why don't you talk about the war?" she asked.

He raised his eyebrows. "There's a change in subject."

"There's an avoidance of the question."

He pressed his thumbs into the arch of her left foot and found a sore spot she hadn't known she had.

"There's nothing to say." He rotated his thumbs and pressed harder.

She held in a moan.

"I did things, saw things," he continued. "They're ugly and I don't want you to think about that stuff."

"You're protecting me?"

He gave her a slow smile. "Something I'm really good at."

"I don't need protecting. We're friends. You can talk to me."

"Not gonna happen."

"Do you talk to anyone?"

"I was debriefed, I saw a navy shrink because it was required. I'm done."

"I don't believe that. You can't ignore what happened."

"Why not? It's the monster under the stairs. Eventually it starves to death."

She wasn't sure it was that simple.

He shifted his hands to her other foot and massaged her arch. "There are times when it gets bad," he admitted, "but not many. I was lucky. I didn't have it like Gideon or even Angel."

He raised his head. "Do you know a woman named Taryn? She's tall, with dark hair. Great dresser. Hot."

Isabel stared at him for a second, then carefully pulled her feet free. "Excuse me?"

He grinned. "Not for me. Angel noticed her the other day. It was like watching a leopard separate an animal from the herd. I wondered if she was up to the chase."

"I don't know her well enough to be sure, but if I had to guess, I would say if anyone can handle our leopard friend, it's her."

"Good. I hope he does something. I doubt Angel's been with anyone since . . ."

Isabel waited. "Since what?"

"Nothing. It's his thing. I shouldn't talk about it."

"You're so annoying."

His grin turned knowing. "Want to spank me? I remember you're into that."

"They were shape-wear and you know it."

"I do."

He grabbed her wrists, and before she knew what had happened, he pulled her out

of her chair and onto his lap. She sat strad-
dling him, her arms on his shoulders, her
face close to his.

"We always seem to end up here," she
murmured, right before she kissed him.

"It's because you're demanding. I can
barely keep up."

She wiggled against his obvious erection.
"You seem to be keeping up just fine."

"That's because I can't resist you."

As Isabel lowered her mouth to his, she
wished his words were true and that this
was much more than a game they played
for fun.

"It's me," Isabel called as she opened her
sister's front door.

Maeve appeared in the living room, her
hair mussed, her clothes stained. There were
shadows under her eyes.

"Thanks for coming," she said, sounding
exhausted. "It's been a hell of a night."

Maeve had called a couple of hours ago
and asked if Isabel could stop by the store
to pick up a few things. Three of her four
kids had gotten food poisoning. They'd been
up all night and Maeve had been awake with
them. With Leonard out of town, everything
had fallen to her.

They walked into the kitchen.

"When does Leonard come back?" Isabel asked as she pulled out bottles of ginger ale and a box of crackers.

"Late tonight. I'm counting the minutes."

Isabel glanced at her watch. It was barely after ten in the morning. "Look, Paper Moon is closed today. I can stay. Bring me up to date with the kids and I'll take over while you get a nap."

"I'm fine," Maeve told her. "Really. You don't want to be alone with my kids."

"Only three, right?"

"Yeah. Griffin's fine and he went to school."

Just then four-year-old Kelly walked in. She wore pj's and looked nearly as tired as her mom.

"Mommy, I'm hungry."

Maeve smiled. "That's a good sign. How about some ginger ale while I get you some crackers? If they make your tummy happy, then you can try some banana."

Kelly nodded, then looked at Isabel. "Hi, Auntie Is."

"Hey, munchkin." Isabel crouched in front of her. "You had a bad night, huh?"

Kelly nodded and leaned against Isabel. "I got sick in my bed."

Isabel picked up the girl and hugged her. "Poor you." And Mom, she thought, know-

332

ing Maeve would have had to deal with the cleanup.

"Come on," she told her sister. "Let's get the other two sorted out. Then I'm taking over."

Maeve hesitated, then nodded. "I wouldn't say yes, but with the baby and all, I really need to get some sleep."

They checked out the other two, both of whom were asleep. Isabel promised to wake Maeve if either stirred, then shooed her sister off to her room and returned to the kitchen with Kelly.

Once her niece had finished her ginger ale and a few crackers, Isabel checked on the laundry. Sheets were piled up, with one wet load sitting in the washer. She pulled clean sheets out of the dryer and tossed them in the basket, then put the wet stuff in the dryer and put in a new load of dirties. After starting everything, she carried the basket back to the kitchen and kept Kelly company while she folded.

Her cell rang and she pulled it out of her pocket. A quick glance at the screen had her smiling.

"Hi, Mom. Where are you?"

"Hong Kong," her mother said. "It's loud. I'm buying you and your sister silk blouses."

"Which will only make us love you more,"

Isabel said with a laugh. "I'm with your granddaughter. Want to say hi?"

"Absolutely."

Isabel pushed the button for the speakerphone and Kelly told her grandmother about the three siblings getting sick. When she went off to watch cartoons, Isabel released the speakerphone.

"Maeve's sleeping," she told her mother. "She's exhausted but didn't eat whatever the kids did. I'm helping out."

"I'm glad you're there," her mother told her. "I miss you both. How's the store?"

"Excellent. Those new designer clothes have already sold. They're bringing in a lot of money."

Her mother sighed. "And that's not enough to convince you to stay? You could buy us out over time and . . ." There was another sigh. "Your father is telling me to stop pushing."

"I appreciate your faith in me, but you know my plans."

"I do. And I'll be quiet now."

They chatted a few more minutes, then hung up.

Three hours later, Maeve staggered into the family room. She blinked as she looked around. "You shouldn't have let me sleep so long."

"Why not?" Isabel asked. "You needed it."

The three kids were stretched out together under a blanket, watching a DVD. They smiled sleepily at their mom but didn't get up.

"Everyone has had ginger ale, crackers and soup. They're all tired and are going to watch the movie. Come on. I'll make you some lunch. You must be starving."

Maeve followed her into the kitchen. Isabel opened the refrigerator and collected the fixings for a sandwich, but before she could start making it, her sister started to cry.

Isabel rushed to her side. "What's wrong?" she asked, crouching next to her. "Is it the baby?"

Maeve shook her head, her blond hair swaying with the movement. Tears spilled down her cheeks.

"You cleaned the kitchen and did laundry," she said, the words slightly muffled.

"Okay," Isabel said slowly and patted her shoulder. "I'll get you some water."

"Thanks." Maeve wiped her face. "I'm sorry. It's just I'm so tired, and when Leonard's gone, I fall apart. He doesn't travel much, but he had to take a continuing-education class and the one he wanted was only available in person in San Francisco."

Isabel got a glass and filled it with water, then returned to her sister's side.

Maeve took it. "Last night was so awful and then you showed up and took care of everything. I really appreciate it."

"I'm happy to help." Isabel told herself she needed to spend more time with her sister, to be there when she could.

Maeve wiped her face and took a drink of the water. "I love my life. Really I do. Leonard is the best man in the world and my kids are great, but sometimes I get so envious of you."

"Of me? Why? I'm a disaster."

"You're not. You're single and don't have many responsibilities."

"Or ties. I'm divorced and I don't even have a cat to keep me company."

"But you have a career."

"I work in our parents' business. That's not going to put me on the cover of *Fortune* magazine."

"No, but your new business will. You have it all."

"No, you do."

They stared at each other and started to laugh.

"Better?" Isabel asked gently.

Her sister nodded.

"Good." Isabel walked over to the counter

and put two slices of bread on a plate.

"I talked to Mom earlier," Maeve told her. "They're having a great time. She says they should have done this years ago."

"She's probably right."

Maeve sighed. "I hope Leonard and I are like them. Always in love."

"You've survived four kids so far. I'm pretty sure you're going to make it."

Her sister winced. "I'm sorry. That was insensitive."

It took Isabel a second to realize what she meant. "My relationship with Eric was doomed from the start. The mistake was not recognizing the problem to begin with." She paused, then turned so she was facing Maeve. "I'm going to tell you something, but first you have to promise not to tell Mom and Dad. I don't want them to have to deal with this until they're home."

Maeve's blue eyes widened as she nodded. "Sure."

Isabel turned back to the sandwich. "Eric was gay."

After her sister was done sputtering and calling him names, Isabel explained what had happened.

"I don't believe he didn't know," Maeve fumed. "He had to have had an inkling. That doesn't just happen. It's not a lightning strike. I can't believe he betrayed you like that."

"I'm getting over it."

"With Ford?"

Isabel finished with the sandwich and carefully sliced it in two, then carried the plate over to the table. "I guess it's too late to ask if you're okay with that," she said quietly.

Maeve reached for the food. With her other hand, she waved the comment away. "Oh, please. We were done over a decade ago. Have at him."

Isabel put the supplies back in the refrigerator, then joined her sister at the table. "He's a pretty great guy."

"I remember." Maeve grinned. "Don't tell him but the sex wasn't all that. I wasn't his first time, but he was mine and all I remember thinking is 'I thought it would take longer than this.' "

Isabel grinned. "We're not really dating."

Maeve finished chewing and swallowed. "What? Sure you are. I've seen you two together. You are definitely dating."

"We're fake-dating." She explained about Denise and how Ford had begged.

"Not that I don't approve of a man begging," her sister began, "but, Isabel, be careful. I've seen the way you look at him, and you're not in a fake relationship."

"That's what I've been thinking, too. I didn't want to fall for him, but he's so funny and easy to be with. He's thoughtful in little ways that are so unexpected."

"All perfect if this was a regular relationship, but trouble when it's not. Are you sure you're leaving? Maybe Ford is worth sticking around for."

"I'm not changing my plans for him," Isabel said firmly. In part because she really did want to open a business with Sonia, but also because she had a feeling Ford meant what he said. That he wasn't interested in love. Which meant sticking around would only lead to heartache.

CHAPTER SIXTEEN

"You can't avoid my mother forever," Kent said.

Consuelo studied the display in the window of Morgan's Books. "I can and I will."

Kent grabbed her hand and gently twisted it behind her back, bringing her up against him. She had to tilt her head to continue to stare into his eyes.

She could have broken the hold a dozen different ways, could have had him in any number of holds that would cut off air or blood flow. She wondered if the knowledge of how to do that would ever fade. If she would ever be like the other women who walked through town on this perfect fall day. Or if she would always feel different.

"She's interested in the woman I'm seeing," he said.

"Then I can send her regular email updates."

He smiled.

People smiled all the time, she thought, unable to brace herself for the kick in the gut she always felt when he did that. Kent's smile was special. It made her feel as if she were the center of a very amazing universe. One where only good things happened.

She knew the folly of believing that, but she couldn't protect herself. Not where he was concerned. If only her heart were at stake, she would probably be fine. But when she was around him, she felt as if he held her entire being in the palm of his hand. How could she trust him not to crush her into dust?

"Oh, look," she said brightly, pointing. "Your sister-in-law has a new book out. Let's go buy it."

"If you'd like." He bent down and lightly kissed her mouth, then guided her into the store.

Five minutes later, she had a bag with Liz Sutton's latest murder mystery. Kent had insisted on paying, which was just like him.

"You should consider an eReader," he said when they were back on the sidewalk.

"I like books." Someone passing by said hello, and she paused to return the greeting. "This town is so strange. People I've never met before talk to me like they know me. But the weirdest part is I'm starting to like it."

"But do you like me?"

He was joking. At least, she thought he was. She glanced at him and saw questions in his eyes. They came to a stop again, this time by a bench. Kent pulled her onto the wooden seat.

"Of course," she said. "Why would you ask?"

"You're elusive."

"I'm completely open." She pressed her lips together, realizing that was far from the truth. "I mean to be."

"Well, then," he teased. "That must be enough."

She looked at her hand in his. His fingers were logger, broader. He was tall and strong, which was nice. If she broke her leg, he could carry her for a long time.

The ridiculous thought made her think of Felicia. She would think Kent was good to have around. That his combination of intelligence and strength would add to the social unit. That even if he wasn't a traditional warrior, he would be a formidable opponent.

She laced her fingers with his. "Your family scares me. I know Ford and he's fine, but the rest of them . . . They've lived here their whole lives. They're close. Traditional."

"Are you worried you won't fit in?"

"Some." All, she thought. "I wouldn't want to embarrass you."

"Not possible. I've seen you eat and you know how to use a napkin."

She laughed. "Thank you for your faith in my table manners." She kept his hand in hers but angled toward him. "I don't want your mom to tell you to stop seeing me."

"She wouldn't. You're adorable. Besides, I'm thirty-four. She stopped getting involved in my love life a couple of decades ago."

Consuelo raised her eyebrows. "Are you sure? Because just a couple of months ago, the woman had a booth with applications to be your girlfriend."

He grinned. "Oh, yeah. I forgot. But she's learned her lesson."

"Has she?"

"Even if she hasn't, I'll protect you. Besides, I'm the one putting it on the line if we hang out with my family. They're going to tell you stories about me."

"That sounds fun. What kinds of stories?"

She figured he would admit to a childish prank or say he hadn't started dating until college. She didn't expect him to clear his throat and admit, "When I was younger, I was kind of a dog when it came to women."

Consuelo had a feeling her shock showed. "What does that mean?"

He shrugged. "I figured out girls were pretty cool in tenth grade. I had something of a reputation. In college, I, um, took advantage of the target-rich environment. I'm not proud of what I did," he added hastily. "I'm different now. More mature. When I was in a relationship, I was always faithful. I never cheated on my ex-wife." He looked both embarrassed and proud as he admitted to his past.

"An unexpected side of you."

He nodded. "It's being a math teacher. People assume I'm shy around women. I get a little nervous at the beginning, but once things get going . . ." He paused.

"Go on," she urged, intrigued.

"I'm going to quit while I'm ahead."

"Afraid your mouth is going to write checks your, um, other parts can't cash?"

"Something like that. It has occurred to me that you're completely out of my league."

He was joking, but she knew he was right. Being a sex god in high school didn't compare to her past.

"Any tattoos?" he asked.

The unexpected question jerked her out of her worries and brought her back to the man in front of her. She smiled. "Two."

His eyebrows rose. "What and where?"

"I'm not telling."

"Building anticipation. I like that."

She laughed.

Kent put his arm around her and drew her close, then leaned in and kissed her. She let herself relax as her eyes slowly closed. His mouth was warm and sure as it settled on hers.

They were out in public — nothing was going to happen, which was both good and bad. Good because for some reason the thought of having sex with Kent terrified her and bad because being close to him made her want him.

Even as his lips lightly teased her own, she felt heat growing in all the usual places. She hadn't been with a man in a long time. She hadn't been with a man she liked in a couple of years. She wanted to lose herself in the act of connecting with a man and not have to worry about extracting information or making her escape. She wanted to make love in a house in the suburbs and wake up to the sound of birds chirping or kids laughing rather than make her way back to a dark and empty safe house.

She drew back and stared into his face. His eyes crinkled as he smiled at her.

"Have I mentioned you're totally hot?" he asked.

She grinned. "Not lately and I was wondering if you'd changed your mind."

"No. You're still amazing." The smile faded. "Not just because of how you look. I want to make sure you know I like who you are."

She hoped that was true.

She took his hands in hers. With the right training, he could become a killing machine. Funny how that thought would never occur to him. He wouldn't hit a woman, wouldn't shame her. Based on how Reese grumbled about the rules at home, she knew Kent was fair and reasonable, even when angry.

"Maybe I should meet your mother," she admitted. "She did a really good job with you."

He laughed. "Interesting logic. I'll give you a couple of days to be sure before I set something up."

Of course he would.

"Tell me it's going to be beautiful," Madeline requested, sounding doubtful.

Isabel pulled the white dress from what seemed like an impossibly small box. "It is. Four hours of ironing from now, it will be perfect."

It was Wednesday morning and they'd just gotten in a big shipment of dresses. While it would be nice if they were sent in hanging boxes, stuffed with tissue and arrived in perfect condition, that wasn't true. Most came folded, which meant wrinkles and creases and plenty of fluffing.

"I see I'm going to be busy for the next few days," Madeline said with a grin. "That's good. Shipping day secures my employment."

Isabel laughed. "Absolutely."

Later in the week they were due to get veils, silk wreaths and a few tiaras, but nothing compared to the work of getting a gown ready for her bride.

"The secret is never to let the client see her gown straight out of the box. She'll never recover from the shock." Isabel carefully unwrapped a beautiful silk gown with plenty of lace and layers. Yup, she and Madeline would be working late this week.

Thanks to her grandmother's planning, the back room was big enough to hold a long garment rack. As each dress was unpacked, it was hung up. A few of the wrinkles would fall out on their own, but the rest required gentle ironing and steaming.

"It's fun to see what's new," Madeline

said, pulling out another dress. "The changes in the styles. Some are subtle, but there are still differences from year to year."

"As long as we have variety," Isabel murmured. "I hate it when stores focus on a single style, like strapless ball gowns. Even though I love them, they're not going to look good on everyone. Every bride deserves to be beautiful."

"You're good at that," Madeline told her. "Finding the right dress for the right client."

"Years of watching my grandmother. She would take hours with a bride, talking to her about what she wanted, looking at pictures of different dresses, then having her try on dozens. It was an event." She remembered being here then. "A bride would book the store for a whole morning or the entire afternoon. Sometimes they had food brought in."

"You could still do that," Madeline said. "A few clients would enjoy that."

"It would be fun." Isabel hung another dress on the rack. "There are a lot of changes I'd make here. Not that I'm staying."

"Are you sure you can't be tempted?"

"Yes. I'm still going back to New York."

Isabel said the words with more firmness

than she felt. In truth, she hadn't thought about leaving in weeks. She still hadn't connected with Sonia, but didn't feel as frantic about that. She knew Ford was the reason and told herself to be careful. That he wasn't the least bit interested in her staying. Still, it was appealing to think about.

The phone rang. Isabel carefully lowered the dress she was holding back into the box and reached for the receiver.

"Paper Moon," she said. "This is Isabel."

"You *have* to get over here right away."

"Patience? Are you okay?"

"I'm fine," her friend said. "But I'm serious. Shut the store and get here now! Bring Madeline."

Patience hung up.

Isabel replaced the receiver. "That was strange," she said. "Patience wants us to come over right away. It sounded urgent."

Madeline rose. "Okay. I'll put out the sign."

Isabel checked the back door to make sure it was locked, then followed the other woman to the front of the store. After grabbing her purse and keys, she made sure the We'll Be Back in Ten Minutes sign was up. After closing and locking the front door, they hurried toward Brew-haha.

Two short blocks later, Isabel raced into

the store only to find several women, including Charlie, Dellina and Noelle, standing at the big window, looking out toward the park.

Patience practically danced over. "Look," she said, pointing.

Isabel ignored the instruction. "Are you all right?"

"I'm fine." She grabbed Isabel's arm and dragged her to the window. "Look!"

Isabel turned her attention to the street with no cars currently in view. There were the usual pedestrians, a man on a bike and three men in the park.

"So?"

Charlie glared at her. "So? Seriously? Don't you know who they are?"

Isabel looked again, then shook her head. "No. Should I?"

Charlie sighed. "Why do I even try?"

"I want the blond one," Noelle said, pointing. "He's dreamy."

"Dreamy?" Charlie scoffed. "What is this? Nineteen fifty? Kenny Scott is known for his speed and catching ability. They say he has magic hands."

Noelle leaned against the window frame. "I could use some magic hands in my life. I wonder if he rents out."

Dellina pointed. "I like that one." She

turned to Charlie. "What's his name?"

"Sam Ridge. Kicker. He's scored more points than . . ." She shook her head. "You don't care about his football career. Stop talking to me."

Isabel turned back to Patience. "That's it? You dragged me over here to look at football players?"

"Of course. They're finally here."

The front door opened and two old ladies walked in. Isabel recognized Eddie and Gladys. They pushed their way through the crowd and pressed their faces against the window.

"Nice ass," Eddie said. "Think they'll take their shirts off?"

"It's sixty-two degrees out there," Isabel pointed out.

"They're men. Let them show us they're tough."

Isabel shook her head. "You're all insane."

Patience grinned. "Come on. It's fun. How often do we have three hot football players move to town?"

"We have bodyguards," Isabel told her. "That's enough. We don't need those guys."

"Oh, they're pretty," Taryn said, walking into Brew-haha. "And if you ask them nicely, they're good at lifting and toting."

Noelle turned to her. "Are they all single?"

"That's what they tell me." Taryn walked to the counter. "Can I get a latte, or do I have to wait until the show is over?"

"I think I can steam milk and watch at the same time," Patience told her.

Isabel took a second to admire Taryn's royal-blue suit. It matched her eyes perfectly and contrasted with her dark hair. Black suede pumps completed the outfit.

"You really know how to dress," Isabel said, thinking her own black dress served a purpose. The bride never felt upstaged. She knew that was important, but looking at Taryn made her want to wear something more interesting. Maybe one of the new designs Dellina was always bringing in. At least she had her shoes, she thought, glancing down at the bright red pumps she'd slipped on that morning. Ridiculous but beautiful.

"I have an image to uphold," Taryn said. "Clothes might not make the woman, but they help. My shoes intimidate the boys, much like yours would, and that's good, too."

She took the latte from Patience and paid her, then crossed to the growing crowd by the window.

"They gonna get naked?" Gladys asked.

"Unlikely," Taryn murmured. "They're

exploring. Maybe, if we're lucky, they'll do some push-ups."

Isabel heard distinct sarcasm in her voice, but Eddie and Gladys didn't seem to notice.

"Wonder if they like older women?" Eddie asked. "I could teach that tall one a thing or two. Or maybe he could teach me." She and Gladys giggled.

Taryn stepped closer to Isabel. "Those old ladies are a little disconcerting."

"You get used to it," Isabel assured her in a low voice. "They show up at events like this. I heard that a couple of years ago the town had male models in for a calendar to raise money for the fire department. Eddie and Gladys brought chairs and stayed for the whole event."

Noelle walked over to them. "I'm feeling nothing," she said, sounding disappointed. "I'm ready for something, I can feel it, but these guys aren't doing it for me."

Taryn smiled. "Kenny will be disappointed to hear that."

Noelle glanced toward the window. "I don't even care which one is Kenny. Are there more men moving to town? Because this is getting ridiculous."

Dellina strolled over. "I want to do more than look," she said brightly. "Is Sam single?"

"Yes, but he's annoying. Just so you're warned."

Isabel looked at Taryn. "You're really not interested?"

"Yawn," Taryn said. "It is physically impossible for me to be less interested. I know them far too well to want to be romantically involved with any of them." She shuddered. "No. We're close. I adore them but I would rather date a fence post. At least it wouldn't argue."

Isabel and Madeline walked back to Paper Moon. When they got there, Ford was waiting by the front door, looking all masculine and sexy. When he saw her, he raised an eyebrow.

"Really?" he asked in a low voice. "Ogling football players? I guess I shouldn't be surprised. After all, you promised to love me forever and look what happened there."

Madeline giggled as she let herself into the store. "I'll leave you two to work this out," she said, then disappeared inside.

Isabel put her hands on her hips. "How did you know?"

"Unlike you, Patience is concerned about Justice's feelings. She called to tell him what was going on and he told me."

She held in a smile. "I'm sorry you had to

find out that way. About the other men I was watching."

"Ogling. There's a difference. I'm very disappointed in you. I expect better from my fake girlfriends."

While she enjoyed the teasing, there was a part of her that wanted his words to be true.

"I'm sorry," she told him. "Patience called and asked me to come over. I didn't find out why — I just went."

"Oh, sure. Blame it on Patience." He stepped closer to her. "I can see we're going to have to have a serious talk about your behavior."

"You're probably right." She batted her eyes at him. "Maybe I should be punished later."

"That goes without saying. I'm thinking a tongue-lashing at the very least."

She shivered as she remembered what Ford could do with his tongue, then dropped her head in mock submission. "Whatever you think is best."

He pulled her close and kissed the top of her head. "I don't want to have to have this conversation again."

"Of course not."

As he hugged her, she felt the vibration of his chuckles. "You're good at this," he said quietly. "How do you feel about escaped prisoner and the warden's wife?"

She grinned. "I think I could get into it."

"That's my girl."

"Actually, we might need to reverse those roles. Your mom called me again to set up a one-on-one."

"Talk about a buzz kill!"

"I know. There's only so much longer I can put her off."

He kissed her. "I have to get back to work. See you tonight?"

"I'll be the blonde."

"Thanks for clarifying."

Isabel walked into Paper Moon and sighed. Her fake-dating situation was getting complicated. The obvious solution was to end things, but she just plain didn't want to.

Before she could return to the back room to help Madeline with the rest of the gowns, her cell phone rang. She pulled it out of her bag and pushed Answer without checking to see who was calling.

"Hello?"

"Hey, Isabel."

"Sonia." She crossed to one of the chairs and sat down. "I haven't heard from you in a while. Did you get my messages?"

"Yeah. Sorry. Life's been crazy here. I've been meaning to call."

"I'm glad you did. We have a lot we need to be doing and talking about."

"I know. Well, sure. That's why I phoned, so we could talk." Her friend cleared her throat. "Look, I don't know how to say this. It's why I haven't returned your calls. I've . . ." Sonia paused. "I've gone into business with someone else."

Isabel stiffened. "What? What are you talking about? We had a deal together. We had plans."

"I know. I know. I should have said something before. It's just . . . I didn't want to wait. You're not coming back until February, and that's a long time."

"It's five months. With everything that has to be done, it's not that long at all."

"Right, but there are other things. She has more money to put in the business. We can start bigger and not take so long to get noticed. I want that. This is my dream, Isabel. I have to do this. I'm sorry if you're disappointed."

"Disappointed? I came back here to earn more money to put into *our* business. I came back to brush up on retail so I would be more of an asset. We discussed that. We discussed everything."

"I know that but retail is risky and this is a better bet for me. Do you really have to be so harsh about it? I was hoping we could stay friends. Can't you just be happy for me?"

For her? Isabel wanted to ask about her own dreams, but she knew Sonia didn't care about that. She had made it very clear she didn't care about anyone but herself.

"Good luck with everything," Isabel said, knowing she sounded bitter but unable to care. She ended the call before Sonia could respond.

CHAPTER SEVENTEEN

Ford stared helplessly as Isabel wiped away tears.

"It's so unfair," she said, her lower lip trembling as she spoke. "All of it. Now I know why she's been avoiding me. She knew. All this time she knew she was going into business with someone else and she never said anything."

They were in the living room of her house. A relatively large room with big windows, but Ford felt as trapped as if he were locked in a five-by-five cell. He didn't know what the hell he was supposed to do to make her feel better and he couldn't walk away.

Madeline had called him less than half an hour ago. She'd said Isabel had gotten a call and had left the store in tears. Madeline hadn't known what had happened, but she'd been worried about her boss. Ford had come running, only to find Isabel as devastated as Madeline had suggested.

"I can't believe it." She crushed the tissue in her hand, then looked at him. "I can't believe it."

There was raw pain in her eyes. He desperately wanted to fix the problem, only he couldn't begin to figure out how.

"I'm sorry," he said, dropping to his knees in front of her. "I'm really sorry."

She nodded. "I know. It's nothing about you. It's me. God, what's wrong with me? First Eric and now Sonia."

"You're not the reason either of them acted the way they did."

"I know that in my head, but my gut tells me something else." She lowered her head and he saw tears fall onto her fingers. "It's like the death of a dream."

She raised her head. More tears spilled from her blue eyes. "No. It's not *like* the death of a dream. It *is* the death of a dream. We had everything planned. It's why I came back."

She shook her head. "Okay, part of the reason is Eric. I wanted to get away from the city, but still. I thought . . ." She swallowed. "I believed in her. In what we were going to do, and she dumped me for someone with more money."

He wrapped his arms around her and pulled her close. He knew there was something he was supposed to be saying — he just didn't know what it was.

"She wasn't your friend," he murmured, holding on tight and wishing that was enough. "A real friend would never do this to you."

"I kn-know." Her voice caught as she burrowed into him. "That makes it worse. I lost my business dream and a friend all in the same conversation. Why didn't she tell me before? Why didn't she hint?"

She drew back and stared at him. "Is it me? Did I make this happen?"

He felt her pain and wanted to rip out his own heart, if that would help. He wanted to find the Sonia bitch and — He swore, knowing he couldn't take out his temper on a civilian. Especially a woman.

"It's not you," he told her, touching the side of her face. "You did what the two of you agreed to. You followed the rules."

"I keep doing that," she said dully. "And getting screwed. Maybe I need a new plan."

She got up and walked to the window. She crossed her arms over her chest and turned back to him. "Have you ever wanted something this much, only to lose it?"

He rose and shook his head.

"It sucks," she told him. "It sucks a lot."

He believed her and a part of him envied

her ability to feel that kind of passion. Because the truth was he'd never wanted anything all that much. What he desired came easily, and when he was tired of it, he walked away. He'd done it all his life. A revelation that didn't help Isabel at all.

Isabel turned back to the window. Ford didn't have any answers, and she should stop badgering him for them. She was about to tell him she would be fine, when someone knocked on the door.

"I'll get it," Ford said quickly and hurried to the front of the house. Seconds later he reappeared with Patience at his side.

Isabel brushed away her tears. "Calling in reinforcements?"

He shrugged. "I was afraid I couldn't handle it."

"You did great."

Patience hurried to her. "What happened? Are you okay?"

Isabel told her about the call and what Sonia had said.

"That's unbelievable," her friend said. "What a bitch."

"That seems to be the general consensus."

Patience led Isabel to the sofa, then looked at Ford. "I'm okay to stay the rest of the day." She turned back to Isabel. "He's getting that trapped, uncomfortable look."

"I'm not," he said defensively.

Isabel managed a smile. "You did great. Thank you."

"You sure?"

"Very."

She crossed to him and kissed him. "Thank you for not running screaming from the room while I was crying."

He hugged her. "I'm sorry."

"I know."

"See you later?"

She nodded and he left. "Want some tea?" she asked her friend. "It seems to be the right thing to do in a crisis. Make tea."

"Sure."

They went into the kitchen. Isabel put water on to boil and dug out a selection of tea bags. Patience found two mugs and put them on the counter.

"Now start at the beginning."

Isabel repeated the phone call, then sucked in a breath. "It's so unfair. I've been calling her for a few weeks now and I never heard back. I should have guessed something was up. But Sonia would often get busy and disappear. She was posting on Facebook, so I knew she was okay. I thought it was a creative thing. I didn't get that she was screwing me the whole time."

She felt her eyes start to burn. "I was so sure we were going to make something brilliant together. Start our business and take the fashion world by storm. Maybe not hurricane strength, but at least a decent wind event."

She tried to smile, but her mouth refused to cooperate. "I feel like an idiot."

Patience moved closer and touched her arm. "You didn't do anything wrong."

"That's what Ford said."

"He's right. You trusted a friend and she betrayed you. If she was having second thoughts, she should have said something."

The water started to boil. Isabel poured it into the two mugs. Patience dropped in the tea bags.

"It's the second half of a one-two punch," Isabel admitted. "There's also the humiliation factor. My husband leaves me for another man, and my business partner dumps me for someone with more money. I'm the common denominator, so I must be doing something wrong."

"You're not," Patience insisted. "You're trusting people you love. If they betray you, the fault is theirs. You and Sonia had a deal. She broke it. I know it sounds harsh, but maybe it's better to find this out before you put your money on the line. She sounds like the kind of person who would run off at any point in the deal. What if you'd opened the store and then she'd left?"

Isabel hadn't thought of that. "I would have been left with a store and no designer."

"Exactly. That would suck more."

They walked back into the living room and sat down.

"I'm so confused," Isabel admitted. "About what I'm supposed to do now. How am I going to trust anybody? But I also know *not* trusting isn't a good thing, either. I don't want to live my life in a cave, bitter and scared of how someone might hurt me."

"Good, because the only caves I know of are on Heidi's ranch, and she ages her goat cheese in them. I don't think you'd enjoy that. I would guess the smell would be difficult to take, day after day."

Isabel managed a slight smile. "Thanks for putting my cave-living dreams in perspective."

"You're welcome." Patience squeezed her hand. "I'm sorry this happened. But at the risk of being annoyingly cheerful, you have options."

"Options that will lead to more disappointment," Isabel grumbled. Right now she felt as if she would never figure out how to make a decent decision ever again.

"That's my little ray of sunshine," her friend said with a gentle smile. "Okay, you're not going to open a store with Sonia in New York. There are hundreds of other places you could do it. Pick a city."

"I don't have another designer to work with." Isabel leaned her head back against the sofa and sighed. Nothing was ever going to be right again.

"I didn't realize there was just the one."

Isabel straightened. "One what?"

"Designer. Sonia's the only one?"

"Very funny."

"I have a charming sense of humor." Her friend shifted toward her. "I've seen *Project Runway*. Season after season they bring us brilliant designers. There are hundreds or thousands out there. You just have to find one. Or maybe five. Maybe it's better not to have a partner right now. You could start with Dellina's friend. Her clothes are great. They're selling."

Isabel saw her point. "That's an option, except Sonia was kicking in cash, too. I don't have enough money to start a boutique on my own." She paused, wondering if she could stand to risk another partner. Between Eric and Sonia, she was feeling extremely unliked.

"What about Paper Moon?" Patience asked.

Isabel stared at her. "I don't want to sell wedding gowns for the rest of my life."

"I know that. But you don't have to. It's successful and there's an income stream. That would help. You could add to the business. Bring in a few designers. Expand the business. The space next door is for lease. So lease it, open a wall and sell wedding gowns and designer clothes. I'm sure your parents would be thrilled to keep the business in the family, and you can probably trust them not to break your heart."

Isabel stood up and walked away from the sofa. When she reached the fireplace, she turned back.

"I never thought of staying," she admitted. "Fool's Gold isn't exactly the fashion capital of the world. My parents would be thrilled."

"There are advantages to being here. We have a big tourist trade. There are plenty of women in town. Plus, you've sold everything from Dellina's friend you've put in the window and that's without trying."

Not leave? She'd always planned to leave. To go back to New York. To make her mark. To stay here would be . . .

What? Settling? It didn't feel like settling.

She liked the town. She had friends she trusted and her family was here. She had to admit that spending more time with her nieces and nephews, not to mention her sister, would be nice.

"I'd have to get my own place," she murmured.

"Easy enough to do. You said Madeline loves working in Paper Moon. Having her there would free up time to do what you really love." Patience rose and crossed to her. "You don't have to decide now, but at least think about it. I know you're sad, but this isn't the death of your dream. You're being shifted into a different direction. Sometimes that's not a bad thing."

Isabel hugged her. "Thanks for listening," she said.

"That's what friends do. And the second it's five o'clock, we're getting drunk. Because that's the other thing friends do."

Isabel laughed. She was still hurt and confused, but she didn't feel so lost. Maybe she would decide to leave after all, but she had options. Choices.

She walked with her friend to the front door and then out onto the sidewalk.

"You'll be at Jo's tonight right at five," Patience said. "That was a statement, by the way, not a request."

"I'll be there."

"Good."

They hugged again, and then Patience headed toward Brew-haha. Isabel kept on going toward Paper Moon. As she smiled at people she knew, she wondered about the other complication. The one she couldn't really talk about. Not yet.

If she didn't leave Fool's Gold, what was going to happen with Ford? Because she had a bad feeling that whatever she'd felt when Eric had left her didn't begin to measure up to what it would feel like if Ford walked away.

Consuelo studied the collection. "I'm not seeing a lot of romantic comedies," she said as she looked over the titles.

The neatly lined-up DVDs and Blu-ray movies sat on shelves by the TV in Kent's basement. There were plenty of action movies and a large collection of kid movies, but little else.

She looked at Kent. "You realize I can't find a single title that reflects the female point of view."

"We're not big on chick flicks in this house," he admitted. "But if there's something you want to watch, I can get it."

"You're willing to sit through *Sleepless in*

Seattle?"

He smiled. "I've sat through worse."

"There's an endorsement." She ran her finger across the spines. "These are okay, but they usually get the action sequences wrong. Or the bad guys are terrible shots. I see that on TV all the time. Our heroes can kill them with a single bullet, but the bad guys fire and fire and nothing happens."

"Maybe the bad guys need more training."

She shrugged. "I guess it would make for a short series if the lead guy was taken out in episode two."

She turned her attention back to the titles. They'd come down here to pick out a movie for after dinner. Kent had invited her over a few days before, all the while making it clear this was a date. Reese was spending the night at Carter's house. It was just the two of them.

Consuelo was willing to admit to a few nerves, but only to herself. She found dating complicated. Real dating. In the service, she'd occasionally hooked up with guys, but not often. In her line of work, a relationship had seemed impossible, and she was just enough like most women to not love casual sex. There were times when she wanted to be held because she was important to a man and not simply as a means to getting laid.

But this was Kent, which meant a traditional date. As he'd yet to do much more than kiss her, she wasn't sure what, if anything, was going to happen tonight. She supposed if she wanted things to go further, she could make the first move herself.

Except she didn't want to. She wanted . . . to be wooed.

Ridiculous, she thought, scoffing at the weakness the desire exposed. She didn't need anyone. She was self-sufficient. A warrior.

"Hey, come back."

She turned and saw Kent standing next to her. His dark eyes were concerned as he studied her face.

"What?" she asked.

"You were looking pretty pissed about something. I knew you'd gone away."

His ability to read her surprised her. "How do you know I wasn't annoyed with you?"

"I haven't done anything yet."

She smiled. "You're right. I did go away. Sorry."

"Want to talk about it?"

She shook her head. There was so much she couldn't say. Not just the classified stuff. Those secrets were easy to keep. It was the rest of it — what she'd done. He understood the broad strokes, but that wasn't the same as really knowing. Not that he could, because she wouldn't tell him, and if she did, they were back to the classified issue.

"Stop," he said quietly. "Whatever you're thinking, stop."

She blinked at him.

"I can feel you withdrawing," he told her. "Don't do that. Stay with me."

"I'm here," she assured him.

She could see he was worried. There was tension in his shoulders. He was frustrated by what he didn't know and too much of a gentleman to push for an answer. An impossible situation. She didn't know how he stood it.

Not knowing what else to do, she closed the distance between them and put her hands on his chest. "Kiss me."

He wrapped his arms around her and obliged.

As always his mouth was firm but gentle. His lips claimed hers with restrained passion. He wanted her, but he wouldn't push. He wouldn't take. When he moved his tongue against her lower lip, she parted for him.

With the first stroke, she felt the burning heat of arousal between her thighs. Her breasts ached. She wanted to tell herself it was because she hadn't had sex in what felt like forever. But she knew that wasn't the reason. The real reason was she hadn't made love with someone she liked in years. Not since she was much younger and willing to trust.

He drew back. "Stop it," he told her. "Stop going away."

He felt that? Could sense her mind drifting?

"I can't help it," she admitted, unsettled by his ability to read her. She both wanted more and was terrified by the implications. "You frighten me."

"Not possible. How can I do that?"

She turned back, aware her emotions had come to the surface. Control seemed tenuous at best. But this was Kent and she couldn't lie.

"You like me," she admitted. "You know as much as I've ever let anyone see and you like me."

He looked confused. "I don't understand."

She waved at him, indicating his face and his body. "This is who you are. You have flaws and good qualities. Your life is predictable. You call your mother, give to charity. I've been trained to reveal nothing. To give the appearance of being someone I'm not. I survived by being tough."

"Not exactly pillow talk, but okay." He stepped toward her. "I trust you, Consuelo. You're right. I like you a lot. You're complicated, but I can deal."

There it was. Acceptance. He knew there were secrets and he didn't care. He trusted her.

She wanted to argue, to tell him he was wrong. That she wasn't trustworthy. Only she knew in her gut that she would never do anything to hurt this man. She couldn't. It would be easier to cut out her own heart.

Walking away was the easy answer, she thought. So simple and what she knew. The harder path was to stay.

She glanced at the stairs, then back to him. Without saying anything, she took his hand.

She led him to the main floor and then down the hall to the master. Once there, she closed the door and turned on the lamp by the bed. Then she faced him.

A half smile tugged at his lips. He stood by the bed, his stance relaxed, his posture straight. As if he had all the time in the world.

She'd worn a long-sleeved knit dress and high heels. She stepped out of the heels, then undid the side zipper and let her dress drop to the carpet. That left her wearing a push-up bra and a thong.

Kent's eyes widened. She watched him swallow, try to speak then shake his head.

"Holy shit," he muttered.

She laughed, feeling the last of her concerns fall away as easily as the dress. Maybe there were issues she had to deal with, but that was for another time. Right now she wanted to make love with Kent. She wanted his hands on her body and his tongue in her mouth. She wanted to stop thinking and start feeling.

She put her hands on her hips and tilted her head. "Well?"

"Okay, then."

He unbuttoned his long-sleeved shirt and shrugged out of it. Shoes and socks followed. He was in good shape. Not overly honed like the men she worked with, which she liked. Kent looked like what he was. A suburban dad with a sexy edge, she thought, as a shiver of desire slipped through her.

He stepped out of his jeans, leaving him in surprisingly small briefs. The dark cotton fabric sat low on his hips and barely contained his impressive erection. The muscles deep in her belly clenched.

"I would have guessed white," she said, pointing to the briefs and walking toward him.

"I think these are more fashion forward."

She laughed and continued moving until she was nearly touching him, but not quite.

"You're incredibly beautiful," he said, staring into her eyes. "And your body. Jeez. Can I just . . ."

He hesitated, as if not sure asking was okay.

"Anything," she said, curious as to what he would touch first.

His hands settled on her hips, then slowly, so slowly, circled around to her butt. He cupped the muscled curve and squeezed. His eyes drifted closed as his fingers dug in deep.

She leaned into him. From what she'd observed, men fell into one of three categories. Breasts, butts or legs. As she was short and small busted, she was left with a great ass. Looked as though she'd found the right guy to appreciate it.

She wrapped her arms around his neck. He bent down and kissed her. She parted immediately, welcoming his tongue with her own. She tilted her head, wanting him to kiss her deeper, and he obliged.

He moved his hands up her back to her bra. He unfastened it easily and the small lacy garment fell away.

She eased back and brought his hands to

her breasts. "So you weren't lying about what happened in high school."

He brushed his thumbs over her tight nipples. "I gave lessons on how to unfasten a bra one-handed. I'm out of practice. I hope you won't hold that against me."

Before she could answer, he eased her back toward the bed. She settled on the mattress, and he moved next to her. He leaned over her and kissed her again. As his tongue teased her own, he put his hand on her belly. He traced her rib cage before exploring her breasts. He cupped the modest curves and then used his thumb and forefinger to rub her tight, sensitive nipples.

She arched her back just a little, wanting more of that. Kent read the signal. He kissed his way down her throat, nipped the skin right above her collarbone, then settled his mouth over her breast.

He drew her nipple in gently and circled it with his tongue, then withdrew slightly and blew on her damp flesh. She shivered with delight.

"How do you like it?" he asked, before licking her other nipple. "Hard? Soft? Something in between?"

The question stumped her for a second. For so long sex had been about a mission, about getting information. If there was any pleasure, that was incidental, and often accidental. But this was different. This was about sharing.

"Harder than you were doing," she told him. "Just go for it and I'll tell you if it's too much."

He glanced at her and grinned. "You just keep getting better and better."

He settled his mouth on her breast again, sucking harder. As he drew in, he used his hand to rub the other nipple, to mimic the actions of his mouth. His teeth lightly grated against her tender flesh, taking her to the place where pleasure grew until it was a hairbreadth from pain. But before she could stop him, he'd backed off. Just enough.

He repeated his actions, arousing her until she squirmed with the desire for more.

"Kent," she breathed. "I need you."

He reacted more quickly than she would have thought possible. One second she was getting desperate, then next her thong was flying through the air and his fingers were exploring the very heart of her. He slipped through her swollen, slick flesh, found her clitoris and circled it.

His pace could only be called masterful, she thought, opening her legs wide and letting him take control. Fast enough to keep her on the road to climax, but not so fast she felt rushed. He pressed over and around, every now and then pushing just a little harder, getting to the very core of those sensitized nerves.

Her breathing came quicker. It had been so long, she thought, her mind starting to shut down. She needed this, needed to have him push her over the edge.

Muscles tensed as he went around and around. She pumped her hips in time with his movements, her breathing quickened. He shifted, replacing his fingers with his thumb, then slipping two fingers inside her.

On the second stroke, she felt herself starting to climax. The unexpected speed shocked her nearly as much as the intensity. It was as if every cell participated, filling with tension and then releasing. She felt herself cry out and couldn't quiet the sound. He kept touching her and she kept coming, and maybe for the first time ever, she wasn't in control.

At last she was done. Kent withdrew his fingers but kept touching her lightly. She didn't know what to think, what to say. She was drained and embarrassed, yet completely under his spell.

She finally opened her eyes and saw him watching her with an expression of pride and worship that touched the deepest, loneliest place in her heart. His arms came around her, and she went into his embrace, secure in the knowledge she would be safe there.

"I'm pretty sure I said 'holy shit' already," he told her, one hand stroking her back, the other settling on her butt. "So saying it again makes me boring. But my mind is mostly blank, and that's the best I can come up with. You're amazing. I want to keep doing that. Only I have other things I want to do, and I don't know which to do first."

She pressed her belly against his swollen cock. "I think we should start with this." She raised her head and smiled. "I want to be on top."

His erection surged as soon as she said the words, and he was already scrambling out of his briefs. But instead of lying down, he touched her cheek.

"There, uh, hasn't been anyone in a while. So this isn't going to be my finest performance. Just so you aren't disappointed."

She smiled and kissed him. "I'm still having aftershocks. Disappointment isn't possible."

She pushed him onto his back, then looked at him. As he'd said, there were a lot of things they could do. Different positions and techniques she'd picked up over the years. But that was for later. Right now she just wanted to feel him inside her and please him as much as he'd pleased her.

She straddled his waist, then eased back slowly. He reached between them and guided himself in one hand, while holding her hip with the other. She pressed back and down until he was inside her. They both gasped.

He filled her to what felt like her stomach. She straightened, letting her body stretch to accommodate him, then wiggled to accept all of him.

He swore.

She laughed.

"Why don't you stay like that for a second?" he said, his jaw clenched. "I'll work on control."

"Sounds like a plan." She held in a smile. "But if I do this, is it a problem?"

She raised herself slightly and then settled back down on him. He groaned.

"I can play, too," he told her.

"You're trying *not* to play. That's different."

"So that's how it's going to be," he said, his gaze intense. "All right. Let's see about that."

He moved his hand between them and pressed his thumb against her swollen clit.

But instead of holding still, he circled it against all those suddenly hungry nerve endings.

Five seconds ago she would have sworn she was incapable of coming again for at least twenty-four hours. Suddenly she was breathing fast and desperate.

"Don't stop," she said, grinding her hips down. "Keep doing that."

"I swear." His voice was practically a growl.

He kept his word, rubbing her harder and harder, but suddenly it wasn't enough. She rose on his penis, then sank down. Her eyes fluttered closed as she rode him, her release tantalizingly out of reach.

"More," she murmured. "More."

With each rise and fall, he filled her completely. Friction left her gasping. Again and again. Then it was there and she was so close. So close.

She came with a scream. This orgasm lasted longer than the one before. She leaned forward so she could brace herself on the bed and pump back and forth. At some point Kent wasn't touching her center anymore. He was holding her hips, helping her keep pace. She opened her eyes and saw him watching her, saw the moment he went over the edge.

They came together. He shoved in deep and she clamped her muscles around him. They stayed like that until they were both still.

With quiet came reality. Consuelo had a vision of herself going up and down, her breasts pounding, as she screamed for him not to stop.

She'd lost complete control. Twice.

A hand touched her cheek. She forced herself to open her eyes and found him watching her. A self-satisfied smile turned up the corners of his mouth.

"So," he said. "You're a screamer."

She slid off him and lay back on the bed. "I'm not. I'm very quiet and controlled in bed."

He chuckled. "Yeah, I could tell." He leaned over her and lightly kissed her. "So I was thinking I'd make you come with my mouth, and then we could do it with me behind, because hey, have you seen your ass? Then dinner?"

She felt the moment of choice. Where she could let her past define her or she could give herself to this glorious man. She flung both arms around him and hung on tight.

He pulled her against him and whispered, "You know I like the screaming, right?"

"I know."

CHAPTER EIGHTEEN

Isabel walked through the empty store next to Paper Moon. It was owned by former champion cyclist Josh Golden, who had spent the past decade buying a measurable percentage of the town. Rumor had it he was a generous landlord, which was good because it wasn't as if she was swimming in money.

The space wasn't very big. Just a couple of thousand square feet, but there were large windows, and best of all, it shared a wall with Paper Moon.

The previous occupant had left shelving in place, and the hardwood floors were in excellent condition. There were two restrooms, one much more elegantly appointed than the other, and a decent-sized storage room.

She returned to the center of the store and turned in a slow circle. It wouldn't take much to put an opening in the wall. She could use the dressing rooms from the bridal shop, which would save on remodeling. The nicer bathroom could be for customers. She would have the cost of painting and some fixtures, but the lighting was already how she would want it.

She could use the shelves for accessories and wondered how hard it would be to find designers who created handbags, belts and jewelry.

She didn't have a business plan, so she couldn't run the numbers, but there were possibilities. She let herself out, careful to lock the door behind her, and returned to Paper Moon.

She tried to look at the store as if she'd never been in it before. Again, there were plenty of windows and lots of light. There was a little too much red velvet on the furniture and gilding on the chandeliers for her taste, but that was easily fixed.

The basic floor plan worked, and the inventory was current. If she had the space next door, she wouldn't have to make any changes in Paper Moon, at least not for a while. It would provide a nice cash flow.

She knew her parents would be thrilled to have the business stay in the family and that they would let her buy them out over time. Once she got her business plan together, she could run the numbers. She had a feeling with the cash she'd gotten out of her marriage, she could make it work, financially. The question was, did she want to?

Staying meant being with her friends. Staying meant being close to her family. Staying meant the confusion of what to do about her feelings for Ford.

But staying also meant giving up on her dream of living in New York again, of being on the cutting edge of fashion. It meant returning to her hometown permanently, and right now she wasn't sure if that was a good thing or a bad thing — mostly because she'd retreated here after her divorce. She wanted to be moving forward, not going back. She supposed that the biggest issue was if she stayed, she might feel as though she was giving up.

It all came down to making the choice that was best for her, given her change in circumstances.

The front door opened. She turned and saw Ford walking in with two beautiful young women. They were petite, with long dark hair and brown eyes. Their perfect skin glowed in a way that made Isabel feel she should be exfoliating more.

"Hey," Ford said, walking toward her. He had a large garment bag in each hand. "I want you to meet Misaki and Kaori. They're sisters."

"Nice to meet you," Isabel said.

She would guess the sisters were in their early twenties. Misaki had on deep purple harem pants and a black leather vest. Kaori wore a dark red dress with inverted pleats.

"Love the store," Kaori said as she looked around. "Retro, but still elegant." Her gaze settled on a display of a Vera Wang dress. "Man, I'd kill to deconstruct that."

"You want to deconstruct everything," her sister said.

Isabel returned her attention to Ford. "So, um, why are you here and why have you brought these lovely young women to me?"

Misaki grinned and took one of the garment bags from Ford and unzipped it. "We make clothes."

Two dresses and a ball gown spilled out of the opening and suddenly Isabel didn't care about how Ford knew the sisters or why he'd brought them. The garments claimed her attention. The dresses couldn't have been more different. One was all draping and movement, while the other didn't look big enough to fit a fashion doll. Talk about skintight.

The ball gown was made of layers and layers of champagne-colored lace. But the detail work was done in leather.

"That belongs on the red carpet," Isabel murmured, touching the capped sleeve and admiring the clean workmanship.

"I wish," Misaki said. "We haven't had much luck placing our designs in stores. We're too edgy for the department stores, and the one boutique we went into basically stole our clothes and paid us nothing. So we're nervous about trying that again. Ford said we could trust you."

Madeline walked in from the back room and gasped. "I want that. I have nowhere to wear it, and I probably won't be able to eat for a month to afford it, but I want that."

Isabel performed the introductions. Misaki beamed. Kaori pushed her aside. "Mine are better."

She pulled out a suit that was both stern and playful. A fitted jacket, with zippers running down the sleeves. The wool blend was soft, with just enough structure.

"Taryn would buy that in a heartbeat," Madeline said.

"She would buy most of them," Isabel admitted. She looked at the girls. "Where did you come from?"

"San Francisco," Misaki said. "We're supposed to be studying to be doctors. Our parents aren't happy at all. You've heard of the Tiger Mom? Well, our mom makes tiger moms look like slackers. Kaori and I can both play three different instruments. We got into UC Berkeley on full scholarship. But we drew the line at medical school. We just want to design clothes."

"You're good at it," Isabel told her. "I'm impressed. I'll take them all on consignment. Do you have prices?"

Kaori whipped out a pricing sheet, along with a simple, single-page contract. Ten minutes later, the deal was done.

Misaki grinned. "This is fantastic. Okay, we're going to walk around town for a while. Ford, text us when you're ready to go." She linked arms with her sister. "This place is so strange. Like a movie set or something."

They walked out of the store. Madeline took their clothes to the back. They'd already agreed the ball gown would go in the front window and the suit would be displayed in the side window.

Isabel looked at Ford. "Thank you."

He shrugged. "You were upset. I didn't know what else to do."

"You found me designers. That's impressive."

"Their brother is a buddy of mine. He was always talking about them. They were a handful for his parents. I thought I remembered him mentioning they were designing clothes now, so I got in touch with him. I drove out to get them this morning."

She walked into his embrace and held him tight. "Thank you."

"You're welcome." He hugged her back. "You were hurting and I didn't know what to do. It's in my nature to fix things."

She raised her head and looked at him. "You fix good."

He flashed her a smile. "Thanks. They're both excited about New York. Misaki wants to move there, but Kaori says they have a West Coast vibe and have to stay here."

It took her a second to understand what he was saying, and then she got it. Of course. Ford still assumed she was leaving. That even without Sonia she was going to return to New York. Because she'd always said she would.

Only now she was less sure about anything.

She opened her mouth to tell him that she might not be leaving, then pressed her lips together. Not for the first time it occurred to her Ford was perfectly happy with the idea of her walking away.

Consuelo hit the bag hard. She was already

dripping sweat and her arms had started to tremble from exhaustion. Anyone else would call it a day, but she couldn't. Not while she could still think.

Rage burned hot and bright inside her. If she stopped hitting the bag, she would hit something else. She would take out her anger on someone innocent, and that never went well.

For the greater good, she told herself as she hit the bag — left, right, left right.

She'd done it. She'd allowed herself to believe. She'd given herself body and soul to a man, and he'd turned out to be as much of an asshole as all the rest.

Kent hadn't contacted her in two days. She'd spent the night with him, had made love until they were both exhausted and then she'd gone home. And since then, there had been nothing. Not a single word.

She wasn't sure where she wanted to put all her anger. Most of it was directed at herself. For taking the chance, when she knew better. But some of it went to him for making her believe. He'd encouraged her to trust him. Somewhere along the way he'd decided to play her, and she'd practically handed him a script.

Ford walked into the gym. He looked

cocky and proud of himself. She glared at him.

"What?" she demanded.

He came to a stop and studied her for a second, then held up both hands. "Whatever it is, I didn't do it."

"For once you're right."

"Want to talk about it?"

She glared at him. "Do I ever?"

"No."

"Then you have your answer. What are you so happy about?"

He squared his shoulders. "Isabel had a problem and I fixed it."

She gave him a pitying look. "Seriously? You believe that?"

"Sure." He told her about the phone call from Sonia and how her friend no longer wanted to go into business with her.

Consuelo winced. "That sucks. Betrayed by two people she trusted back-to-back. How did you help?"

"I found her two new designers. Sisters. Their brother is a SEAL. They're willing to work with her in New York." He grinned. "Problem solved."

"You're such an idiot." She dropped her arms and started to remove her gloves. "And you have it bad."

"It?"

"You're falling for Isabel. The master of noninvolvement has gotten caught in a net he never even saw." She supposed she should be happy that her friend had found someone. She wasn't mean-spirited enough to wish the whole world be as miserable as her.

"It's great," she added, hoping she sounded sincere. "I like her a lot. She's better than you deserve, but then, you were always lucky."

He took a step back. "I don't know what you're talking about."

"Don't pretend to be an idiot. You're not far enough from the real thing for it to work. You care about her."

He looked confused and uncomfortable. "Sure. We're friends, but we're not really together. We're fake-dating. Because of my mom."

"Not after all this time." She pulled off the first glove, then the second. "You're practically living in her house, aren't you? You spend all your free time with her, you're sleeping with her and it's the best it's ever been."

Like her night with Kent, she thought bitterly.

"We're not dating," Ford insisted stubbornly.

Consuelo walked up to him and poked him in the chest. Hard. With luck, she would leave a bruise.

"You're in love with her, you moron. You probably have been for years. Don't screw this up." She poked him again. "She's great. Ask her to stay. Get married and have babies. It's what you want. It's what you've always wanted."

He shook his head. "I'm not that guy."

"You were born to be that guy. You're just like everyone else in this damn town. Accept your fate."

With that, she turned and walked away. Her eyes burned, but she told herself it was from sweat and nothing else. She wasn't actually crying. She didn't cry, didn't believe in tears. Or wallowing. She'd made a mistake and now she would move on.

The fact that moving on meant she would have to leave Fool's Gold was a problem she would deal with later.

The Fall Festival had been one of Ford's favorites as a kid. It fell on the second weekend in October, when the leaves were turning and all the storefronts were decorated with pumpkins and scarecrows.

There were a lot of carts selling stuff nobody really needed, like honey soap and apple-scented candles. But the women in town seemed really excited about it all and were buying it by the truckload.

What he liked was the food. There were ribs and grilled corn on the cob. Corn bread, slow-cooked pulled pork and, his personal favorite, sweet-potato pie.

"Seriously, you have to try this," Isabel said, offering him a bite of her S'More. "I don't know how Ana Raquel makes it the best thing ever, but she does."

He didn't care about the dessert, but he was relieved to see Isabel smiling again. For the past week, she'd been kind of down. He knew she'd been thinking about what had happened with Sonia.

He tasted the S'More. It was sweet, but not too sweet.

"Nice," he said, handing it back to her.

She grinned. "But not sweet-potato pie?"

"Not even close."

"What is it with guys and pie?"

"Like you don't want any?"

"I'll have some to be polite."

He chuckled and put his arm around her.

Now that she was feeling better, he could stop thinking about how to fix her, which meant he could put more effort into forgetting all the ridiculous things Consuelo had said the other day.

At first her words had made him uncomfortable. He didn't want to lead Isabel on, which he wasn't doing. They'd both been clear on the fake-dating from the beginning. As for him being in love with her — he wasn't that lucky. If he could be in love with anyone, he would want it to be her. But he wasn't. He couldn't be.

He thought about how Leonard was secretly working out every day to impress his wife, and how his mom had mourned his dad for over a decade. His sisters were wild about their husbands, and when Ethan looked at Liz, he knew the rest of the world disappeared.

Why wouldn't he want that? That intensity? That caring? Of course he did. But it wasn't there. Never had been. He liked a woman for a while and then wanted to move on. That was who he was.

"I heard from Misaki and Kaori," Isabel said as she finished her dessert and dropped the paper container into a recycling bin. "They're really excited I've already sold two pieces. They're making more. I really like working with them." She smiled up at him. "Thank you. Bringing them to me was really thoughtful."

"I know. You're lucky to have me."

She laughed and slipped her arm through

his. "I am. I'm still confused about Sonia, but I'll heal. I'll learn from the mistake and move on."

"I have no doubt. You're strong with the Force." He changed his voice to sound like Yoda from *Star Wars.* "There is much power in this one."

She laughed again. "I appreciate the compliment, but I'm not sure it's something I've earned."

"Sure you have. You're forgetting, I saw you grow up."

They walked around a young couple with a double stroller. The little boys inside were obviously identical twins. An older girl sat on her father's shoulders.

"Those letters," she said with a groan. "I knew they'd come back to haunt me."

"No haunting. You were a sweet girl. When you screwed up at UCLA, you took responsibility. You recognized what you'd done wrong and made amends. We can't be perfect. That's what I learned in my training. It's not getting it right the first time — it's learning to do it right and then not getting lazy. That's what you did."

"You're giving me way too much credit."

"No. It's not just UCLA. You stopped writing me when you thought Eric was going to propose. There was nothing between us, but you wanted to do the right thing. I respect that."

"I wasn't sure what to do," she admitted. "It's just when I wrote you . . ." She shrugged, then smiled. "So you're admitting you read them and liked them."

"Yeah, I did. They got me through some tough times." He paused and kissed her. "You always told me to stay safe."

"I worried about you. No one knew where you were or what you were doing. It was scary. Worse for your family, but still."

He remembered how he would tell himself he didn't care about her letters, but that he always looked for them. That when they came, he saved them until he could have some quiet time by himself. That when something bad happened, he went back to the letters. That he wrapped a few in plastic and tucked them in the bottom of his backpack when he went on a mission.

"I made it through," he said. "Now I'm home."

"We're all glad."

A voice cut through their conversation.

"Yes, I know she's an elephant."

Ford stopped and turned toward the speaker. He saw Felicia staring down a tattooed man.

Felicia leaned closer, obviously not intimidated by the man's glare. "Priscilla is a part of this community as much as anyone else. Heidi and her mother-in-law bought a special saddle so the children could ride Priscilla. This is a festival. Rides are a given."

"Yeah, but now no one wants to ride my ponies."

"Wouldn't you rather ride an elephant than a pony?"

The man shuffled his feet. "Yeah. Maybe."

"Then why are you surprised?" Felicia drew in a breath. "But I understand you need to make a living at this, too. I'll move you to the other side of the park. We'll raise the ticket price on the elephant rides to cover an additional ride on your ponies. Then it becomes a two-for-one ticket. How's that?"

The large, tattooed man nodded his head and kicked his booted foot into the sidewalk. "You know they're good little guys. It's not their fault they're small."

"I understand," Felicia said, clutching a tablet in her arms. "Let me get those arrangements going for you." She turned and saw them.

She walked briskly toward them. "Hello, Isabel. Ford. Please don't tell me you two have a problem."

"Not a one," he assured her. "Just enjoying the show."

Felicia drew in a breath. "I swear, he's more worried about his ponies not getting all the attention than he is about losing money. Which probably speaks well for his character. But Priscilla has attention needs, too." She made a noise low in her throat. "This is not a normal town. I suspect it's why I fit in so well, but there are constant challenges. If you'll excuse me, please."

With that she walked away. Ford watched her go.

"I've seen her get men and equipment into places where all the experts said it couldn't be done. If NASA really wants a colony on the moon within the next decade, they should talk to her."

"I don't think she wants to move," Isabel told him.

"You're right. Come on. I'll buy you an elephant ear. All this talk of Priscilla has made me want one."

"That is gross and we just had S'Mores."

"You had S'Mores. Besides, they're the last of the season."

"You get one," she said, leaning into him. "I'll nibble."

He could think of several things other than an elephant ear that he would like her to nibble on, but that was for later. He had big plans for tonight. A fire in the fireplace, some wine. Maybe a can of whipped cream.

He grinned as he imagined a naked Isabel holding the can and asking, "Where exactly is this supposed to go?"

But she would be game, as she always was. Given which team he preferred to play for, Eric wasn't completely to blame for Isabel's lack of sexual awakening. Ford supposed if he had to say, he was a little bit pleased that he'd been the one to teach her how much fun intimacy could be.

"You know we need a pumpkin for the porch," Isabel told him as they walked toward the food carts. "Maybe a couple. I hate to admit this, but I haven't carved a pumpkin in years. Do you know how? I don't want to have the only freak pumpkins on the street."

"It's going to be Halloween. Freaks are a good thing."

"Yeah, but I'm afraid mine would be freakishly bad."

"I know how to carve a pumpkin. I did it as a kid, and sometimes when I was deployed, they'd fly in pumpkins."

"Marking the seasons?"

"As best they could."

Fool's Gold was about as far from Iraq and Afghanistan as a guy could get. He'd thought he would have trouble fitting in, but he hadn't. Mostly because of Isabel, he realized. She'd been his buffer.

As they stood in line for elephant ears, he found himself wanting to ask her to stay. But he couldn't. Not only was New York her dream, but he had nothing to offer in return.

He had to let her go — he owed her. She'd given him the haven he hadn't known he needed.

CHAPTER NINETEEN

Generally the music in the bridal shop was calm while being upbeat. No songs about broken hearts were allowed. Sort of rock-edged spa music. But today Isabel could hear only the music playing in her head. The Clash song "Should I Stay or Should I Go?" played over and over as she checked inventory and ordered samples.

It was the question of the day. Her weekend with Ford had been lots of fun. He was funny and charming and sweet, if slightly obsessed with elephant ears. Being with him was easy. Loving him . . . Well, that had probably been inevitable.

She was willing to state the obvious. She'd totally and completely fallen in love with him. There were a thousand reasons — some about him and some about her past. For years he'd been the person she'd poured her heart out to. She'd confessed all, and whether or not he'd listened, he'd been the one she'd instinctively turned to when things got bad.

She'd wondered about seeing him in person. Would it be better or worse than she'd imagined? Could the man live up to the hype?

She'd discovered that he could and he did. Ford was honorable and caring. The fact that he was terrified of his mother only added to his charm. Isabel understood him, depended on him and had fallen in love with him. The downside was he didn't think *he* was capable of loving anyone. Because he never had done so.

She wanted to challenge him on that. To grab him and shake him until he admitted that he'd been too young when he and Maeve had gotten engaged, and since then he'd never been in one place long enough to fall in love. That he needed to give it a try because without him, her heart would be shattered.

The music in her head started again. *Should I stay or should I go?* A question people had been asking since the most ancient of ancestors had been able to form thought. Because she wasn't just asking about her business; she was asking about Ford. Did she take a chance that he might figure out that she was his one true love?

Because what if she wasn't? What if he really *wasn't* interested in loving her back? What if he knew himself better than she thought?

Isabel shook her head. This was neither productive nor encouraging. She needed to make her decision to stay or go based on her and no one else. If she stayed and it didn't work out with Ford, she would find someone else. Or stay single. Not everybody had to get married to find happiness.

The front door of the store opened. Isabel turned and saw Taryn walk in.

"I got a message you have new clothes for me," the elegant brunette said. "Dellina said she was desperately bitter about the new designers and reminded me to buy local. Do you know what she's talking about?"

"I brought in a couple more designers last week," Isabel told her. "They're young and edgy."

Taryn nodded. "But not Dellina's friends. I get it. I'm going to have to explain to her that I don't guilt easily."

"I don't think she'll be surprised to hear that. Come on. The clothes are over here."

They walked toward the storage room. Isabel paused to point out the suit in the side window. "That's very you," she said.

Taryn moved closer. "I love the zippers. Okay, I'll try it on."

"Did you notice the ball gown in the window? Lace and leather."

"I did and I'm tempted, but I'm not sure where I'd wear it." She smiled. "Not that I always need a reason to indulge myself. What the hell? Sure, bring them all in."

With Madeline not working until later that afternoon and no other customers, Taryn was the only one in the store. Isabel put Taryn in a front dressing room, in the mother-of-the-bride room, so she could still hear if anyone walked in.

She wrestled the suit off the mannequin, collected the other two dresses and walked back toward the dressing area. Taryn had already removed her suit and heels and stood by the dressing room door in a push-up bra and bikini briefs.

Isabel instantly felt inadequate. The other woman's thighs were perfectly firm and defined. Her midsection was lean, with a muscle shadow going down both sides. With her long hair loose and flowing, she looked more like a swimsuit model than an executive in her mid-thirties.

It was one thing for Consuelo to look amazing — the woman worked out constantly. But Taryn had the body of a goddesslike creature *and* spent her days in a regular job. Taryn was not only two inches taller, she was probably a size two or four and Isabel . . . wasn't.

Isabel couldn't decide if this moment of truth meant she should find a Pilates class somewhere or go get a doughnut.

"Try on the suit first," she said, handing it over. "I'll go get the ball gown out of the window."

By the time she returned to the dressing room, Taryn was standing in front of the big mirror.

"I love this," she said, turning back and forth.

Isabel had to admit the woman could wear clothes. The severe construction of the jacket gave it a more masculine air, while the zippers were an unexpected edgy touch. The combination made Taryn look incredibly sexy and dangerous at the same time.

"All you need is a whip," Isabel joked.

"I can keep the boys in line verbally, but I like the idea of a whip for backup. They can be unruly." She turned and looked at Isabel. "What's up?"

"What do you mean?"

"You're not your usual upbeat self. Did something happen?"

Isabel wasn't pleased to be told she was pouting enough for people to notice. "Sorry. Personal stuff."

Taryn stepped off the podium and walked toward her. "Like what? How can I help?"

"You can't, but I appreciate the offer."

Taryn raised perfectly groomed eyebrows, as if she were planning to wait Isabel out.

"I had a business partner in New York. When I left here, I was going to open a store with her. Trendy, upscale. She was the designer. I brought in the plan and retail experience. She found someone else and dumped me."

"I hate breakups," Taryn told her sympathetically. "I'm sorry. But at the risk of sounding sanctimonious, you're better off without her. If she'd do that now, she'd do it later. And then you'd be in a huge financial mess. Trust me. Partners have unintended consequences."

"Like ending up in Fool's Gold?"

Taryn shrugged. "Exactly like that." She tugged on the hem of the jacket. "There are other designers out there. Look at this one. I doubt your friend was a whole lot more talented."

Isabel hadn't thought of it that way. "You're right," she said slowly. "Actually, it's two designers. Sisters."

"Better and better. Plus, there's the one you met through Dellina. So screw the other bitch and start over with a stable of fantastically talented designers. I know it's a cliché, but success is the best revenge." She paused. "Or is it sex? I can never remember."

Isabel laughed. "It's success."

"Oh, well, I suppose they're both enjoyable." She shrugged out of her jacket, apparently comfortable in her body. "What about staying here? You have this store already. It gives you a built-in cash flow."

"I've been thinking about it," Isabel admitted, taking the jacket while Taryn slipped out of the skirt. "Fool's Gold will never be anyone's idea of a fashion capital, but the start-up costs would be less. I'm still not sure. I worry that not going back to New York is too much like giving up. Death of a dream and all that."

"Death of a dream?" Taryn asked, taking the ball gown and stepping into it. "Dramatic much?"

Isabel laughed. "Point taken. I've been wallowing. I guess it's time to decide."

"There are positive aspects to this wretched little town," Taryn told her. "Even I can admit that. The boys love it, and you have a growing population. There's plenty of industry coming in. You could talk to the Lucky Lady people and see if they would let you put a display window in the resort area. That would drive traffic to your store."

Something Isabel had never thought of. Whatever she was going to say next was erased from her mind when Taryn whipped off her bra and handed it to Isabel, then pulled up the dress and slipped her arms into the capped sleeves.

It wasn't that seeing another woman's breasts shocked her; it was that Taryn was so comfortable with her body. Isabel didn't mind being naked around Ford, mostly because he obviously enjoyed what he was looking at. But in a dressing room? Isabel would be the one changing behind closed doors.

Which was a statement about her, she realized. Her fears and how she judged herself. Her friends wouldn't care.

Taryn presented her back. "I can't reach the zipper," she said.

Isabel pulled it up the last few inches, then adjusted the deep V in the back. She hung the suit over the back of a chair and faced her friend.

The dress was amazing. Layers and layers of champagne-colored lace with unexpected edges in black leather. The cap sleeves were young and sweet, yet the front dipped nearly to Taryn's waist and exposed the inner sides of her breasts. At the same time, there was too much fabric around the hips.

"I know someone who does tailoring," Isabel said, going into gown-selling mode. She studied Taryn critically, then reached for the ever-present dish of pins.

"If we took it in here and here," she said, pinning as she talked, tightening the dress through Taryn's rib cage, waist and rear. She eyed the bodice. "Is the front going to work?"

Taryn glanced down. "It's more wide than low. I feel like I'm one quick turn away from a wardrobe malfunction." She turned back and forth, and sure enough, one of her breasts popped out.

"That would make you popular at any event," Isabel murmured.

Taryn tucked her breast back in place. "Tape?"

"No. It's a design flaw. I'll call Misaki and talk to her about putting a band across the front somewhere. The dress has to be anchored. You're wearing it in the real world, not simply walking down a runway. Movement is required."

Taryn nodded. "I think a stripe of black leather right between my breasts would be perfect. Have I mentioned I love this dress?"

The front door opened and Dellina walked in.

"Hi, I brought —" Her eyes widened.

"OMG, look at that dress. It's stunning." She wrinkled her nose. "It's from those other designers, isn't it? Damn, they're good. It's kind of low in the front, though, isn't it? No, not too low. Too wide. Although the side cleavage is very sexy."

"I flash people when I move," Taryn said. "We need a fix."

"So they're not perfect," Isabel told Dellina. "Is that a relief?"

"A big one." Dellina waved her large portfolio and smiled at Taryn. "I have some preliminary ideas based on what you gave me."

"Wonderful." Taryn presented her back so Isabel could unzip her. "We're down to three locations that are a good fit for us," she said as she stepped out of the gown and started to dress. "One of them is in a warehouse. Right next to CDS."

Isabel grinned. "Because the potential sound of gunfire is exciting to them?"

"Apparently." She handed Isabel the gown. "The other thrill of the warehouse is the boys want enough space to put in a basketball court, which I am desperately opposed to, but am once again outvoted." She finished fastening her bra, then held up her hand. "No. I'm wrong. It's only a half court. So why would I complain?"

"A basketball court?" Isabel got a hanger for the gown. "Won't that be loud?"

"And annoying. There's a sound to try to work by, the constant thump-thump of the ball on cement. I'm going to have to kill at least one of them. I see that now."

Dellina laughed. "I do have one basketball-court-free option."

"I wish, but they'll never go for it."

Dellina looked at Isabel. "I heard about what happened with your designer friend in New York. I'm sorry."

"Me, too, but I'm dealing."

Dellina pulled a couple of sheets from her portfolio. "I hope I didn't overstep my bounds, but I did a couple of quick sketches using the space next door for non-bridal clothes. It wouldn't be an expensive remodel, and you can get a lot more in there than you'd think. Especially if you use the dressing rooms you already have."

Isabel took the papers and glanced at the designs. They were clean and well thought out. She immediately saw the potential and how the two stores would flow together.

"I like this," she said. "Give me some time to look them over. Then maybe we could talk. I don't know what I'm going to do, but . . ."

She pressed her lips together. The song in

her head had disappeared, because she did know what she was going to do. The answer was ridiculously simple. Fool's Gold offered her everything she could possibly want. Friends, a new business and a place to belong.

"I'm staying," she said softly, not sure she believed the words, yet knowing they were right. "I'm staying," she repeated more firmly.

"I'm so glad," Dellina said, hugging her. "We have to talk later. I have a thousand ideas about the store."

Taryn watched them both, then looked at Isabel. "You and I should talk, as well. You're going to need capital. However much money you have put away, it's not enough."

Isabel nodded slowly. "You're right. But I can go slow."

"Or you can start with an ass-kicking opening. I'm interested in helping. As a silent partner. I earned my money the old-fashioned way, and there's plenty of it. If I'm going to be stuck in this town, then I might as well have fun. Working with you would give me that."

How unexpected, Isabel thought. "Let's schedule a meeting," she said, thinking she could learn a lot from the woman. And not just about business.

■ ■ ■ ■

Kent didn't understand what had happened. He'd returned from his math competition only to find Consuelo wasn't taking his calls. He'd seen her in the grocery store last night, but she'd ducked out of sight before he could catch up with her.

The message was clear — she'd changed her mind about him. In the three days he'd been gone, she'd had time to think, and he wasn't who or what she wanted.

The truth hurt, he admitted, as he pulled into the CDS parking lot. That night with her had been incredible. He'd thought . . . well, he'd thought a lot of things. Not just that they had chemistry, but that she cared about him. That she liked how they were together and that she wanted more of that.

But he'd been fooling himself. Or she'd figured out the truth. About him and about Lorraine.

Consuelo was sweet and kind despite her tough exterior. She was too nice to tell him what had happened, so she was avoiding him. While he wanted to keep his pride intact, he knew that the right thing to do was to man-up. He would say what had to be said and then let her get on with her life.

He found her in her office. The room was small and utilitarian. There were no feminine touches.

She looked up as he entered, her expression unreadable. He stepped into her office and closed the door behind him.

He'd imagined seeing her again so many times while he'd been gone. He'd pictured her rushing into his arms, holding him tight and never letting go. He'd thought about her having dinner with him and Reese, then sneaking in a few kisses after he drove her home. He'd hoped this weekend they would have a repeat performance of their last night together.

He wanted to be angry, but he knew the fault was his. Mistakes from the past had come back to haunt him.

"Hey," he said as he took a seat. "How's it going?"

"Fine."

She looked tired. Or maybe he was seeing what he wanted to see. That she hadn't been sleeping well because of the decision she had to make. The truth was probably much harsher — that she didn't care enough to sweat his reaction.

"I know what you want to say," he began, figuring there was no point in pretending otherwise. "You're not interested in a regular guy like me. You thought you were, but all that danger and testosterone is more interesting than a man who teaches math to teenagers."

Consuelo slowly rose to her feet. "What the hell are you talking about?"

He frowned. "You sound angry."

"Of course I'm angry. I'm hurt and I should know better, right? The joke's on me for thinking you were different."

"Because of Lorraine."

Her dark eyes widened. "Who is Lorraine? You disappeared for three days and then you *cheated*?"

"What? No. Lorraine is my ex."

"You saw your ex?"

"Of course not. What are you talking about?"

"I get to ask the questions," she snapped. "Where the hell have you been?"

"At a three-day retreat with my math class. Our first competition is next month." He blinked. "I told you in the card I left for you. I stopped by on my way out of town. With everything that happened on our last night together, I couldn't remember if I'd said anything or not. I didn't want you to worry. We were in Sacramento. Sixteen kids and about that many parents."

She pointed to her fairly clean desk.

"There's no card."

Kent studied her for a second, hoping that maybe, just maybe, there'd been a misunderstanding. Something they could get over. Because having her stare at him with a combination of pain and loathing hurt him more than he'd thought possible.

He stood and crossed to the bulletin board by the door. He'd tacked a small envelope there. Now he pulled it free and handed it to her.

Her eyes widened as she stared at the writing on the front.

"You left me a note?" she asked, her voice oddly small.

He nodded.

"When?"

"The next morning."

She opened it slowly and scanned the card inside. He knew the message explained about the math retreat and asked her to call him when she could.

Consuelo swallowed. "I didn't know," she breathed. "I thought you'd just disappeared. I thought you didn't want . . ." She pressed her lips together. "Then if you didn't break up with me, what are you talking about?"

He was still processing the new information. "You were avoiding me because you thought I hadn't called?"

She nodded.

"I'd never do that."

"That's what I thought. So I couldn't believe I'd been wrong about you." He started toward her, but she shook her head. "No. Tell me what you were going to say before."

He swore silently. "I thought you were avoiding me because you'd figured out I wasn't that interesting. That you were disappointed it took me so long to get over my ex-wife. I couldn't face the fact that I was wrong about her. I fell in love with her. I asked her to marry me. I had a child with her and then she left. She walked out on me and on Reese. I get leaving the marriage, but her own kid?"

He started to turn away but knew he had to face her. Had to be completely honest.

"I was forced to realize I'd been an idiot from the beginning. That everything about our marriage was a sham. I was hurt and embarrassed and struggling with being a single dad. I didn't want to face my mistakes, so it was easier to tell everyone I was waiting for Lorraine to come back. Then it became a pattern, and I didn't know how to break it. I couldn't get over her until I was willing to admit the truth about her. About us. And that took longer than it should have."

"How did you finally move on?"

"I guess I got tired of whining," he admitted. "I accepted I'd made a bad decision, did my best to learn from it and prepared to start dating again. What I couldn't prepare for was meeting you."

Her dark gaze never left his face. She drew in a breath, but didn't speak. He knew it was all up to him.

"Look at you," he said, smiling at her. "You're tough and sweet. You care about my kid. You're fair. You don't take anybody's shit. But you're patient with the little kids. Reese talks about how you'll spend a full ten minutes in the middle of class to help a student who's scared."

He managed a slight smile. "I like that you could take my brother. He needs that in his life."

The corner of her mouth twitched, but she didn't speak.

"I know there's stuff in your past," he continued. "I know you did things — some unspeakable things — to help our country, and that you're as proud of that as you are scared to tell me the details." He shrugged. "I'm sorry you went through that, but if you're waiting for me to judge you, you've got the wrong guy. I won't. Not ever."

He thought about his past, how he'd taken the easy road. The one without risk. Maybe it was all so he could come to this moment.

"I know it's fast and you have no reason to believe me, but I love you, Consuelo. I want you in my life, and I want to be in yours. I want to love you and take care of you for as long as you'll have me. I want us . . ." He sucked in a breath. "Okay, it's too soon to say the rest of what I want, but you get the idea. If you're interested."

She stared at him for a long time before launching herself around the desk and into his arms. He caught her as she rushed him, hauling her against his chest. She wrapped her arms around his neck and her legs around his waist; then she started to kiss him.

"I thought you'd left me," she admitted. "I was never going to fall in love, and you broke my heart."

"I'm sorry."

"No. It was me. I should have called and talked to you. I shouldn't have been so afraid." She stared into his eyes. "It's just I've never known anyone like you. I'm so scared you're going to figure out that you can do better and then you'll be gone."

"Never," he promised, then kissed her.

She kissed him back, holding on so tight he knew she would never let go.

She raised her head, her eyes bright with tears. "Yes," she whispered. "Yes, I love you, and yes, when it's time, let's have that other conversation. But for now, we'll hang out and have lots of sex."

He started to laugh then, because how on earth a guy like him found a woman like her was beyond him. But he'd been lucky and he planned to spend the rest of his life being very, very grateful.

"You're an incurable slob," Isabel said to herself as she picked up a monster-truck magazine and two coffee cups. They'd been left in the living room, along with a lot of other stuff belonging to Ford. She put the magazine on the shelf under the coffee table and carried the mugs into the kitchen.

The man could barbecue, he could make her laugh and cause her to see stars in bed, but he left a trail of crap wherever he went. A small price to pay, she thought, nearly tripping over a pair of boots by the bathroom.

She carried the boots into the bedroom.

Sometime in the past few weeks, Ford had basically moved in with her. They were together every night, and somehow his clothes had started appearing in her closets and drawers. She would give him credit for doing the laundry. At least twice a week she came home to a freshly washed and folded pile of panties and bras. Her towels were always clean, as was the bathroom, now that she thought about it.

She set his boots in the closet and pushed them forward so she could close the door. Only they wouldn't move. Something was in the way. She saw his duffel and shifted it. The zipper was open and a banded stack of letters tumbled to the carpet.

Isabel immediately recognized her own handwriting. She reached for the letters and undid the elastic band. The envelopes fanned out in her hand.

These were from when she was in high school, she thought. She bent down and saw three more banded groups of envelopes in his duffel. All her letters? Was it possible he'd kept them?

She sank onto the carpet and opened the top letter. The first thing she noticed was how worn the paper was. The seams where it had been folded were practically translucent. Some of the individual words had faded, and there were smudges on the side from being held.

Every one of them looked the same. Worn,

well read. As if Ford had pored over them a dozen times. No, a hundred. She'd often wondered if he even cared that she wrote, but now she saw that somehow she'd connected with him.

She scanned the contents of the pages, wincing as she saw hearts in the margins or a particularly hideous picture spilling out. She heard footsteps and looked up. Ford stood in the bedroom.

"I was such a kid," she said, waving the letters. "How did you stand it?"

"I liked them. I watched you grow up." He gave her a slow smile. "You turned out good."

He stood there all tall and broad. He wore cargo pants and a black T-shirt. Very "mercenary does Fool's Gold." He was tough and sweet, and she'd fallen for him weeks ago. Between then and now had simply been an attempt to avoid the obvious.

She scrambled to her feet and put the letters on her dresser. "So I have some news."

He leaned in and kissed her. "New lip gloss? What's the flavor?"

She stepped back. "This is serious."

"So's your lip gloss. Is it piña colada?"

"Yes, now listen. I'm staying."

He looked at her as if he hadn't understood what she'd said.

"I'm staying in Fool's Gold. I'm going to expand Paper Moon and add a boutique." She drew in a breath. "Obviously Sonia is a big part of why, but you are, too. I know this was just supposed to be pretend. But it's not. At least not for me." She twisted her fingers together.

"I'm in love with you, Ford. I think I have been since I was fourteen. At the very least, I've been waiting for you to come back. Or us to find each other. Either way, I love you."

She had more she wanted to say, more she wanted to hear, but she didn't get the chance. The affection fled his face and suddenly she was staring at the surprised features of an uncomfortable stranger.

He didn't say anything. Not a single word. Instead he turned on his heel and walked out of the room. A few seconds later, the front door of the house closed and she was alone.

CHAPTER TWENTY

Isabel was unaware of the specifics when it came to the passage of time. She went through nights and days, she showed up at work and apparently made sense, but she wasn't really there. Fortunately, there were no big decisions to be made, no orders to get right. She oversaw fittings and suggested veils and smiled when Madeline talked, but it was as if it were happening to someone else.

Friday she closed the store at six and headed home. The days were getting a little shorter. Lights were on in several of the houses in her neighborhood. She could see happy families gathering in kitchens and family rooms. But when she got to her house, it was dark. No lights, no Jeep with painted flames. Just a silent, empty house.

Ford was gone. He hadn't said anything and then he'd left. She'd said the words he hadn't wanted to hear, and she'd lost him forever.

She walked up the driveway, toward the back door. It was open, as always. Because this was Fool's Gold and nothing bad ever happened here.

Only it had.

She walked into the kitchen and set her purse on the counter. After changing into jeans and a long-sleeved T-shirt, she started back toward the kitchen. Only once she got there, she didn't want to eat. She sighed. Maybe having a broken heart would get rid of those stubborn ten pounds she was always trying to lose.

Someone knocked on the front door. She walked through the house knowing there was no way it was Ford. He would simply walk in the back, as he always did. Something else he wouldn't be doing again. Something else she would have to get used to.

She opened the door and saw Jo standing there with a blender under each arm.

"Hey," her friend said. "We heard and we're here. I have a new recipe for rum slushies. I think they're going to be a hit."

Before Isabel could ask what was going on, over a dozen women spilled into the house, and everyone was carrying either food or alcohol.

Felicia followed with Dellina and Anna-belle. Charlie ushered in Madeline, who hesitated.

"I'm the one who told," she confessed.

Charlie nodded. "Madeline called and said what had happened." She smiled at Madeline. "You would have been a lousy firefighter, but I hear you sell a mean dress and you're an excellent friend."

Isabel looked at Madeline. "How did you know?"

Madeline shrugged. "I've never seen you look so sad and broken. I didn't know what to do, so I phoned Charlie. She arranged all this."

Isabel felt herself fighting tears. She walked over to Madeline and hugged her, then turned to Charlie and did the same. The taller woman held her tight.

"All men are assholes," Charlie assured her.

"Not Clay."

"He's an exception, but we aren't here to talk about him."

Isabel stepped back and nodded. She knew that most of the women in the room would claim their husband or fiancé was an exception, but she was okay with that. Just because her heart was broken didn't mean the rest of the world couldn't be happy.

Maeve waddled in, looking more pregnant every time Isabel saw her. "He's an idiot," her sister said, hugging her. "I'm here for you."

"Thanks."

As always, Jo set up a bar in the kitchen. Drinks were poured, food dished and laid out. There were plates of brownies, plenty of cookies and ice cream. For the salty snackers, bowls of chips and dip were scattered around the living room. The blender went on and off with great regularity, and everyone declared the rum slushies a hit.

By her second one, Isabel went from crushed to crushed and buzzed, which turned out to be a better place. Somewhere around seven-thirty, Consuelo and Taryn walked in.

Consuelo rushed to Isabel's side. "I'm sorry," she said, sitting next to her on the sofa. "I just got the message. I had my phone turned off."

"Enjoying a little new-boyfriend fun?" Dellina asked, then slapped her hand over her mouth. "Sorry."

Isabel shook her head and smiled. "No. Don't be sorry. We are going to drink to my friend and her official relationship with Kent. Because I love you enough to want

429

you to be happy."

Consuelo hugged her. "I can seriously hurt Ford, if you want. I know his vulnerabilities."

"Maybe later," Isabel said, determined to get through the evening without humiliating herself.

Her house was filled with people who obviously cared about her. Whatever she needed, they would provide. She only had to ask. They would be here for her. She was lucky. She only wished it was enough.

Taryn — still stunning in tight-fitting jeans, a silk blouse and boots — strolled over. "I'm confused. I was told to show up, but the reason is unclear."

"Ford dumped her," Charlie said. "He's such an idiot."

Taryn sat on the coffee table in front of Isabel. "Seriously? I've seen you two together. I would swear he was completely into you."

"I think he was," Isabel said, not sure if talking about it made her feel better or worse. "We were having a great time together. I'm the one who changed the rules."

"Did he freak out when he learned you were staying?" Taryn asked. "Men are so damned delicate. I swear, you wouldn't believe the trouble I have with the boys."

"That was part of it." Isabel drew in a breath. Maybe if she told them what had happened, she could begin to heal the gaping hole in her chest.

"I told him I loved him."

The room went quiet. She felt everyone looking at her. She drew in a breath and continued.

"I wrote him letters from the time I was fourteen until I was twenty-four. He was in the military, and I thought I loved him, so I wrote letters. They were silly. I was a kid, and he never answered. But writing them kept him alive in my head, if that makes sense."

Patience nodded. "Of course it does. I'm sure he appreciated them."

"I don't know. He kept them. I found them the other day. They were worn, as if he'd read them a hundred times."

Several women sighed.

"I realized I belonged here. In Fool's Gold and with Ford. So I told him I wasn't leaving and that I was in love with him. And then he left."

She felt the first tear slip down her cheek.

Consuelo grabbed her free hand. "What did he say?"

"Nothing. He turned and left without a word."

"I raised him better than that."

Isabel pulled her hand free and wiped her face, then looked up to see Denise Hendrix walking toward her. Ford's sisters were with his mother, and they all looked sad and upset.

"I'm sorry," Denise said. "I heard what happened. I hope you don't mind me coming to see you."

"No, of course not." It was a little strange, but Isabel had enough rum slushie in her not to worry about a detail like that.

Denise took a chair close to the sofa. "I'm sorry for not believing you. I didn't think you and Ford really were seeing each other. I thought it was an elaborate scheme so I'd stop bugging him."

Isabel's eyes widened. "It was," she admitted.

Denise looked more pleased than upset. "I knew it!" She sighed. "Now I know why you were avoiding me and our tea. Your excuses were starting to get elaborate." She patted Isabel's arm. "I have six children. It takes a lot to fool me."

"I'm sorry," Isabel murmured, fighting tears again. "I should have come to see you while I still could. Now I'm not with Ford and . . ." She held in a sob.

Denise hugged her. "I'm sorry my son is

432

an idiot."

"Me, too."

"None of this would have happened if the three of you hadn't bugged him about getting married," Nevada muttered. "Now Isabel's hurt and Ford is gone."

Isabel turned to Consuelo. "He's gone?"

Her friend shifted on the sofa. "Not permanently. He took a couple of days off. He said he needed to clear his head." Consuelo looked at her. "He'll be back."

"Ford is unlikely to walk away from the business," Felicia offered. "He enjoys his work. He's settled into the town. I'm surprised he would leave you. From the empirical evidence, I would think he was very fond of you." She paused. "Am I not helping?"

Isabel started to laugh. "You're helping a lot. All of you."

She had this, she reminded herself. Her friends, who loved her. Family, a business she was excited about. As for Ford, she would get over him. Eventually.

The cabin by Lake Tahoe had enough of the basics to be comfortable. Most of the time there was electricity. The large open room contained two sets of extra-long bunk beds, a table and chairs, most of a kitchen and a big sofa. There was a wide front porch with chairs and a view of the lake. The area was beautiful, quiet and isolated. Ford cared only about the last two, but the view was nice when he bothered to look.

He owned the cabin with several buddies. They came up here when they needed to get away. When life was too stressful or after one of those missions that came with ghosts. But even after three days, he couldn't seem to find what he was looking for.

Whoever he'd been was gone. Isabel had changed him, and he couldn't go back to who he'd been. He also didn't know how to move forward, which left him in a hell of a pickle.

He knew he missed her. Missed her more than he'd thought possible. More than he'd ever missed anyone. He needed her to breathe, and right now he was a man gasping for air.

But . . . Always but. How could he be with her? She deserved so much more than he had to offer. She needed someone to love her and cherish her. He wanted to say he could do it, but he'd never really loved anyone. Never wanted to stay. When the woman got serious, he got gone. His current location illustrated his inability to break the pattern.

He heard the sound of a truck in the

distance. The intrusion wasn't completely unexpected. He'd known someone would come looking for him. He rose and stretched, then walked down the two steps leading to the gravel driveway and rounded the corner.

Only the guy getting out of the truck wasn't Angel or Gideon. It wasn't even Justice. Instead Leonard stood by the truck, a small suitcase in one hand.

Unexpected, Ford thought, returning to the cabin. He pulled a second beer out of the refrigerator and took it out to Leonard. Then he sat in his chair and propped his feet up on the railing.

The lake was the deepest blue he'd ever seen. The leaves had all changed and nearly half were gone. Winter was coming. Not this week, but soon.

Leonard dumped his suitcase in the cabin, then took the seat next to Ford's. He picked up the beer and twisted off the cap, then took a seat.

"You ready to talk?" Leonard asked.

"Nope."

By the next afternoon, Leonard was obviously frustrated enough to spit nails. Ford was impressed he'd lasted as long as he had. Just sitting. When it had gotten dark, the two men had gone inside, and Ford had grilled a couple of steaks he'd bought at a store off the main highway. They'd eaten in silence, then listened to the radio before going to bed.

But now Leonard was squirming in his seat.

"I'm not going to just *sit* here," he said, glaring at Ford. "I have a family to get home to."

Ford nodded toward the driveway. "I'm not keeping you."

"I'm not leaving without you."

Ford settled more deeply into his chair. "Then you have a problem."

Leonard got up. He'd put on a little muscle, but was still scrawny. Still, he was a good man, and Ford appreciated the effort.

"I'm fine," he said. "You don't have to worry about me."

Leonard pushed up his glasses and glared at him. "I'm not here about you. I'm here because of Isabel."

Ford did his best not to wince at the name. Hearing it made him think about her, which made him ache. Not that he'd been able to forget her for even a second, but still.

"You're walking away from the best thing that ever happened to you," Leonard told him. "Being a part of something important

— a family — is what life's about. You could marry her, be a father. Why would you ever want to turn away from that?"

Ford studied the man. Leonard was telling the truth as he knew it. For him, Maeve and the kids were everything. Ford respected that, even if he would never have it for himself.

"You have a real chance with Isabel," Leonard continued. "But it's not just her I'm worried about. Maeve isn't happy." Leonard puffed out his chest. "I'm willing to do anything to make Maeve happy."

Ford straightened in his seat. He believed Leonard. Love gave a man courage where he didn't have a right to any. Leonard would take him on because it was the right thing to do.

"You're a better man than I'll ever be," he said, rising. "But I'm not going back."

"Why not?"

"I'm not like you. You're right. What I have with Isabel is more than I deserve. She's my fantasy come to life. She's adorable and funny and sweet, but I don't love her. I can't. I've never been in love with anyone. I just don't have whatever it takes to have those feelings."

"That is such crap." Leonard's expression turned pitying. "Seriously? Is that the best you can do?"

"It's true."

"It's not true. You're capable of love and a whole lot more. You're not emotionally stunted. Look at your loyalty to your team. You would have died for them."

"Yeah, but that was different."

"Not the principle. What about with your mother? You were willing to do anything not to have to hurt her feelings. You love her. You love your family."

"You're not getting it. How you love a woman is different than how you love a family."

"No, it's not. The sex is different, but the love is the same. It's giving of yourself, wanting them to be happy. It's doing the right thing and showing up every day. If you can love one person, you can love Isabel."

Ford wanted to believe him. If only it were that easy. "I haven't had a serious relationship since Maeve," he admitted. "There have been plenty of women, but I haven't wanted to be with any of them more than a few days, maybe a couple of weeks. They tried to convince me, but I wouldn't have it. I walked away every time."

Leonard patted him on the shoulder. "That's because you were falling for someone else. The letters. Isabel's letters. You couldn't fall for those women because you were already in love with Isabel. All this time, she's been the one. You came home for her. That's why you picked her to have a fake relationship with. You figured it was the closest you could come to the real thing, and you wanted that with her. It's been Isabel the whole time."

Ford's first instinct was to crush Leonard like a bug. His second was to take a deep breath and figure out if he could be telling the truth.

Was it really that simple?

Isabel finished cleaning the kitchen. Sadly, that was what her Sunday afternoon had been reduced to. She knew she could call one of her friends and go do something, but she wasn't in the mood for company.

The party Friday night had helped a lot. The hangover had been a distraction, too, but mostly she'd been reminded of the love and support she had in town.

She started the dishwasher, then sat down at the kitchen table with a pad of paper. Now that she was staying, she needed to make a list of all the things she had to do. For one thing, her parents were due back in a few weeks. She adored them but seriously wanted her own place. She'd already mentioned taking over the store during their last conversation and they'd been thrilled. Which meant she needed to move forward with getting an estimate on what the renovations would cost.

There was a meeting with a lawyer to draw up partnership papers with Taryn and contracting with all her designers. Maybe even find a few new ones. A thousand things to keep her busy. Unfortunately, none of them kept her from missing Ford.

"Hello, Isabel."

She jumped in the chair, then sprang to her feet. Ford stood in the living room, unshaven, slightly mussed and as gorgeous as ever.

"I know I locked the door," she said. It was something she'd started doing yesterday.

He shrugged. "Locks aren't a real problem with me. I need to show you something."

He walked down the hall and into her bedroom. Once there, he pulled open his duffel and withdrew the letters.

She paused in the doorway, not sure why he'd shown up but determined not to let him know how much he'd hurt her. She would be fine, she told herself. She would get through this, and eventually she would heal.

He flipped through the letters, then held up one. "I got this the day a buddy of mine was killed. I was right next to him when it happened. If the bullet had gone ten inches to the left, I would have been the one who died."

He tossed that envelope on the bed and picked up another one. "Three nights in a frozen shit hole with no food or water. You'd discovered Billy and surfing, and reading your letter took me away to L.A. and something good."

He fanned out the letters, then dropped them all onto the bed. "The reason I don't talk about what happened is I already did. To you. You were there with me, every step of the way. You kept me company when I was lonely. You reminded me what I was fighting for, and in the end, you brought me home."

She didn't know what to think, what to say.

"I watched you grow up, Isabel," he continued. "I know you better than I know anyone. It took your skinny accountant brother-in-law to get me to see the truth, but the reason I've never fallen in love with anyone before now is that I've always been in love with you. I don't know if it happened with the first letter, or the second, but I can tell you by the time you kicked Warren in the balls after the prom, I was yours. I was just too stupid to figure it out for myself."

He shrugged. "If you're still in love with me, I'd like that a lot, because I'm sure in love with you."

She didn't remember moving, but suddenly she was in his arms. He held her so tight, she didn't think she could breathe, but that was okay. She had Ford and he loved her.

She started to laugh, and laughter turned to tears; then he was kissing her, and she was kissing him back.

"I do love you," he murmured, his lips moving against hers.

"I love you, too."

He cupped her face and stared into her eyes. "We can stay here, if you want, but if you need to be in New York, I'll go with you."

She pressed her hands against his broad chest. "No. I want to be in Fool's Gold." She sniffed, then smiled. "By the way, your mom says she knew we were faking it all along."

"No way."

"That's what she told me."

He grinned and kissed her again. "But that's the thing. I wasn't faking after all.

Isabel, marry me?"

She felt happy enough to float. "Yes."

He pointed to the letters. "After all this, I'm going to have to write all of our vows myself."

She smiled. "I think you're up to the challenge."

"I'm up for anything, as long as I'm with you."

ABOUT THE AUTHOR

Susan Mallery is the *New York Times* bestselling author of over one hundred romances and women's fiction novels. Her funny and sexy family stories consistently appear on the *USA Today* and the *New York Times* bestsellers lists. She has won many awards, including the prestigious National Reader's Choice Award. Because her degree in Accounting wasn't very helpful in the writing department, Susan earned a Masters in Writing Popular Fiction. Susan makes her home in the Pacific Northwest, where she lives with her husband and toy poodle.

MRoS